C000114617

For more information, please contact: magic79.jb@outlook.com

First published February 2018

Revised Edition February 2019

For Jenny & Katie

With Love Aways

 **Chapter One**

The tedium of passing traffic rarely held my attention as I had always found other things much more stimulating. In a small seaside town where there always seemed to be something new brewing change was never far away floating in with the sea breeze.

Today however was no exception when the sight of an old blue weathered pickup, patterned with odd spots of rust had me take a second look as it rolled on slowly by where I was stood waiting at the junction.

Friends who knew me would mockingly have expressed that what had really caught my eye was the hunk of the driver sitting behind the wheel. Lamely though and more to preserve my pride I would have replied that my only interest would have been in the collection of dented suitcases and oddments of furniture on the back.

Obviously on the move the load had been haphazardly tied down preventing slippage between the metal panel of the drivers cab and the rear bumper. Interestingly though, neither driver nor vehicle had been seen previously anywhere in or around Cockleshell Cove before today.

As the pickup passed near to where I was standing I noticed a casual hand appear from the driver's window and wave my way before it quickly disappeared the engine demanding a gear shift before the driver had to hold the vehicle steady and negotiate the lines of parked cars.

Inquisitively i looked around to see if the wave had been for anybody else. Surprisingly I had the junction to myself. I might have waved back although I wasn't in the habit of waving at strange men. I couldn't be sure, but I thought that I heard a chuckle from inside the driver's cab. Sneaking up on my blind side I did however recognise the wry smile belonging to a friendly face.

'Hello Sprigg,' the greeting came with sunshine reflecting back from her eyes, 'has waiting around on street corners become so dull that you've taken to soliciting the driver of an old rusting Chevrolet?' Jane's dulcet tone was unmistakable.

Like a naughty child caught red-handed with their hand in the biscuit barrel I felt the shame colour my cheeks.

'I was interest was merely what was in the back of the truck than with the driver. It needs a paint job that much I can tell.'

Jane scoffed, making me realise that my reply had sounded less than credible.

'A paint job my aunt fanny.' She craned her neck following the Chevy as it turned from sight. 'Anybody with the least amount of knowledge would recognise a late forties Chevrolet pickup with a six cylinder, three thousand six hundred horsepower engine beneath the bonnet. The man driving has as much appeal apparently and both have magnetic kerb crawling potential.'

Engines and motors bored me senseless.

'You know perfectly well Jane that I don't find engines, rusty blue, six cylinder or whatever the least bit sexy and your insinuation that I was waiting at the junction acting like a hooker is deplorable. Any tender moments that I choose to share with a man are performed behind closed doors and not inside the cab of a dirty old pickup.'

At least two inches taller than me and annoyingly attractive with or without make-up my best friend Jane Aldridge had been born not only with beauty, but an intelligent streak. Instantly noticeable was her chest which held mens stares twenty paces away. I loved Jane and would fight fiercely her corner, whatever the issue. Like a bubbling cauldron she could however be unpredictable and often I found myself the butt of her entertainment. Without an intake of breath or seemingly paying no attention to what I had just said, she continued.

'My uncle Jim on mum's side owns a mechanics garage. When he's not tinkering with customer repairs he dabbles in imported second-hand American cars and trucks. You should see what he can do with a rust bucket like that Chevy, it's nothing short of miraculous.'

Jane checked her watch and licked her lips.

'You know Sprigg, if you didn't walk around with your eyes shut half the time you would have noticed a banana yellow paint job cruising the beach front road between the cove and Addlesome Bay. The owner has a personal insignia called *Surf Board Steve,* he's worth getting to know.'

With a shrug I indicated that I wasn't interested and that included surfers, yellow paint jobs or cruisers called Steve.

'Seeing as you know so much,' I explored, 'what do you know about the driver of the rusty blue Chevy?'

Giving me one of those all familiar smirks Jane smiled. 'Depends on how much the information might be worth?'

Deviously intelligent and sure of her game, Jane knew that she was on a winner.

'The usual I suppose,' I replied, knowing that this morning's treat would be on me if the information provided proved useful.

Jane clenched her hands victoriously into two tiny balled fists.

'That'll do nicely Sprigg. I can tell you that the driver is not from these shores. His skin tone isn't false and he packs more muscle than any other man in and around the town.'

There was a brief pause as she contemplated the value of what she had to unveil.

'Does our deal include a top up?'

I conceded and agreed that it did.

She continued. 'In which case I can tell you that the reason you saw him driving through town today was that he is taking up residence at the old lighthouse.' Jane grabbed my arm and yanked me across the junction towards the coffee shop. 'This has made getting out of bed early all worthwhile.'

'And you would know all this, precisely how?' I asked.

'Insider knowledge and the Chevy was heading out towards the coast road, which we both know is a dead end leading to the lighthouse.'

Pushing me over to our usual seat beside the window, we looked up at the menu board above the counter although we had already decided our order.

'First we secure breakfast, then if you are still interested I might consent to tell you more.' Jane was enjoying this.

Forever the tease Jane was no different than the first day that we had met at primary school. Our bond was unbreakable and as girls we were much closer than boys, moulding our likes into one another's wardrobe, picking up habits good or bad and shedding tears along the way through puberty, before reaching womanhood.

Jane Aldridge however was exceptionally gifted knowing every trick in the book which she could use to good advantage in any given situation, including bribery and corruption which I have to say she generally kept for her husband Dave, hitting initially his wallet before expecting her needs to be fulfilled in the bedroom.

Betty's Butter n' Bake was our Saturday morning haunt where the inviting heavenly aroma of freshly baked pastry and rich bean coffee was a temptation too hard to resist. Settling ourselves down on the worn brown leather settee we juggled the plates of warmed almond croissants on our knees, gently blowing over the creamy froth that covered the hot chocolate.

The fresh ground coffee was our normal tipple, but as I was paying today Jane had decided to push the boat out and order hot chocolate, adding that a little indulgence did nobody any harm once in a while. Putting aside all decorum she devoured her croissant in record time immediately going onto the second.

'Did you miss breakfast?' I asked, with a shake of my head.

Chewing continuously, she nodded.

'I've no time on a Saturday for breakfast. The deal at home is Dave deals with the kids while I hit the shower. This is my day to be free of household chores, cooking and washing. Getting together with you Sprigg is the one treat that I look forward to each week.'

Dabbing the side of my mouth with a napkin I had no such regular schedules for chores. I did my housework as and when they became a necessity. That I suppose was the beauty of living alone as I could pick and choose the time and place.

Having devoured the second croissant Jane was then engaged with trying to extract a stray segment of almond from between her upper incisors using the fold of a napkin.

'So,' she leant my way, dislodging the last of the almond, 'for somebody not overly interested in motor engines our regular dark horse had her eyes glued firmly on the driver of the Chevy.'

She took another mouthful of hot chocolate.

'I have known you the longest Sprigg and generally you are over cautious in such situations waiting until the horse has bolted before you close the stable door.' She looked around at the few men sitting with their wives at the tables near to the counter. 'Some men however are worth chasing. Take some advice and lose the shackles, cast aside those doubts that could your judgement and let your hair down girl and live a little.'

To help emphasise the point of freedom, she pushed her elbows in close making her chest wobble from side to side which succeeded in catching the attention of the Saturday boy who was working the coffee machine behind the counter. His saving grace was that the counter top was high, higher than the top of his belt line.

Peering over the rim of my porcelain mug I studied my best friend wondering if she possessed the gift of being able to read people's minds. Yes, I had been thinking about making personal changes and the Chevy driver had caught my interest. Now I was doubly interested especially as he was living at the lighthouse. Looking away so that she wouldn't notice I recalled the moment that he had driven past.

'I like my life the way it is,' I replied, 'it moves at an easy pace, is uncomplicated and since returning to Cockleshell Cove from London I have managed to find a harmony here that I would hate to lose.'

Jane however wasn't going to be so easily ignored. 'You'll end up the second oldest virgin in the town!'

'Who's the first?' I asked, wiping the froth from my upper lip.

'Kevin Toomey.'

The exasperation in my sigh was clearly evident. 'Jane, Kevin Toomey has a mental condition!'

She laughed. 'Well if you don't hurry up, he'll get laid before you do.'

A couple of male workers in for a bacon sandwich looked over our way.

Jane was impossible. Knowing that the Saturday boy was still watching us she adjusted herself rummaging around under her tee-shirt, forgetting that I had lost my virginity in London.

Three years spent in the capital studying commercial design and art had left me emotionally drained and scarred. The time alone had also taught me how fragile some relationships could be and that some men considered bedding a woman to be just a conquest, another notch on the bedpost. Coming home with my pride dented, I still felt vulnerable.

At night lying in bed I would marvel at how I had managed to avoid the alcohol influenced drug scene and the wild weekend parties. Looking back on the experience, the time between then and now had blurred the memory and long had the ink dried in my diary.

'I thought a dark horse was supposed to be surrounded by mystery Jane. I quite like that idea, the same as I like keeping my life private. That awful chapter in London was over a long time ago and I have since turned the page.' I put down my mug. 'Falling in love is an emotional minefield and so often the stakes of expectation are set far too high. I'm not saying that I won't ever commit myself again, but first I would need to know that the man was genuine, unlike Antoine.'

Licking the creamy froth seductively from the side of her mug, Jane was smiling across at the boy behind the counter.

'Whatever you say Sprigg, only don't deny that mister muscles behind the wheel of the Chevy didn't stir up your internal juices this morning. At the end of the day you are no different to me, Penny or Vanessa.'

Heaven forbid I was anything like Jane, the others maybe. On another table two elderly women had been listening in on our conversation. Looking my way one of them gave me an encouraging wink combined with a thumbs up gesture much to Jane's amusement.

'Now see what you done,' I whispered, 'that's exactly what I mean, my love life is not my own anymore. Not everything in life revolves around sex Jane. I believe that a real relationship has to be nurtured and allowed the time to grow, to mature together. It wasn't everybody that went around back of the school bike shed or the coastguard station for a quick fumble and some satisfaction!'

With a mischievous glint in her eye Jane winked back at the two women before leaning across the coffee table coming closer to me.

'Not everybody crosses their legs when sitting on the headland and a sudden breeze whips up the beach. Knickers or no knickers sometimes you gotta go with the flow. The same as not every boy loses an erection when the waters cold and as the saying goes Sprigg *let the force be with you* which doesn't necessarily mean that you shut the drawbridge before the last knight has crossed the ramparts.'

I didn't know where to hide my blushes. Even without looking his way I could feel the eyes of the boy behind the counter burning my way wondering whether I had any knickers on. Nearby the two elderly women were remembering days gone by when they had sat on the headland themselves on a breezy day, what happened then was their memory.

Considering the possibility of ordering another round of hot chocolate Jane was surprisingly a little more discreet with her next bit of advice.

'I was simply implying Sprigg, that now and again it's a good thing to feel a stirring in your loins and when a good looking man drives by in a powerful truck, push out the assets given to you and have them guess what else you have hidden underneath. Window shopping is not an indication that the last item in the sale is necessarily for you and neither does it mean that you don't check your purse to see if you have enough change left to buy the goods!'

Somehow I just knew that the two elderly women would be in agreement. As for the Saturday boy behind the counter he was still trying to unravel the mystery as to why the knight had to cross the drawbridge. Whether it was the additional glucose from the chocolate or something else I couldn't be sure, but Jane was on top form this morning.

'A little bit of mystery now and again is what makes you feel good Sprigg and keeps this dull life of ours ticking over nicely. Believe me when I say that a certain rush of blood can be as good as any damn Saturday morning chocolate with or without cream.'

Running the tip of her tongue around the rim of the mug for any last remnants of chocolate or cream the advice was flowing thick and fast.

'Get a man down where you want him and I guarantee that he will come bouncing back up twice as eager to please. Remember all good ripe fruit needs plucking.' She put her mug down with a purpose. 'Right, I'm ready for another what about you?'

'I thought that we were supposed to be on a diet?'

'I am, it's just that I only indulge once a week and starve myself the remainder.'

I was desperate to steer clear the conversation away from my private life, sex and men. Diets on the other hand were also taboo. It was odd because I sensed an underlying tension in Jane despite her being so jovial, as though she was masking something much deeper.

'Is everything okay between you and Dave?'

She looked around before giving her head a slight shake

'We've sort of reached that point in our marriage where the charisma has somehow gone up in a puff of smoke vanishing quicker than a magician's rabbit and the old wand is lacking all initiative.'

I sat open mouthed, startled by her admission.

She jabbed herself in the chest. 'And this old witch has misplaced her book of magic spells to help. Just recently it's been lights out at bedtime, listen to the owl hooting outside before we turn over for eight hours of uninterrupted sleep. That's not the Aldridge way Sprigg.'

Like a ball of cannon shot the revelation was unexpected. It hit me smack bang centre of my stomach. I had never thought of Dave and Jane's marriage as going stale. Like rabbits they enjoyed a very active sexual existence and had been at it since they had been caught behind the bike shed by the school caretaker and later chased away from the coastguard station.

'That's troubling,' it was all I could think of to say in the circumstances.

In a whisper I asked. 'Has Dave been to see the doctor only they can prescribe Viagra in such cases or alternatively, there's a marriage guidance who could help.'

As serious as Jane could ever be she looked up from the bottom of her empty mug.

'We've already been.'

I was shocked, I had never meant for them to actually seek help, it was more a passing comment. Dave and Jane nearly always sorted disagreements in their own special way.

'We saw this dishy man over in Breakwater only Dave hardly opened his mouth other than to utter three words and that was at the end of the session, when he said to me 'are you ready'.

Jane paused collecting her thoughts.

'I know my old man better than anybody Sprigg and he can be as stubborn as a mule with a thick impenetrable hide at times, but lately his silence is what really concerns me as much as the lack of sex.'

'It's a bit early to be suffering a midlife crisis, isn't it?' I replied.

'We'll that's what I thought, although suddenly it's like our eighteen years of marriage has meant nothing and gone up in a puff of smoke.' She shook her head discontentedly. 'Like a stranger has thrown a bucket of cold water over the flames of our passion.'

Breaking my croissant in half, I gave Jane the other half hoping that it would stop her scraping around the inside of the mug with her spoon.

Ever since I had known both Dave and Jane, they would fight like cat and dog then patch things up soon after with a good session of uninhibited sex. Despite her reservations on the subject I was convinced that they would do the same now. I saw the marriage guidance counsellor as a mere fad to achieve the end to an argument. Dipping the end of her croissant in my chocolate she promptly popped it into her mouth.

'You're an artful bugger Sprigg,' she said, 'only you've cleverly managed to steer me away from you by bringing in my problems.' Jane adopted an inquisitive expression once again. 'So let's get back to the Chevy forty nine.'

Accepting that I had no escape, I got in first. 'He looked younger than me.'

'Not his age you daft bugger,' Jane replied, 'the Chevy was manufactured in nineteen forty nine. Matthew Van Janssen is just shy of his late thirties.'

'You tramp Aldridge, you knew his name all along.'

I had always looked upon Jane as being like an older sister. A sibling that I had never had or enjoyed. Robert, my older brother was always away doing scout camp or things with the boys his age and was never around to talk or help, when I needed help. Jane was my confidante and with whom I could entrust my inner most secrets.

At the counter I ordered two more hot chocolates, getting a wry smile from the boy behind the counter. I could almost read his thoughts as he prepared our drinks in fresh mugs. Maybe it was dangerous giving Jane more sugar, but the Saturday outing was our way of relaxing after the long week. Returning with the drinks Jane was ready to spill some more interesting facts regarding the new owner of the old lighthouse.

'Our Chevy driver belongs to the rugby club where Dave is a member. According to my old man, Matthew Van Janssen is hot property, pursued by women, married or unattached. Originally from Holland he was raised by his grandparents albeit that his birth parents are both still alive.

'During the day when he is not moving house or cruising around in his pride and joy, he creates sculptures, designing and specialising in the bending, twisting and moulding of metal into fine works of art.

'Rumour has it that many of his pieces end up abroad with private collectors or can be found in established art houses, expensive luxury hotels and notable galleries. Some even go to celebrity restaurants in Hollywood. A recent resident of Ashburton Grange he has decided to make Cockleshell Cove and the lighthouse his home.'

'And is he attached?' I asked.

'Word has it only to his cat.'

I thought it slightly strange that somebody so handsome was without a female companion. Going around gathering up the empty items of used crockery the boy from the counter was rather wary of being too close to Jane.

'Now look what you've done,' I said, 'the poor boy is petrified of you!'

'Get away, he'll meet a lot worse than me before he leaves school. The kids nowadays are much more resilient and promiscuous. Some of the things that my two tell me will turn my grey roots white. Anyway, don't change the subject, what's the plan of action?'

'There's the rugby club dance next weekend!' I reminded her.

Jane gave it the big thumbs up.

'That'll do nicely. Dave is supposed to be working behind the bar and young Charlotte from number twenty five is babysitting Annabelle and Scott. We would have a whole week to plan our strategy.'

I didn't like the sound of that as Jane's planning sessions could end up disastrous for me. 'Like what exactly?' I asked.

Sipping the rim of the mug because her chocolate was too hot to drink Jane gently tapped the side of her head as she put her strategy in order of preference.

'A battle plan Sprigg. Firstly we need to check out your wardrobe one evening this week, then come the morning of the dance we need to get your hair done with Trudy.'

Looking at my reflection in the window I didn't see any reason as to why it needed doing. 'What's wrong with my present style?'

'Nothing really, although you've a few loose ends that need tidying up maybe fluffing up the volume will help.' Jane checked by pulling my chin left and right. 'And wearing your hair up always makes a woman look much more intelligent and alluring.'

I pulled up the sides and checked myself in the reflection, I wasn't entirely convinced that it made any difference.

'I could end up looking like an old frump.'

I turned my head back and forth, but it made no difference to how I looked. Next, I thought Jane would have me wearing a front buttoned blouse with a frilly ruff up to my chin or a dress that was so low it would be practically down to my navel.

Pushing her breasts together to sort herself Jane's cleavage resembled a deep ravine from the sun kissed Alps. Behind the counter the Saturday boy exhaled loudly then rushed through to the safety of the kitchen out back. Laughing as he went Jane pulled her hands away. Seeing that I was looking, she smiled.

'If you've got them show them, that's my motto.'

Jane was never this bad, I blamed the extra mug of hot chocolate.

'Succulent fruit has to be plucked from the tree otherwise they just become wind falls.'

She pulled me over grabbing hold of my wrists.

'Get the right man on your side and he'll know when to go harvesting. Isn't that right ladies?'

Jane looked across to where both the elderly ladies had interrupted their own conversation to engage with ours. They both nodded approvingly.

'The harvest season doesn't last long young lady so grab the opportunity when you can, why think of it as Eve giving Adam the first bite of the apple and the rest will take care of itself.'

Chapter Two

Matthew Van Janssen emptied the back of the Chevy arranging the few items of furniture, suitcases and boxes that he had elected to bring with him from Ashburton Grange into two stacks in the lobby of the lighthouse so that they could be sorted later. As long as they were inside they would be safe and secure.

'What do you think girl?' he asked, as Rosie the black cat purred her approval, pirouetting around his ankles.

When the local estate agent had telephoned him with prior knowledge of the impending sale stating that the current owners were eager to sell the lighthouse the metal sculptor had without hesitation jumped at the chance to be the new occupant owner. The beach headland with its one hundred and eighty degree panoramic view had long been a favourite haunt since his arrival in the picturesque county of Dorset almost eight years to the month.

With Rosie following close behind they did a circuit together of the lighthouse taking in the rocky headland, the long hedgerow at the rear and the farmer's fields beyond the leafy lane before arriving back at the opening to the coastal path that followed the curve of the sandy beach all the way back to the town of Cockleshell Cove. What struck them both, man and cat was the peace and quiet, the unspoilt picturesque headland, which would prove to be the ideal location to work and relax.

Coming from Damerscoot Hoorn in Holland, just shy of fifty kilometres from the capital of Amsterdam, the metal artist had quickly forged a laudable reputation for himself with customers requesting commissions as far away as America, New Zealand and Johannesburg. Studious collectors of art recognised his talent and were prepared to dig deep into their pockets, paying handsomely for his bronze statues, his crafted sculptures and many of the unusual pieces that he designed himself. Often they were prepared to wait months for a commission piece to be delivered knowing the quality of his craftsmanship.

The air tasted salty at the headland, engagingly fresh and helped clear the dust of the move from his nostrils as Matthew stood on the rocky edge below which was a short outcrop of rocks, water pools and unspoilt sand where the tide had ebbed back out.

Stretching hard he felt the resurgence of being there fill his lungs and invigorate his entire body with the warming rays of the sunshine. The move had taken longer than he had anticipated, but at last it was almost over. Standing where he could see all Matthew felt rejuvenated, alive. There were times when he thought that this day would never arrive. Now the priority was to make the chance of a new start work.

After an hour, lying back on the grass supported by his elbows with Rosie at his side, the cat had closed her eyes and was enjoying her new found freedom as much as he. Shimmering over the crests of the waves and rising up over the headland the breeze was warm and inviting. Behind them the lighthouse stood tall and whitewashed, the focal point of the cove and navigational landmark for passing ships. The only downside, if there was one, was that the lamp in the beacon room had been inoperative for a good many years. It was already on his list of things to do.

Stroking the back of the cats head, Rosie woke and purred. 'I love it here already, what about you girl?' Responsively she rolled her head confidently in the palm of his hand.

In the far distance they could see the moving silhouettes of people on the beach exercising their dogs or enjoying a paddle in the water and beyond that the sea wall which gave protection to the small armada of fishing boats moored in the harbour. The town was far enough away not to be a nuisance and Cockleshell Cove was just how Matthew Van Janssen had imagined it would be.

Gathering together a handful of loose pebbles he threw them as far away into the sea as he could skimming the tops of the waves before they disappeared. Rosie watched sensing that the peace which was long overdue had at last arrived.

Matthew was about to launch another pebble when the ringtone of his mobile phone shattered the silence. He wanted to ignore the call, but there was every chance that it would be from Carlos, his agent informing him of another commission. Reaching around back of his jeans he withdrew the phone from the pocket and flipped open the protective cover. Instantly, he saw the name recorded on the screen. Matthew felt his shoulders slump and his heart become heavy.

'Have you moved again?' the voice at the other end asked, accusingly.

Anna Van Janssen, his younger sister was unimpressed and before he could give any reply she launched into her normal tirade of abuse.

Closing his eyes in an effort to shut out the world, Matthew sighed long and hard.

'Yes Anna and before you ask, no I am not going to give you the new address.'

There followed a muted silence before his sister resumed the conversation.

'You promised Matthew, you promised that we would be together forever. You promised, do you not remember!'

He rubbed his temples which ached hearing her voice using one hand, forefinger and thumb massaging the tension inside his head. Why did Anna always wreck everything he wondered. She not only haunted his dreams, she kept him awake at night and made Rosie extremely uneasy.

'The hospital is the best place for you Anna and the treatment programme will allow you time to get better, to heal. I cannot help you, you know that.'

He had repeated the statement time and time again, but Anna refused to accept the truth regarding her condition or situation. Had anybody been close enough to have heard his words they might have thought his response harsh, possibly even heartless, although they were not. Matthew had been advised by the doctors to remain detached and that by taking a positive stand the message would eventually get through to his sister. The move to Cockleshell Cove was him being positive.

The silence proved Anna wasn't listening to reason. She retaliated angrily.

'You promised Matthew or have you forgotten that I am your sister. I hate it here and these morons have no idea of the torment that I am going through being away from you.' She added a pleading squeak to her voice. 'Let me live with you and I promise to be good!'

It was a hollow guarantee and he knew Anna was only playing him. She had always been good at manipulating men whatever their age, although in his case Matthew had learnt his lesson the hard way. Anna was the dark cloud on his horizon.

He replied calmly, but with a sternness in his voice.

'No Anna, this is a new start for me and I am not going to have anything distract me from my projects. You have got to work through your problems and be strong. Focus on getting well.'

From the other end of the phone came a derisory grunt of dissatisfaction. False hope as the doctors had advised could set back the treatment by several months.

'If you continue to fight the doctors and the nurses then you will never get free of the ward. You should find a compromise and soon things will get better. Remember Anna, what grandma used to tell us when we were little, she would say *'a pauper needs to find a coin before they begin to shed a tear for what they did not have in the first place'*. I am going now Anna, goodbye.'

With her ear glued to the phone Anna could hear the crying sound of the seagulls in the background. 'You're near the coast!' she hissed angrily.

Looking up at the bird flying about overhead he would have launched another pebble the seagulls way, but the bird was too quick to have been so easily scared away.

'Lives are always constantly changing Anna, as do relationships even those between a brother and sister.'

'Noooo...' her reaction was emotionally charged with a mix of rage and pain.

Matthew stared out to sea determined not to let Anna get to him, not today of all days. Today was about starting all over again, afresh. From the way that his sister was reacting her treatment was obviously still progressing unsuccessfully.

'Do you so easily forget that I am your sister Matthew and what of the promises to look after me when I came to England, do you chose to ignore me?'

Matthew was silent again unable to reply.

'One day soon I will make you remember!' It sounded like a threat, not a promise.

'We made promises to each Anna when we were children, a long time ago, but we are adults now. As I said things change.'

Fighting hard to think and keep her limbs moving the effect of the sleeping draught was slowly beginning to enter the blood stream, introducing calm into her day. The more Anna Van Janssen struggled to stay awake and alert, the quicker the drug flowed around her body. Slurring her words she began to speak more softly.

'Help me Matthew, please,' she begged. 'We could build ourselves another home together just like the one that we built when we were young. Surely you remember the hut that we built down by the river?'

Moments later the call was interrupted as the mobile fell from her hand and down onto the bed covers as Anna felt the curtain of sleep descending over her eyes. She lay her head down and succumbed to the power of the drug that the nurse had given her. Only she would know the places that she visited or walked through in her dreams. The torment however would never cease nor would the voices inside her head, the voices that controlled her when she was awake.

Realising what had taken place Matthew pressed the *call cancel* setting. He felt the relief wash through him. It was becoming increasingly difficult speaking to Anna nowadays and the unpredictable way in which she reacted always seemed to be influenced by her medication. Despite everything the pain of responsibility for his sister continued to cut through him like a knife. Looking out to sea it was a burden that he had no idea how to dispel.

Stroking the back of Rosie's neck the cat reacted by purring, trying to put him in a better place having been party to the call and realising that it was from his sister. Retracting her claws, Rosie was also less tense now that she had gone.

Ashburton Grange had been constantly tinged with uncertainty and a period of high emotion, but here at the headland even Rosie had felt the calm which surrounded them both. Here they had a chance to relax without the mad woman about. That was until she recognised the voice at the other end of the line, then it brought the nightmare back. Rosie also needed solitude and peace.

A strong gust from the rocks below threw up a sudden cloud of spray, dust and sand particles causing both animal and man to protect their eyes. They took it as an omen to make tracks back to the lighthouse.

'Come on Rosie,' he invited 'I think it's high time that we unpacked some more boxes.'

Standing up Rosie arched her back and stretched out her limbs feeling the resurgence of energy flow through her. Moments later she ran ahead wanting to get to the door first.

Walking a short distance behind Matthew was still having trouble with his thoughts. Anna had been a relentless interference, a perpetual nuisance having followed him over from Holland soon after he had arrived in England. At first he had been angry, demanding that she go back home, but as always he had relented and allowed Anna to stay sharing his home. Soon after though, she began to annoy him again. Just the little things that she did would irritate him and get under his skin, but they would be enough to fester and grow.

The days soon became weeks turning into months adding resentment to their sibling relationship. The more Anna saw how it was affecting her brother the more she planned and schemed. The climax culminated when she took an exaggerated amount of paracetamol tablets, cunningly knowing that too many pills would not kill her, but would get her the attention she craved. However, what she had not bargained upon was her brother's response, becoming both indifferent and resentfully embarrassed.

 **Chapter Three**

Following the downtrodden path back along the cliff edge Matthew was suddenly aware of a dog running wildly below darting left and right over the fine sand and foraging amongst the rock pools actively looking for tiny crustaceans. Coming up fast behind the dog was a young woman, the very same that he had seen standing on the street corner in town earlier that morning. He observed her as she awkwardly negotiated the uneven surface.

'Ollie wait,' Sophie called out, more a command than a request. Ordinarily the collie would have obeyed, but the rock pools were far too tempting.

Stepping around a deep pool she was aware that somebody was watching her from up above. The man waved and she responded with a similar gesture. Looking up at the sun however caused her to lose her footing on secure ground and the next thing that she knew Sophie was heading face down into the water. Somehow though in falling and lunging for the dog she managed to grab its lead. When she pushed herself back up, kneeling to assess the severity of her embarrassment she found that she was drenched from head to waist. Looping the lead through her belt she got back up.

'Do you need any help?' Matthew called out concerned that he might have been the cause of her fall and that she had hurt herself in doing so.

'No, thank you I'm fine, although if it's okay with you I would rather take Ollie back along the lane rather than back up the beach, it would mean cutting through your grounds.'

'Come on up,' he replied, walking back to where the head of the stone steps had been carved into the rock face.

Sophie took the zig-zag steps up to where Matthew Van Janssen was waiting. Wiping the salty water from her face she was aware that she must have looked unimpressively like a damp squib. More annoying was that before she had left home she had made sure that her hair looked good.

'Are you sure that you're okay,' he asked, reaching down so that he could help her up the last few steps. 'Watch the top step only I noticed earlier that it's worn smooth and has become slightly loose of its mount.'

Through an entanglement of wet hair she managed a smile. 'Thank you, I do feel such a fool though. I've lived on Cockleshell Cove long enough to know how slippery it can get down amongst the rocks.'

'It's easily done.' He pointed at several holes dug into the grass. 'And watch out for the rabbit holes. I never expected it to be this hazardous this end of the beach.'

Eager to be free of his lead having spotted Rosie up ahead Ollie suddenly lurched forward successfully slipping his lead from Sophie's wet wrist. His escape however was thwarted by Matthew's quick reactions who dived down to the grassy ground and grabbed hold of the loop in the lead before Ollie had gone more than a few metres. Returning the favour Sophie was immediately down on her knee and holding out her hand.

'I am very sorry. Are you alright, are you hurt?'

Matthew sat up and brushed the dust from the legs of his jeans.

'I'm fine really, although Ollie is a lot faster than most opponents I tackle.'

She remembered that he was a rugby player.

'He is a lively young thing for a collie and sometimes even I find it hard to keep up with him.'

Brushing away the grass blades from his tee-shirt, he knelt again and ruffled the underside of the collie's chin, which pleased the young dog.

'You moved into the old lighthouse today?' she added into the conversation.

Matthew gave a chuckle. 'News certainly travels fast in these parts!'

Sophie nodded. 'It does in Cockleshell Cove.' She was a sodden mess and her pride had been severely dented, but he didn't seem to be put off by her appearance.

'And it was you standing at the junction.' He replied. 'I did wave, but I wasn't sure that you realised I had.'

She brushed his tee-shirt where he had missed a few blades.

'I wasn't sure if the gesture had been for me or somebody else?'

He shook his head. 'Well, I'm pretty sure that there wasn't anybody else about when I looked.'

'Do you always make a habit of waving at strange women,' she asked taking back the lead, wishing that she had phrased it better. 'What I mean is that I didn't mind, but I am a stranger.'

'Not now you're not. Anyway I had heard of you from a friend.'

She was about to ask how he knew when Ollie took advantage of her lack of concentration. Wriggling free this time he charged clear of them both.

'Let him go, he'll come to no harm.' Matthew quickly advised.

Rosie saw the dog heading her way. Standing her ground she raised and arched her back in readiness. Sophie called, but her shout was ignored, lost in the air.

Matthew gave the command *'stop'* and surprisingly Ollie did. Running up behind Sophie regained control of his lead and wagged a scolding finger at the collie telling him that he was a bad dog.

'Maybe I should take him home before he causes any more trouble.'

Protectively Matthew came to Ollie's rescue.

'He's really only doing what comes natural. Most dogs will chase after a cat although if I were you I would be more concerned for Ollie's safety than Rosie. She knows how to handle herself and in a scrap Ollie would come off the worse, trust me.'

He held out his hand as an introduction.

'I should have done this at the top of the stone steps. I'm Matthew Van Janssen, although to friends I'd rather just plain Matt.'

Sophie slipped her hand into his. He was strong and yet surprisingly gentle.

'Sophie Sprigg.' She responded.

'Would you like a coffee and a dry towel for your hair, I've not quite unpacked all the boxes, but I think I know which will have clean linen.'

'That sounds really good and thank you. I promise that we won't overstay our welcome!'

Matt called Ollie to his side and amazingly the collie obeyed strolling across to where he was waiting. Rosie watched guardedly settling herself down by the front door.

'Come on boy,' Matt called 'let's get you a drink as well.'

Their coming together although not quite as Sophie had intended had however happened. She looked like a drowned rat not that it seemed to matter, but more interestingly she had succeeded in getting an invite into the lighthouse. Running her fingers haphazardly through her hair Sophie astonished herself, her brazen approach coming to the fore like never before. Maybe, she thought it wasn't only Jane who had been affected by the additional sugar intake that morning.

'He's a very healthy and friendly dog have you had him long?' Matt asked as they neared the front door.

'Ollie, oh no he's not mine he belongs to a girlfriend. I was just taking him for a walk along the beach because she needs to visit a sick aunt. Problem is the little devil knows the beach so well that he made straight for the rock pools. He likes to go hunting for sea snails.'

Matt smiled inwardly to himself there was always a sick aunt whenever women looked for an excuse to come sniffing around. Taking an old towel from the back of the Chevy he proceeded to rub Ollie dry while Sophie tied the lead to the nearest fence post.

'He seems to like it here.' Matt remarked as Ollie sat himself down when dry. Sophie was concerned that he had settled himself fairly close to where Rosie was also sat. Surprisingly neither animal make any attempt to worry the other.

Pushing open the impressive front door Matt invited Sophie in. 'Come on let's find you a towel now.'

'Are you going to ruffle my hair like you've just done with Ollie?' she asked, her eyes peering up at him under her eyebrows.

Matt laughed in response 'only if you wriggle about!'

The lobby was a mess stacked a metre high with cardboard boxes, wooden cases and oddments of furniture that had been unloaded and left where he had laid them down.

'Are you sure that I'm not gate crashing your first day here in your new home?' Sophie asked.

Matt gave a shake of his head, smiled and gestured that she take the staircase up to the floor above. 'The box with the towels are in the kitchen above.'

On level ground he stood a good six inches taller than her. Also noticeable in different light was that his skin was very slightly weather beaten and tanned like that of a Viking. Sophie admired his muscle tone having noticed how he had grabbed hold of the lead diving down to the ground. Taking in the atmosphere of the kitchen she waited as Matt rummaged through a tall cardboard board. Watching him lift out the contents he reminded her of a Viking stepping down from a wooden craft having just landed on our shores, having come across the sea to plunder and pillage the land, killing the men and enslaving the women. Silently a sigh of ecstasy escaped between her lips.

Pulling a towel from a laundry basket Sophie could only stand and watch. Handing it over, he quickly delved into another box beside the cooker pulling out a kettle, milk and sugar, coffee and two mugs. 'There,' he said, 'that was easy.'

Wrapping the towel about her damp hair only her face as visible. She liked the split levels of the interior and how the lighthouse was cosier inside than she had imagined it would be. Down in the lobby she had noticed a door at the side wondering what lie beyond.

'Do you like it,' Matt asked.

'What?' she replied, consciously aware that her tee-shirt was very damp and now clinging tight to her body and that the cotton bra beneath was doing nothing to conceal her chest.

'The old lighthouse.' He replied.

'Oh yes, this building has always been a favourite of mine. It's an artist's dream set against the headland, the rock face and the trees behind. As a young girl of ten I would walk the beach to the headland just to go hunting sea shells. Even when it's breezy you can think up this end of the beach.'

Her description pleased him because it was as he saw it.

'When you're dry, I'd be only too pleased to show you around. There's four levels, the old beacon room with the lamp that doesn't work, two bedrooms, a bathroom, lounge and the kitchen and beyond the lobby door is my workshop.'

He shifted boxes aside so that they had somewhere to sit and drink the coffee.

'You must be tired Matt. It's been a long day?'

'Once the bed is made, I'll get a good night's sleep and start the real unpacking tomorrow. This place will soon look like a home.'

'I don't mind making the bed if you wanted to unpack some of the kitchen boxes.'

Sophie had uttered the proposal before thinking through the implications. She had not meant it to sound like she was keen to see where he would sleep that night.

Handing over his first mug of coffee in the new home, it resembled liquid mud, brown with a frothy middle and floating undissolved granules of coffee. Matt added two sugars and a splash of extra milk to make it more acceptable. Sophie smiled approvingly, at least it was wet and warm, a little like she felt.

'What I meant by my offer Matt, was that I make a good bed and in return for stopping Ollie running off, I would be only too happy to free up some of your time. Moving can be tiring and the last thing you want to find at the end of the first day is that you've forgotten to make the bed.'

She crossed over to the window to look down and check on Ollie. She was surprised to see both Ollie and the cat asleep under the warm sunshine.

'This really is very cosy Matt.' She paused. 'And there's something here, something special within the lighthouse. You feel it as soon as you enter.'

'Like a welcome spirit?' he suggested.

Sophie nodded breathing in the ambience through her nose.

'Yes, like something puts its hands around you and holds you safe!' She shuddered, not knowing if the lighthouse agreed or whether the damp had caused the shiver.

Matt smiled as he sipped his coffee. He liked her interpretation of his new home. Putting the key in the lock and pushing open the front door he had instantly felt the calm hand of the lighthouse as it had gently guided him around making him feel welcome.

'Have you had Rosie long?' Sophie asked.

'She was rescued from the clutches of a disinterested owner in the first year of my arriving in England. We've been inseparable since. Rosie likes home comforts, but she is very independent. She likes the peace as much as I do.' He didn't elaborate.

Almost on cue Rosie jumped the last step of the wooden staircase padding across to where Sophie was sat on a wooden box. Circling her ankles she purred like an old electric pump. Sophie reached down stroked her head and made a fuss of the cat.

'She likes you. Rosie is a good judge of character and she can tell when somebody is kind to her.' The black cat continued to interlace herself around Sophie's ankles purring affectionately.

Having made it known that she approved of Sophie being at the lighthouse Rosie took herself back down the stairs to the lobby below where she settled again outside close to where Ollie was still sleeping.

Glancing down from above Matt saw the two animals lying side by side.

'Just like old friends they also seem to have hit it off.'

Sophie wondered if he was also referring to her as well. So far things were going well, much better than she had anticipated it would.

'Would you mind if I used the bathroom Matt, only I really do need to do something with this damp tee-shirt?'

Aware that her nipples were beginning to harden she was losing the battle with her bodily self-control.

'Sure,' he replied, with an admiring smile 'up to the next level and on the right beside the master bedroom.' He took a clean rugby shirt from the linen basket and handed it over. 'This was only laundered at the beginning of this week. It's dry and will stop you from getting a cold!'

She took the shirt and thanked him going up to the bathroom. If he had noticed he had politely saved her blushes.

Slipping out of the wet tee-shirt she looked at her breasts through the thin bra, her nipples were hard and excited. She rubbed them dry with the towel hoping that they would go down by the time she went back down to the kitchen. Just being close to him set her body alight. Sophie looked at herself in the mirror. She had never felt this way and so soon, not even with Antoine. Was it being here she wondered with Matt or the lighthouse, she didn't know.

Dabbing the bra dry as best she could she pondered, leave it off or keep it on. She put it back on. Throwing the sports shirt over her head it was miles too big, but surprisingly soft on the skin. Ruffling her hair into some sort of style she went back down.

'It certainly looks better on you than me!' he said.

Sophie gave him a quick twirl. 'It's nice and warm, thank you.'

Taking hold of her wet tee-shirt he went up to the top of the lighthouse where he hung it over the metal railing of the gallery balcony where the afternoon sun would partially dry it. Returning to the kitchen he found her drinking the last of the coffee.

'It'll need a good wash as it's got some oil on the sleeve from the seaweed in the rock pool. I suggest you keep the rugby shirt on and give it back when we see one another again.'

'Thanks Matt.'

He'd made it abundantly clear that he wanted to see her again. Sophie felt a warm glow pinch her sides. Jane would be incensed that she had not come on the walk with Ollie.

'You're obviously not from here Matt, where do you originally come from?'

'Damerscoot Hoorn in Holland, it's not that far from the capital. It's a relatively small village, much the size of some around Dorset. Damerscoot Hoorn however was too small for my liking and everywhere there everybody knew your business. I like my life to be private.'

'Is that why you moved here, to England I mean?'

'No,' he hesitated for a moment then decided to be honest. 'I ran away Sophie. I took a morning ferry across the sea to England and I have never looked back. I was running away from a bad situation.'

'Oh, I'm sorry Matt, I didn't mean to pry into your private life.'

'You didn't pry and I wouldn't have said anything if I wasn't comfortable in telling you, but strangely enough I am!'

She felt a warm glow sweep through her body, Matt made her feel at ease and he was easy to be with. After Antoine, Matt was a real man.

He continued divulging more about his life in Holland.

'My grandparents had tried in vain to reason with me and have me stay, but my head and mind were spinning. I felt like I was spiralling out of control so running was the only option left.' He looked out of the other kitchen window at the sea. 'It feels suddenly different being here, like the whirlwind that has been my life of recent has ceased revolving. You're right Sophie, there is something really good about this lighthouse.'

'And Rosie,' asked Sophie looking down at the cat below 'does she feel the same?'

He nodded and smiled. 'I think so. We'll talk later and I'll ask her only we tend to talk through problems and sort things together.'

She chuckled. 'I've got a friend like that called Jane, she does most of my sorting.'

Matt leant back relaxed, he liked her company and Sophie was easy to be with. For the first time in eight years he found himself being able to converse with somebody on his level of understanding.

'I left Ashburton Grange believing that my life needed change so when the old lighthouse became available I had to have it. I've been handed a second chance. I admit that I've not been into town much, but I hear it can get lively during the summer months!'

'It can and does sometimes. Cockleshell Cove has always held me spellbound. Many of the holiday makers that come here think that we're a sleepy little seaside town. It's not until they leave they realise different. I also believe that as an old smuggling haunt, the place has a magic all of its own. Dorset folk are like none other that I have met. They're a friendly bunch and always willing to help, although perhaps like your village a little nosey. I like my life private too.'

Studiously he watched her move from one window to another.

'This is going to sound corny, but I feel that I know you and yet we've only just met. Maybe it was in another lifetime!'

Sophie smiled. It was an interesting chat up line.

'Maybe I was a former wife and I've come back to find where you hid the family treasure.'

Their laughter was without inhibition and each wondered why they so easy with one another.

'A ghost or not the previous owner told me that lighthouse has a secret or two to tell. Nothing tragic or dark, but more a romantic sea-faring myth. On certain nights a young woman is said to walk the gallery balcony with a lantern waving the light back and forth at the sea keeping an all-night vigil on the lookout for her husband, lost at sea. A fisherman who went out, but never came back.'

'Jack Scurvvy. Yes, I've heard of that tale as well. I didn't realise that it was here that she waved the lantern, I'd heard that it was from the headland.' Sensitive to such phenomena Sophie expected a chill to run down the length of her spine. To her surprise there was no reaction. 'It doesn't feel haunted to me Matt, if anything it feels homely.'

He grinned. 'I'll let you know if she appears. I'm not frightened of ghosts only the living kind. Would you like to see the lighthouse?'

'Yes please. I've always wanted to see inside and especially the old beacon room, then your workshop.'

'I should have shown you the workshop when we came in. The previous owners had it built to be a storeroom only they hardly ever used it. With a separate chimney at one end it's ideal for the autumn and winter seasons. I intend growing some bushes and climbing roses either side of the front door as the exterior looks a little uninviting. You will especially like the top of the lighthouse.' He didn't say why.

Pushing aside the heavy oak door Sophie stepped through into a rectangular shaped room immediately catching of the fireplace. Up above a set of outside doors was a single window borrowing light from the headland. Matt switched on a set of spot lights instantly transforming the workshop into a metal wonderland. Propped up against the walls were tools of various shapes and sizes, together with supplies of metal in an assortment of colour and texture.

'Did you move everything here by yourself?' she asked.

'The previous owners were very good to me, they allowed me access to the store before the date of exchange. I've been gradually bringing my stuff across from Ashburton Grange. I've one more trip to make to collect some more metal and then I have escaped forever!'

The expression on his face was strange. She wondered if it was the shadow cast by the spotlight or whether his frown was hiding something else.

'My dad had a workshop once although nothing as grand as this, come to think of it, it was more a large shed at the bottom of the garden.' She shook her head remembering the memory. 'After school and at weekends I would go down there with him and tinker about playing with the wood mainly. My dad would tell me that it was his little piece of heaven. You've so much metal, you must have been collecting bits and pieces for a very long time?'

'Some came with me from Holland, although most of what you see is from local suppliers. There are a few pieces however that I keep back for very special occasions. I have a delivery Monday bringing in a new batch, hence the space by the doors.'

Stacked neatly into the corners and either side of the fireplace were bits of his previously crafted work, bronze statues, metal gates and garden ornaments, each different although skilfully made.

'Pieces like these,' Sophie said, moving along the line 'must take ages to create?'

'Sometimes, although I never think about it when I'm working. Some days, I'll maybe work all day and finish a project late into the night. It all depends on how quickly the client wants a piece finished. That as they say is the nature of the beast.'

'And leisure time Matt, do you have any?' Sophie needed to know. If there was little available then there'd be no point in pursuing Matt as suitor, if all he ever did was work, eat and sleep.

But Matt was already ahead of her thinking. 'Like walking the beach?'

'That and maybe a meal out or who knows, perhaps watching the stars!'

His grin was pleasing. 'Now those sort of interests I can and will always make time for. What about you though Sophie, what do you find to do in your spare time?'

Matt was good at throwing the subject back at her.

Pulling the excess of his rugby shirt tight around her waist using it as a cloak she breathed in the smell of oil, metal and burnt coals. When she had walked the beach that afternoon with Ollie she had only intended the excursion be a recee and maybe get a glimpse of the new owner, see the lighthouse from the headland. Things however were moving faster, much faster than she had planned. Perhaps Jane was right and it was time that she let her hair down and begin living dangerously.

'I part own a small shop in the town with a friend. Our speciality is mainly stationery goods, greetings cards, art supplies and craftwork.' Configuring the room size in her mind, she made comparisons. 'Our entire shop and stock room would fit into this workshop space. Generally business is good and we manage to keep our heads above water although Vanessa, my business partner is more adventurous and wants to be rich. That might never happen in Cockleshell Cove. In my spare time I dabble a little in oils although I prefer walking the beach or watching the stars.'

Matt looked interested. 'So do you buy or sell paintings?'

She chuckled. 'No, nothing as extravagant. I'm an artist, although I'm not Rembrandt or Turner. Most of what I paint is local scenes, landscapes like the headland and lighthouse.'

'I'd like to see them sometime.'

His request sounded genuine unlike some men that she had met in the past who thought that showing an interest in her art would get them through the front door of her house and later under the bed covers.

'I am always interested in the creations of other artists,' he continued 'so often an idea will originate from somebody else's inspiration. Do you have any in the shop?'

'A couple although they're paintings that I done a long time ago.'

Sophie pointed to the corner. 'What's hidden under the dust sheet?'

Pulling away the cover he revealed his most recent creation, a bronze woodland stag. Matt altered the spotlights so that the light captured the beast in all its glory.

Sophie stood with her mouth open, amazed.

'Wow Matt that's beautiful. I love it, really I do.' She stepped closer. 'You've captured the dignified stance just right!'

He pulled aside two more dustsheets, unveiling a metal hare with its ears pensively upturned as though expecting a hunter to shot at any moment.

Under another sheet was the statute of a winged angel, the wings which were turned downward and inward gave protection to a little boy and a girl. Some art critics might have considered the trio a sad representation of human despair, but as Matt explained the piece was bound for Rome and due to sit in the lobby of a convent where the nuns went out daily to help feed the poorer families of Italian society. In awe of the creation Sophie touched the children's faces.

'I call it *'Salvation'* what do you think?' Matt asked.

Sophie's response was softly delivered, thoughtfully pensive.

'The name is just perfect Matt. I've not seen anything as beautiful for a long time. It's a pity that not more people, other than the nuns will actually see it.'

Looking at the stag and the hare Sophie was in awe of his talent.

'Now I understand why sometimes you need to work all day and night!'

There was one last dust sheet left, Matt pulled it away having left it purposely till last.

'This is different and the client was very explicit in what he wanted me to create. I would really appreciate your honest opinion. I've already made mine, but yours will be interesting to hear.'

Sophie looked at the various metals which had been cut to size, twisted and interlinked very meticulously, but Sophie had a problem with what she saw.

'What is it?' she asked.

Matt laughed not surprised by her reaction. 'I think it's supposed be an angel climbing free from a waterspout although to be honest I'm not entirely sure. I just followed the drawing supplied by the client. Carlos told me that it will stand to one side of the client's swimming pool.'

'And is it finished?' she asked.

He nodded as he redirected the spotlights once again.

'With the right sort of lighting it could look very effective, especially late evening.'

Under the glare of the workshop lighting it did come to life, but it wasn't her favourite piece.

'You've not said what you think.'

'Honestly Matt,' she looked once more at the waterspout 'I much prefer the angel and the children. I like the stag and the hare too, but this last piece, the angel and the waterspout, this isn't you!' She was a little worried that they had only just met and here she was criticizing his work. He did ask though.

Under the soft lighting her tousled hair, unbrushed and a little wild complemented the colour of her eyes only adding to her natural beauty.

'To be frank,' he replied 'I totally agree with you. I have one final coat of lacquer to apply, but after that it's finished and I'll be glad to see the back of this particular commission. You're right Sophie, it's not me.'

He changed the lights around so that they fell upon the children protected by the other angel. She smiled and walked back over. This was what she liked.

'I have another commission to start next week which I could do with some help with, would you be free anytime?'

'Show me the old beacon room and I'd gladly help.'

When she stood at the top of the lighthouse with its panoramic view it was like looking out on a picture, on a clear day like it was today she could see for miles. Beyond the horizon was another adventure and way down back along the beach she could see people walking along the sea wall. The beacon room was her favourite of them all.

'The night sky and the abundance of stars must be simply breath-taking just lying here watching.'

'Help me with my latest commission, then maybe after supper we'll find out one evening!'

Was Matt toying with her affections, she didn't think he was. Sophie however had been hurt badly by Antoine, the question was, was she prepared for another fall, she wasn't sure. The buzz of the afternoon and being with Matt was like electricity charging up and down inside her body. Inside the lighthouse everything seemed so right and was Elizabeth Scurvvy the friendly ghost that she'd heard about. There was so much to know, so much to find out. Magic or no magic she was prepared to explore all.

Heading back down she said it was time to make the bed and then she really did have to go to get Ollie home in time otherwise Penny would be worrying that the two of them had got lost. Matt would have offered to take them both back into town, but the passenger compartment was still dirty from having moved his belongings that morning.

Waving goodbye, stating that she would be in touch soon, Ollie and Sophie headed off down the leafy lane with her wearing his rugby shirt. The sports shirt would need an explanation when she reached Penny's as would why the walk had taken so long. With each stride Sophie went through various scenarios, each sounding as unconvincing as the next.

Chapter Four

Lying on top of the bed with her head on the pillow Sophie gazed up at the stars beyond the window tracing the astral realm with the tip of a finger, amazed at how many stars were out unlike other nights when dark clouds left the night haunting and mysterious. She wondered if any one of them held her destiny.

Not given to whims of clairvoyance or unrealistic prediction she had long resisted the urge to visit the sultry fortune teller whose booth sat at the end of the pier and whose crystal ball was reputed to have seen all, past and present. What Sophie needed reassurance on was the future. Having safely despatched Ollie back with Penny and avoided the awkward questions that had been asked, she had promised to reveal why she was wearing Matt's sports shirt over a lunch date the following week.

Checking out the time on the clock, the hour was late and her eyes felt very heavy. She felt her thoughts dull as her mind began the process of slowing down making way for eight hours of uninterrupted sleep. Sophie was almost gone when an annoying hum at the side of her head told her that she had a call. Yawning wide she reached out and grabbed the mobile. The name on the screen read *Jane Calling*.

'Are you alright?' Sophie asked, concerned that something was wrong.

'You brazen hussy.'

Typical Jane and launching into the conversation without a greeting. At least she was okay.

'Just how lame can the excuse be, that you get to take poor Ollie for a long walk knowing that the beach ends at the headland. I thought you said that you would keep your oestrogen levels under control until the rugby club dance!'

Breathing in through her nostrils Sophie engaged her brain, thinking fast.

'It was Ollie who decided the route not me. We were down on the beach and he made for the rock pools, you know what he's like for hunting about. Matt just happened to be on the edge of the cliff when I caught up with the hound from hell. Anyway, how come you found out so quickly, when I left Penny promised that she wouldn't say anything?'

She didn't say, she sent me a text message instead only it happened to include that you returned wearing Matthew Van Janssen's sports shirt!'

Swinging her legs out from under the quilt Sophie slipped into her fur lined slippers, this wasn't going to be one of Jane quick calls.

'When I reached out to grab Ollie I slipped and fell face first into a deep rock pool. You know how treacherous that end of the beach can be when the tides just gone out. I ended up looking like a drowned rat so Matt kindly gave me one of his shirts to prevent me catching pneumonia. And before you ask nothing happened other than we had coffee together and he showed me around the lighthouse.'

'Yeah right,' the reply was curt and loaded with suggestion. 'Like an eagle doesn't hump a female marsh harrier when the old man's out looking for nesting material. I've come to the conclusion Sprigg that you're not just a dark horse, you're the whole bloody corral put together. Tell me was it good?'

There was a tinge of envy in Jane's tone.

'Nothing overly exciting other than coffee and discussing his commission work. I assure that was all.'

'But, its Matt now, you got that in fast. Only his rugby mates call him that.'

'Well, Matthew is rather conventional and artists prefer less formal references.'

There was a muttering from the other end of the end, too quiet to be heard. 'And I hear that you used your wily charms and demure pout to see his workshop creations. Don't you know, you normally have to pay to get to see a Matthew Van Janssen's creation?'

'We have a mutual interest in art, that's all. We are just friends Jane.'

Jane crashed her head back down hard on the pillow making it dent in the middle. Next to her the space in the double bed was cold and untouched. She reached across consciously feeling nothing.

'I'm sorry Sprigg it's just me, I'm feeling a little sorry for myself. I am pleased for you although bigtime envious. Lately this bedroom has seen more action from the spiders spinning webs than it has me and my old man. Before I phoned you, I was looking back at what I have achieved in my life. I could write down my accomplishments on the back of a stamp. It amounts to fuck all. Truth known, I'm envious of your lifestyle.'

'Oh come on, surely not!'

'Why not. Look at you, you took yourself off to London and got a diploma in art. You part-own a shop in Cockleshell Cove and you can damn well do what you like, when you like. What have I achieved, a quick fumble with my boyfriend behind the coastguard station one dark night and a month later I discover that I'm pregnant. Now I have a husband that doesn't come home until late, two kids and a *fucking* non-stop singing budgerigar. It took just one stupid mistake to launch me down the slippery slope. In some ways I can't blame Dave for not wanting to be here.'

Sophie was concerned, she had never heard Jane so low. She wondered if she her maudling was due to a bottle of red wine. Jane continued.

'I asked him what was wrong before he went out, but all he would say in response was that he was going through a mid-life crisis.'

There was a pause as Jane wiped her eyes with the back of her hand.

'Bloody hell Sprigg we're only bleedin' thirty three, it's hardly what I would call mid-life. My mother has never forgiven Dave for getting me pregnant. Christ you'd think being a catholic she'd realise that it takes two to tango. Listening to her go on sometimes, it's no wonder my father did a runner!'

Sophie was at a loss as to how she could help. 'Your mum loves you, Dave included and come to that so does he. You've never been in any doubt Jane, that he absolutely adores you and the kids.'

At the other end of the line Jane was crying uncontrollably. 'Well then why ain't he here when I need him so desperately?'

Again Sophie didn't have the answer. Jane sniffed hard.

'I'm really sorry Sprigg, but be an angel in my hour of need and tell me about you. Tell me more about the muscle bound hunk from Holland.'

'I would rather talk about Dave because I know more about him than I do Matt.'

There followed another long sigh and more sobs.

'So would I Sprigg, but my old man ain't here and he's keeping things close to his chest rather than on mine. I could shove a stick of dynamite up his arse and light the fuse, but he would still refuse to tell me anything. Midlife crisis or not I am gonna beat it out of him soon.' Jane paused. 'If I didn't know any better, I would say that he's getting his afters elsewhere!'

Sophie could feel the tension in the air as Jane poured out her troubles. She felt pretty useless at the other end of the phone. Her thoughts went to when they were much younger, when she, Jane and Dave, Penny and Vanessa had all grown up together. There were times when Dave could be as moody as Jane and even a little cantankerous, but there had not been a day go by when he had not grafted hard for his family, giving them everything that they needed, a nice house, a new car for Jane every third year and good holidays twice annually and abroad. Sophie wasn't in the least convinced Dave was over the side.

'You're just going through a rough patch Jane, a lot of couples do when they been together as long as you and Dave.'

'You mean the marriage blues?'

'Definitely not. That's when there's no love left and you two have a boundless amount stored away in the wardrobe. Someday soon the clouds will part and let the sunshine back in. Your love is still there, it's just going through a slight hiccup.'

Jane wiped the sobs away looking across at the bedside clock. 'Proper little poet you've suddenly become.'

Sophie ignored the cynicism.

'Trust me Jane, you'll come through this much stronger and raring to give the relationship more than you had before.'

She closed her eyes and thought of Matt. 'And think of the sex, it will be better than ever!'

Jane laughed. 'And just when did you become a marriage guidance councillor Sophie Sprigg?' Tinged with a hint of sarcasm, it was good to hear Jane laugh even if she was hurting inside.

'Don't forget,' said Sophie 'that I had a ring side seat when my parents went through a similar episode. The pain of their separation still lingers in the background and every so often it bubbles to the surface every time there's a birthday or anniversary due or Christmas is looming.'

'Sorry Sprigg. Yes, I do remember. That was a tough time during our last year at school. I remember that they came close to getting a divorce, but somehow they got through it.'

'That's what I'm saying Jane, if they made it work again then so will you and Dave.'

Sophie realised by bringing it up, that the breakup still hurt.

'It's probably why I steer clear of any long term relationship.'

Jane nodded. 'I wish you were here now so I could cuddle you Sprigg. You know how much I adore your mum and dad.'

She breathed deep and stopped sobbing.

'You're right. Dave and me, we'll get through this somehow, but if I find out that he's playing away, so help me I will kill him!'

That was better Sophie thought, Jane was more positive when she was angry.

'He's not playing around though,' she replied giving her tone more emphasis to sound convincing 'believe me he's not. And if by a streak of luck my mister right pops up any day soon then I would want my man to be as good as your Dave.'

'Do you mean that?' Jane asked, surprised.

'You know I do. Dave's solid, dependable and honest.'

'Alright. Jane responded. 'I'll give him the benefit of the doubt, although my guts are churning over like a dog gnawing on a juicy bone. God help him though, if you're wrong!'

Time to change the subject thought Sophie.

'He's really handsome, up close I mean.'

Jane blew her nose to clear her heads of dark thoughts.

'Who Dave, have you lost your senses?'

Sophie chuckled. 'No, you fool not Dave, Matt.'

'Are you trying to make my night any worse?'

'No, of course not I was just saying it out loud that's all.'

'Well, there are a lot of hungry loveless women out that would agree with you. Rumour also has it that chiselled like a Greek Adonis he has muscles in all the right places, although he is surprisingly gentle.'

The description sent a wave of intrigue through them both. Sophie was the first to respond.

'And how would you know that?'

Jane however wasn't without a reply. 'Well you've worn his sports shirt, didn't it feel soft next to your skin?'

Hanging on a coat hanger and over the handle of her wardrobe the sports shirt had pride of place in her bedroom. It had felt good next to her skin, soft and warm, and much better when she had got home, removed her bra and walked around the house with it on.

'I'm telling you that we just shook hands when I left to take Ollie home.'

The groan down the line was long and pained.

'Jesus fucking Christ Sprigg is that all you did, shake his bloody hand!' Jane thumped the back of the pillow with her head several times wishing that Sophie was there so she could beat some sense into her best friend. *'No matter carry on.'*

'He has the softest, most intelligent eyes not the kind that blow away the top layer of your clothing, but deep and thoughtful eyes that add soft lines to his work. And like me, he's been seriously hurt in love, maybe that's our bond, who knows.'

Jane scoffed. 'Bond my arse and you'd know that just by holding his hand. The last time that I read anything remotely interesting on touching, it was called tantric sex. When a couple are supposed to be turned on by fingertips touching. Dave and me tried it last Christmas only it didn't do a bloody thing for me and the silly sod nearly broke one of my false nails pushing so hard.'

Sophie laughed at the thought and especially as Jane was so particular about her nails. Slowly Jane was responding and becoming her old self again. She added a little extra to the tale.

'Given a moment longer it might have worked before he broke my nail, but sitting crossed leg he developed an almighty erection, something mission control would have been proud to have. In the end I said *'fuck this'* and jumped him!'

Sophie couldn't do anything for laughing. Laying back on the bed her thoughts were of Matt. She imagined him doing similar.

'I saw his workshop too, it's amazing.'

Jane let out a groan that sounded like she was in agony.

'Mother of Mary, Him and the Holy Ghost, you really do need to get out more often Sophie Sprigg. A good many females this side of the county would have torn their clothes from their body once they were inside that lighthouse and begged him to take them there and then without any recrimination.' Holding onto the top of her head, she sensed the air of frustration would end with her being defeated. 'So what was it like?' she asked.

'What, what was what like?'

'His bloody workshop!' Jane yelled dropping her jaw onto her chest.

'Amazing. There was a stag, a hare and an angel with two children beneath the angel's wings. His creations are like poetry, poignant and impossible to forget.'

Jane felt a headache coming. She accepted that she could swear until she was black and blue, but nothing and nobody was ever going to change her friend. Sprigg was like an angel with a defective chastity belt.

'It's a pity then that some of that talent doesn't rub off on my Dave. The only poetry that he ever wrote was scribbled on the back of the bog door at school and even then his spelling was never up to much.'

Jane looked over to the empty side of the bed. She also listened out for signs that her children Annabelle and Scott might be awake. Had they, she wondered been listening at the bedroom door.

'So did you mention the dance?' her voice went down a decibel, maybe two.

'It completely slipped my mind, but I suppose that's what happens when you help iron out the wrinkles in a man's bed linen, all thoughts of dancing tend to fly out of the window.'

Jane, rolled on the bed laying on her belly, completely naked. 'So you did get as far as the bedroom then.'

'Yes, but nothing happened. I ironed his sheets and together we made the bed.'

'Please tell me that it's a double bed?'

'Yes, why?'

Jane clasped her hands together and thanked god for small mercies.

'It helps Sprigg, believe me it helps.' She smoothed the sheet where she had been lying on it removing the creases. 'You did lose your virginity in London didn't you?'

'You know I did, I told you so. Why?'

'I was just thinking of something funny that was all. I remember when Dave and I were courting and his family went away for a long weekend. Saturday morning arrived and I snuck around to his place. Taking the ladder propped up against the garden shed I climbed up to his bedroom window which was wide open.' She felt the memory sink in the pit of her stomach. 'What greeted me was not a pretty sight I can tell you. The slob still had on his socks, underpants from the day before and a string vest, a bloody string vest no less.'

'So did you climb in?' asked Sophie, eager to hear what happened next.

'You've got to be joking. If the socks, string vest and underpants weren't bad enough, he was sprawled unconscious across some dirty old sleeping bag and sleeping between his legs was the family dog. I left the ladder propped against the window ledge to let him wonder who had left it there. Why do you think we've never had a dog as a pet?'

'You still went with him behind the coastguard station and later you married him.'

'Believe me Sprigg, there have been times when I believe that I should have taken the dog home to meet my mother and not Dave.'

Sophie wondered if Matt had any such vests in his wardrobe.

'The time spent in London was it serious between you and Antoine?' Jane asked. The question was out of the blue and caught Sophie by surprise.

Sophie hadn't thought of her French lover since he had gone back to Marseille. As soon as Antoine's studies were complete and he received his degree in English Literature and Classical Art he had fled the country quicker than the arrival of the mistral.

'At one point I did think it was serious. We'd share pizza together, a bottle of cheap wine and make love or that's what I thought it was. However, on reflection it was probably just a shag, another notch on Antoine's bedpost.'

Sophie swallowed the saliva at the back of her throat. She felt angry.

'Looking back I was so naïve, young and impetuous. I wanted to try everything, but the taste of bad wine can leave an empty hole in the pit of your stomach. Just before I came back to Dorset I heard through the grapevine that he had a long-term girlfriend back in France.'

'*Men can be such bastards.*' Jane whispered.

'Maybe, maybe not. It was a lucky escape really, but the experience left me very wary.'

'And Dutch gods, where precisely do they figure in the lucky stakes?' Jane asked.

'At this moment in time Matt's holding the ace card. I'm fortunate that his bedroom is on the second floor and there's no ladder.'

There was a sudden click at the front door as the latch was engaged. 'I gotta go Sprigg, Dave's home, bye love you.'

Jane cancelled the call and turned out the light pulling up the duvet cover. When Dave crept into the bedroom he smelt fishy. Jane screwed up her nose making out that she was asleep, even tantric sex was out tonight.

Plugging in the phone charger Sophie settled herself again ready for sleep.

From her bedroom window she could just see the very top of the lighthouse. She wondered if Matt was watching the stars or whether he would be down in the workshop working into the night. If they had been together she knew exactly where she would have wanted him.

Chapter Five

Anna Van Janssen sat on the bed with her knees pulled up tight against her chest, rocking slowly back and forth, dispassionately tugging at the loose strand of hair that was hanging down over the left side of her face.

She focused her interest on the activity opposite where a uniformed nurse was having problems with the bedtime needs of an elderly patient. By rights Anna should not have been on the ward with its locked doors and barred windows, her place was at home with Matthew, wherever that was now.

'It's not fair,' she mumbled to herself as she continued to rock, her forehead furrowed, her head bent forward so that the staff could not see her watching. 'Matthew's treating me so rotten, but I know that he still love me.'

The mutterings were heard by the nurse at the bed opposite. She stopped what she was doing to make sure that nothing was wrong. 'Are you okay Anna, did you want something?'

Anna looked up and shook her head decisively from side to side. Looking along the parallel line of beds on either side of the ward she watched other patients being put to bed. Creating a physical arc with her outstretched hands and arms Anna encompassed the entire ward.

'Look at them,' she continued to mumble 'each one as incompetent as the next and beyond anybody's help. They should all be put out of their misery.' She continued rocking. 'By rights, I should not be here.'

She watched with interest as the elderly female patient rolled the medication around inside her toothless mouth before swallowing the pills. Satisfied that the old woman was settled the nurse turned out the light over the bed head.

Anna continued with her mumbling as the nurse rolled the trolley back up the ward towards the office. 'It's not my fault that I jumbled up my medication. It was the pills which made me do all those nasty things to Matthew, but I know that he forgives me, that he still loves me.'

Scrolling through her list of recorded numbers she activated the call, but annoyingly it went straight to her brother's voicemail. Anna threw the phone down onto the bed in frustration. 'Why wasn't he accepting her calls?' she wondered. Dark and malevolent, deep and spiteful thoughts went through her mind as she imagined her brother lying in the arms of another woman, a stranger when it should have been her. Almost instantly she heard the voices feeling the ache both sides of her skull. When Anna succeeded in getting away from this place she was determined to show her brother what it was like to be with a real woman. Catching sight of the nurse heading her way with the medicine trolley she hid the mobile phone beneath the pillow.

'Time for your ten o'clock meds Anna.' The nurse joyfully announced. According to the ward clock she was slightly early.

With a smug grin Anna swung her legs over the side of the bed and waited patiently for the nurse to count out the different coloured pills. Why were so many nurses overweight she wondered? This woman in particular had a slack posterior, hairy chin and the over application of make-up was struggling to disguise her lack of beauty.

She watched the nurse dropped three pink, one yellow and two blue pills into a small plastic beaker. Checking to see that she had the correct dosage, she duly signed the med chart before tipping them into Anna's open palm. For once Anna was rational and compliant.

'That's much better Anna,' remarked the nurse with a confident smile 'it's so much easier when you don't fight us back!'

Anna returned the smile popping the pills into her mouth one at a time making gulping motions to look as though she was taking them down. When the last blue tablet went gulp the nurse closed the trolley lid.

'After a good night's sleep Anna you will feel more refreshed and ready to face a new day. If you continue to behave that nice Dr Meacham will come and pay you a visit tomorrow. We'll tell her how co-operative you've become. Who knows maybe in time she will consider re-evaluating your treatment which could speed up your discharge.'

Resting her head down on the pillow she watched the nurse push the meds trolley back to the office where she joined the other nurses in the tea room, soon they would be handing over to the night shift. Under the cover of the dimmed lights she tip-toed across to the bed opposite with the six pills in the palm of her hand.

'Here Philly, take these,' she whispered encouragingly 'these are much better than what the fat nurse gave you. They will make you sleep for a long time.' The old woman looked at Anna with wary hesitation in her eyes, but Anna had been planning this moment for days, she wasn't going to be thwarted, not now. 'Swallow the pills and I will give you a bag of your favourite sweets.' In one decisive gulp they disappeared.

'Are you going for a walk in the garden again Anna?' the elderly patient asked, struggling to keep her eyes open. Softly caressing the old woman's hand until she fell asleep Anna soothed the path of her slumber ignoring the question. When the woman's breathing changed and she lay unconscious Anna went back to her bed where she lay on top, waiting. Soon she thought, soon she could leave.

In the tea room the nurses passed around the biscuits.

'Anna appears to be calmer this evening.'

They nodded in unison. Pouring the tea the medication nurse smiled.

'The night staff should finally get some peace on their shift, only the pills that I've given Anna would knock a bullock out for the night.'

*****

Ascending the spiral staircase to the old beacon room Matt took extra care not to spill the whiskey in his glass tumbler. With his foot he nudged the airbed centrally to the old lamp before sitting down. On all sides the room was flanked by millions of sparkling stars, seemingly watching him as he watched them.

Bringing together the tips of both forefingers and thumbs he looked through the tiny hole that had been created peering up at the moon. The naked beauty of the lunar planet blanketing the sea below in a shimmer of small incoming silvery waves.

The day had been a strange mix of moving house, the call from Anna and then an unexpected visit from Sophie. Of the three Sophie's visit was the most pleasing and he liked her company. Looking at the few lights still on in the town he wondered if she was asleep. Distracted by other thoughts he should have given his mobile number. Sipping at the whiskey he heard Rosie pad up the stairs and begin a nightly exploration of the fascinating room in the moonlight.

Matt lay back with his hands behind his head thinking about Sophie, her long dark hair casually resting on her shoulders and the way that her eyes connected with his whenever she smiled, a nice smile. Watching Rosie looking up at the moon, he realised that unintentionally Sophie had in one afternoon managed to penetrate his normally impenetrable armour. He also had told her things that he'd not told others.

Thinking back he took his memory back to when he had met Helga ten years earlier on a street corner very similar to the one where he had seen Sophie that morning before she had met her friend and disappeared into the coffee house. He nodded to himself, Helga was nothing like Sophie.

An interesting observation, a significant difference was that Sophie admired and respected his creations, his artwork and also liked where he lived. Helga had never found the time to be encouraging or admire his talents. All that mattered to Helga was how much each piece would fetch on the current market.

Sipping the whiskey he felt it slip down his throat and warm his chest. There was something about the lighthouse that made him feel comfortable and secure after just one day, Rosie too was calmer. Instinctively understanding his thoughts and silence the cat sat at his side so that he could stroke her head.

'I like it here girl what about you?' he asked. The black cat purred as she nuzzled her head into his lap repeating the action time and time again. 'Things are going to be a whole lot different, I promise you.' If Rosie could have talked, she would have agreed.

Saying it, Matt didn't just believe it, he actually felt it. Possibly for the first time in years he saw a future with promise, with real dreams and maybe a relationship. Swallowing the last of the whiskey he was determined to make it different.

With Anna out of the way there was a chance that things could be different. Staring at the bottom of the empty glass was like looking into a crystal ball. The moon threw a white light into the glass vessel that seemed to change shape as he turned it one way then another in his hand. Matt felt his thoughts travelling. Anna had become a constant irritation, always interfering, forever scheming and disparaging of his previous relationship and with Helga.

The dissention, when it finally arrived had been when Helga had met Johan. Their friendship had flourished and with the help and influence of Anna grown stronger. Soon the rift between Helga and Matt had fallen into a deep chasm and soon Helga saw everything that he did as boring, unromantic.

Matt had tried to salvage the relationship, but resentment had crept in on both sides like a virus without a cure. Matt worked long and arduous hours, making it easier for Johan to pounce and seize his opportunity with Helga. Within a few weeks Helga was gone having vanished from his life forever. Lying at his side and unanswered his mobile had lit up several times. Thankfully he had changed the mode to silent, ignoring all calls from Anna.

With Helga gone, Matt loaded his Chevy and drove to the port where he took the ferry across to England, a broken man with a damaged heart. That day he had vowed never to fall in love again. It was still a mystery why Anna had followed him so soon after Helga leaving. He refilled his glass and continued looking at the moon.

He toasted the memory of his grandparents, very special people without whom he and Anna would not have survived their early existence. Ignored by their biological parents, both he and his sister had found the love that they craved through their grandmother and grandfather. Why then, he wondered was Anna trying to destroy his life turning up at every place he found to live in. She was like a bad dream that would not go away.

He swilled the whiskey around in his mouth remembering the day before Christmas when the situation with Anna had suddenly reached an ugly, unpleasant climax. Resembling an unwashed, dishevelled and hungry down and out she had turned up again without an explanation as to where she had been or with whom. Out of pity and feeling responsible Matt had taken her in, but as expected Anna had planned everything in advance and two weeks later when he was asleep she had climbed into his bed naked.

Having participated in a hard fought rugby tournament that afternoon Matt was exhausted. He woke to find her stimulating his erection while kissing his neck. Throwing her from the bed Anna had become instantly aggressive and verbally violent, minutes before she attacked him.

The family doctor had prescribed medication to calm her mood swings, but over the next week Anna had made a cocktail of the medication growing ever insufferably wanting, demanding that he have sex with her day and night.

The final humiliation had come when he had refused her advances escaping from the bedroom and going into the hallway to call the police. Coming up fast from behind Anna had smashed a large ceramic vase over his head knocking him senseless. When the police arrived they found Matthew insensible and Anna astride her brother attempting to have sex with him.

With fragments of the broken vase lying about as physical evidence and her brother injured and unconscious she was arrested after a struggle and taken into custody where she was assessed by a psychiatrist. The very next day Anna was committed to Ashburton Mental Hospital indefinitely.

Anna hated being confined, locked up and having to spend her day on a psychiatric ward where most of the other inmates were elderly women. From the onset she had been aggressive and would adopt acts of violence to get herself noticed, self-abusing herself and attacking the other patients, nursing staff and doctors. Prescribed a heavy dosage medication Anna was volatile, needing constant supervision.

Diagnosed as suffering from a severe personality disorder the doctor in charge of the hospital believed that her problems had derived from a childhood trauma almost certainly the victim of rejection by her parents. The condition had left a distinct hatred mainly against women. Had it not been for their grandparents they would have both been fostered out. From an early age Anna had developed an unhealthy fixation for her brother Matthew, believing that he and she should be together, not just as siblings, but lovers.

For the duration that Anna had been living with Matthew and Rosie, the cat had despised her. Always wary and hiding, Rosie had kept out of her way as much as possible.

With just the night lights illuminating the long ward the sound of snoring, grunting and tormented dreams punctuated the silence. Anna had tried Matthew several more times, but for whatever reason he still wasn't answering. Breathing deep like the doctor had advised she kept herself calm. Soon two of the three nurses on duty would be going for their two o'clock break at the canteen. Soon Anna would depart too.

*****

Pushing the glass tumbler to one side Matt settled down with Rosie on his lap. They could sleep under the stars tonight and save the bed for another occasion. In the old beacon room the air was still and peaceful. Laying his head against the cushions that had been supporting his back he stroked Rosie, thinking of Sophie. Like a warm breeze she had arrived leaving her mark not just on him as a person, but on his heart.

 **Chapter Six**

Jane looked anxiously at her watch as it was so unlike Sophie to be running late. The week had flown by surprisingly uneventful with Sophie busy in the shop and Matt sorting the lighthouse, adding the finishing touches to the stag. In the Aldridge household communication was at an all-time low unless they were talking with the children.

Running for all she was worth Sophie suddenly appeared.

'I am sorry Jane, I lost all track of time.'

Expecting Jane to be irritable Sophie was surprised to find her calm and composed.

'No problem, I left the house early before the kids were up. Dave volunteered to look after them this morning and free up some girlie time for us both. Are you ready to have some fun?'

Sophie smiled. 'Yes, definitely. How are things at home?' she enquired.

Jane fluttered the fingers of her right hand. 'Tetchy and now we're speaking in one syllable responses. There are times when I could launch a saucepan at my old man's head. It's the damn secrecy that's driving me close to the edge and I haven't had sex for almost two weeks now!'

Sophie wanted to laugh, but the look in Jane's eyes was one of desperation. Sophie thought it wise to remain silent steering clear of the subject.

'Are we ready?' she asked.

'I was ready minutes after eight this morning.' Jane replied.

Nearing the hairdressing salon Sophie suddenly felt hesitant. At the door she held onto the handle, refusing to go in. 'Are you sure that this is one of your better ideas Jane?'

'In you go Sprigg,' pushing her through the door Jane was in no doubt 'before I do something you will regret later.'

'But, I like my hair the way that it is. Matt likes it.' The first part was true, the second a lie because she didn't know what he liked.

'Call it atonement for taking poor Ollie on an extra-long walk just so that you could get yourself close to the headland. Penny told me that Ollie has been acting odd since you took him there.'

Sophie smiled, it was probably the excitement of meeting Rosie.

Jane wasn't finished. 'And you, you thrust yourself upon a poor defenceless man trying desperately to get his life together. You make his bed, but you don't end up in it. What kind of signals are you sending out Sprigg. Having your hair done today will hopefully help some.'

'The signal, as you put it Jane, was one to say that I am no easy lay, that I have principles.' Seeing Trudy, the stylist listening Sophie gave her a wry smile.

'When we're ready ladies,' the hairdresser implied, 'only I've got a busy appointment book today!'

Muttering under her breath Jane wasn't prepared for any of Sophie's educated truck, not today. 'An easy lay, fuck me an easy lay is a hen producing an egg, not some frustrated shop girl that hasn't seen a man naked for almost two years!'

'Why don't you open the door and announce it to the street outside, they didn't quite hear down at the corner shop!' Sophie hung her coat on the peg.

Jane raised her eyes skyward, then looked at Trudy.

'It would be easier with chickens!'

Sophie frowned. 'Discretion Jane, that's the way forward.'

Placing her coat next to Sophie's, Jane turned to the stylist.

'God give me strength, do something with her bloody hair Trudy before I cut her throat.'

Sophie sat in the adjustable chair provided as Jane plonked herself in a chair behind next to a pile of magazines. Throwing the protective nylon sheet around and over her top the stylist pumped up both sides of her hair checking for volume and length. Poised ready with comb and scissors Trudy had a wicked thought about men.

'You know the last time that I saw a naked man, he had a daisy stuck up his arse!'

Sophie closed her eyes shame-faced. As usual Jane had managed to lower the tone of the conversation in record time.

'Nigel's stag do?' Jane asked, nodding.

'That's right. Jason Conrad's boy is getting married today and it was his stag night on Thursday. Ben and I were on the way home when we came across young Nigel. He had been stripped naked, bent over and his rear end used as a flower pot!'

Looking at her reflection in the mirror Sophie felt compelled to ask. 'That's awful, what did you do?'

'Ben called the fire brigade of course.'

'Why, couldn't you do anything to help?' Both Sophie and Jane knew Nigel Conrad and his older sister Felicity.

'We had no option other than to call them, Nigel was chained and padlocked to the lamppost!'

Ignoring their laughter Sophie felt sorry for Nigel, she had a fear of hen parties and how they too could get out of hand.

'He must have been terribly embarrassed.'

'Not as embarrassed as he's going to be, come the reception later this afternoon. Ben took a photo of Nigel on his mobile which he sent to Clark David, the best man.'

Trudy continued pulling at strands of hair. 'So what am I doing today?' she asked.

Sophie nodded Jane's way. 'She thinks I need to be more alluring. I'm not sure how having your hair done will do that, but if you've any ideas then go ahead.'

Trudy cast her eye across at Jane then winked.

'Would this be a ploy to win fair heart of a certain Matthew Van Janssen?'

Sophie's turned her head around fast to look at Jane.

'You're unbelievable Aldridge, how many other's know about Matt?'

Jane's expression was a mask of innocence.

'When I made the appointment in the week I had to tell Trudy something so that she some background information. You have to think of a hair stylist as like an artist, they need inspiration to create a masterpiece.' Jane got up and walked next to where Sophie was sat. 'And if she's going to work her magic on you Sprigg, she needed all the help that we could give. Think of it as our contribution to getting you laid.'

Sophie looked at Trudy who raised her eyebrows sceptically. Jane had returned to her seat again.

'We're going to a rugby club dance, not some knocking shop annual ball.'

Starting with the split ends Trudy intervened. 'That's what Ben said it would be. Lots of single blokes plus the usual hounds from the town. All made up and ready for action.'

Sophie was aghast. 'You're going too?'

'What and miss all the fun, you bet I am. The annual dance is the calendar highlight and not to be missed. We go to see who get off with who.'

Jane grinned. 'Just watch what you say Sprigg, remember who's cutting your hair!'

Sophie felt her cheeks flush and tried to make amends. 'I'm sorry Trudy, I didn't mean to imply that you was part of that group!'

It only made things worse as both Trudy and Jane laughed.

'*Fuck* Sprigg, you're hopeless,' said Jane, 'Trudy knows exactly what you mean.'

'Okay then,' Trudy insisted 'make amends and tell me about Matthew Van Janssen, what's he like up close and personal?'

'Handsome, infinitely kind and very attentive to detail.'

Trudy stopped snipping. 'I bet he is, Ben tells me that most of the blokes at the club are envious of what he's got. Even the name has suggestive overtones!'

Jane looked up from her magazine. 'Yeah, that and her making his bed, only she doesn't test it to find out just how well he's equipped.'

Whatever Sophie said was only going to make things worse and worse still outback where Trudy had her stockroom, Teresa the Saturday girl had her ear glued to the door, this was much better than working at the greengrocers.

Jane wasn't finished. 'Getting hold of the tackle, isn't a rugby term Sprigg...' She stopped momentarily and a wicked grin masked her expression. 'Although it could be. When my old man is about to climax, he shouts. 'Now... now... now... Jesus I can't hold it much longer. *Fuck me* I'm sure the bastard thinks he's back on the rugby pitch!'

Sophie was no prude, but there were times when visiting the hairdresser was worse than a biology lesson at school where discussing pre-sex education had many of the girls flush crimson. Trudy inhaled deep expanding her well rounded chest and tried to restore some dignity.

'So is he going to change anything at the lighthouse?' she asked.

Sophie shook her head. 'Not that I know. He only moved in a week ago, but he does have plans. I suppose we will have to wait and see if anything develops.'

'And if any does develops, will that include you?'

Jane looked over the top of the magazine.

'Maybe, but time will tell and probably I'll be the first to know.' She watched the mirror and saw Jane go back to the article that she was reading.

Trudy reached for a back comb.

'You know I love Ben, I always have, but what I wouldn't do with a man like Matthew Van Janssen for one night. I've watched him on the rugby field and everything is just so perfectly formed.'

'Me too,' added Jane 'trouble is that at some time you'd have to come up for air!'

Swinging the chair around Sophie found the implication disagreeable.

'You shouldn't be talking like that. What would Dave, Annabelle and Scott think if they heard you say such a thing?'

Jane shrugged. 'Dave would probably say, it would save him the trouble of satisfying me.' She pondered. 'And with things lately in the bedroom stakes, he'd be right.'

Clipping the hair up at the back Trudy was ready with some genuine advice.

'You know Sophie, men like Van Janssen don't grow on trees. He really is a prize catch, only if you don't make a move on him soon, somebody else will. There are a lot of hungry women queueing for the chance to leap into his bed. You've got to show the opposition that you mean business and that he is yours.'

'How?' Sophie asked, ignoring Jane as she looked up and groaned.

'Getting laid by him would be a damn good start.' Jane promoted. 'Once a man has tasted the freshness of a mountain spring, tap water tastes unusually bland.'

Sophie was about to protest, but Trudy was in agreement.

'Stoke the fire and let the flames of passion burn through girl, after that there'll be no turning back.'

'Unless the fire's just ash.' Remarked Jane, her head stuck back in the magazine.

'Ignore her,' prompted Sophie 'she's going through an early marital mid-life crisis in her mid-thirties.'

'A mid-life crisis,' Jane scoffed 'that's *fucking* rich. The way things are at the moment my old man will be lucky if he makes forty.'

Trudy saw the opportunity for some more gossip. 'No change then since you was in here last?'

Jane shook her head and put down the magazine.

'There are times when I could have burnt down the coastguard hut and raised puppies instead.' She raised a hand to stop Sophie interrupting. 'Men are like kettles, they get furred up and think that come forty they've hit the magic midway term of their life. They view the latter stage as all downhill. *Fuck* I'm the one that's go to worry about everything going bulging and south, not that lump of lard!'

Sophie quickly came to Dave's defence.

'He could have something serious on his mind that he's trying to sort through and when he does he'll be back again and twice as good, see if I'm not right.'

Jane wondered if there would be another side. Heaving up her bosom she wasn't going down without a fight. 'As long as these two magnificent specimens don't drop below the kidney line, they'll be called upon to give service for some time yet. My children might be the cause of my cellulite and the state of my rear end, but when I'm on my back who's gonna be looking at the top of my legs when they're gorging on my rack.'

Sophie was speechless. 'Jane how could you. Annabelle and Scott didn't cause any of your cellulite that was natural body progression.'

'Bollocks,' replied Jane. 'With both of them I had a bad craving for tubs of creamy cheese laced with anything fruity, pineapple or orange, mango and even strawberry jam. Dave started the process and I ended it.'

She got up, turned around to flaunt her rear. 'Look at it, it's like a bloody jelly!'

Trudy secretly scanned herself in the mirror. She and Ben had no children, but her backside was already bigger than Jane's. Sophie looked on astonished and shaking her head, Jane was still in very good shape. She put the sudden attack of self-criticism on Jane's low esteem.

Looking over the top of her spectacles Trudy checked the style. It needed a few more minor snips and then it was done.

'All we're saying Sophie is that Matthew Van Janssen has been hot property for some time.' She tapped the appointment book with the end of her comb, 'I have at least half a dozen women booked in for afternoon appointments, single women and all hoping to make a good impression this evening.'

She picked up a viewing mirror and showed Sophie the back view. 'If you weren't such a good friend, I would have made this hairstyle look like a cruft's reject.'

Trudy gave herself an approving nod. 'Jane's right, this style will knock the competition for six.'

'You make it sound like I'm going to war!' Sophie exclaimed approving of her hair.

Jane quickly jumped in. 'That's just it Sprigg, you are going to war and that's what happens when you date a man who is in demand. You've got to hit the competition hard and below the belt if that's what it takes to win.'

Trudy put the mirror aside back combing every so often, gently pushing Sophie's head forward to deal with the neckline. 'There are some emotional wars and men are worth fighting over Sophie.' She reached for the can of hairspray, but Sophie wanted the style left in its natural state.

'The enemy later will be dressed to kill with their best arsenal on show. Plunging necklines, unyielding dresses that are so tight they will hardly be able to breathe and every one of them fearless. Remember at school when we ran the hurdle race together, tonight the hurdles are the human. The old trout brigade will be out to win so you've got to sprint that bit harder to win Sophie. Leap first and don't look back, that's always been my motto. I had to do similar when I realised somebody else had her eyes on Ben.'

Sophie looked surprised. 'So how did you win that battle?'

'At the time I was waitressing in a restaurant in the town only it's no longer there. Ben turned up one evening with Sharon Tuddy, my arch rival. When the chef wasn't looking I added some ex-lax to her plate. I delivered their meals with a smile. Halfway through the main course her stomach started jumping through hoops. Sharon rushed to the bathroom and remained there a good quarter of an hour before she came back out. Throughout the meal she revisited the cloakroom several more times. In the end she begged Ben to take her home. He told me that they ended up having a row outside her house and she blamed him for ruining the evening. Walking away from the house he saw the bathroom light go on as she revisited the loo. He never went out with her again.'

'That was very underhand!' Sophie replied.

'Everything's fair in love and war Sophie. You just have to gain the upper hand by whatever means possible.' Trudy stepped back announcing she was finished. 'This will knock em' dead.'

'So there's no truth in the rumours about Van Janssen being gay then?' Jane had been unusually quiet listening for the past five minutes.

'Well if he does bat for the other side, there would still be a queue of women wanting to straighten him out!' Trudy winked back at Jane.

Sophie refused to listen, knowing that it could never be true not of Matt. From beyond the stockroom door they heard Teresa giggling.

'Matt's as straight as any man I know.' She replied, the fires of indignation setting her eyes hard and determined. 'How much do I owe you?'

Standing behind her Jane was laughing loudly.

Chapter Seven

From the hairdressers they made their way to the coffee shop where they grabbed the leather settee by the window ordering the normal chocolate and croissant.

'So what else do you know about Matt,' Sophie asked, 'other than Dave plays rugby with him?'

Jane's expression was sympathetic.

'That he had the dirty done on him back in Holland. His fiancé walked out on him and straight into the arms of another man and that he has a fruit-cake wayward sister who is currently banged up in Ashburton Mental Hospital. He bought the lighthouse for some peace and quiet and that he dotes on his black cat Rosie.'

'Is that it?' Sophie asked, suspicious that Jane kept back snippets for a rainy day.

'Matt's a workaholic and other than rugby practice he's very much a loner. You did well getting in the lighthouse on the first day.'

'Maybe he just needed a friendly face about the place.'

'Wise up Sprigg, with your looks you would knock any man dead at fifty paces. You have got to start believing in yourself sometime and what Trudy said about the competition tonight, she wasn't joking. Several women have already thrown themselves at Matthew Van Janssen that Dave knows about, but he's rebuffed them all. You on the other hand have something special that he obviously likes.'

Sophie couldn't think what exactly. 'What precisely would I have to offer Jane, which no other woman cannot?'

'Love Sophie, real love.'

It sounded odd coming Jane and especially in her present circumstances. Jane went on. 'Love is a rare commodity in this day and age believe me. Men and women play at being in love, but really they just go through the motions, have the big wedding before banging out a couple of kids.'

It sounded a little twee, but Jane had more to add.

'Several years down the line things change and they end up in the divorce court blaming one another for having lost a decade of their life. It's a poor excuse. You're not like that Sprigg you're kind, sensitive and exceptionally grounded. If you do find the right man you'll give it all to him and more. From what I've heard about Matthew Van Janssen he doesn't strike me as a man to shy away from responsibility.'

Sophie liked it when Jane was serious and not messing about. She liked it when she was funny which invariably she was, but the times that they could have a sensible conversation were the moments to treasure.

'He's probably just being cautious that's all Sprigg. Dave told me that he was hurt real bad in Holland.'

'So what would you do, if you were me?' Sophie asked, seeking advice.

'I would go along to the dance tonight and make damn sure that he knows you're interested big time. I am not suggesting that you drag him out back of the clubhouse and shag him senseless as soon as you see him, but give out the right signals, the ones that tell a man that you want him for who he is, no strings, no promises. Men like to feel in control. It's part of the game.'

'Which is what, I've been out of the game for a long time Jane?'

'Something a whole lot more tangible than just friendship. Most normal relationships, other than those that start behind the bike shed start out where the couple build on the first date, cementing bricks for the future. You up the pace when you both feel that it's right only not before. If you have any doubts ask Dave, he'll vouch that dropping your guard even for a moment can have seriously far-reaching consequences.'

Sophie affectionately squeezed Jane's arm. 'You really are the best when it comes to advice.'

'However,' Jane replied consciously, 'should you see my old man out back of the rugby club with some old tart, then you give me the heads up and I'll cut of his balls.'

At that precise moment the waitress arrived with their hot chocolate and croissants. When she had gone Jane concluded.

'Sure there are times when we both wish we could turn back the clock, but life isn't like that Sprigg. You have to grab what you can when you can and you make the most of it. That's why I can't understand what's got into Dave. He was always so romantic, attentive and talkative. It's like some unknown entity suddenly turned off the switch.'

Sophie left her hand supportively on Jane's arm.

'Trust me Jane. I have no idea what Dave is up too, but one thing I do know about your husband, he would never do anything to hurt you or the kids!'

'I just hope you're right.'

Jane fought hard to hold back her emotions as the tears began to well again. Sophie hugged her ignoring the concerned looks from the other tables. *'I love the daft bugger more than I love life, I can't lose him Sprigg!'*

'And you're not going too,' Sophie whispered, ' be patient a little while longer and he'll come through this crisis, you'll see.'

Jane pulled away wiping her eyes with a tissue. She smiled and huffed. 'Thanks Sprigg, I don't know what I'd do without you.'

They cut the croissants in half and licked the cream floating on top of the hot chocolate.

Jane chose to change the subject.

'I thought that was an awkward moment back at the hairdressers when Trudy said that she'd squeeze herself into last year's dress.' The laughter cut through the inside of the coffee shop.

'So why do you think I was so apprehensive about her doing my hair this morning,' Sophie replied 'Trudy's eyes have been progressively getting worse. Sometimes I'm not sure how she manages to keep the salon going.'

'She goes instinctively by touch!' responded Jane, although it wasn't very reassuring.

'So tell me honestly Jane, is tonight going to be a blood-bath?' Sophie was serious. 'You know that I've never been any good at fighting?'

Jane chuckled remembering the fights at school involving Sophie had always been fought and won by Jane.

'Don't worry Sprigg, I'll be there should anything kick-off and Trudy, blind or not is pretty handy in a scuffle. Just be mindful that the tarts going along to the dance are only the cheap perfume, false tits and no-brain brigade. Remember also, you've already made his bed so you've ticked off one of the boxes. Trudy.'

'You wouldn't really cut off Dave's bits would you?' Sophie asked.

'Cut 'em off… I would feed them to the dog down the road!'

They were almost at the bottom of their mugs when Sophie observed Jane musing over her thoughts. 'A penny for them?' she asked.

Jane shook head in disbelief. 'My mind is like a bloody merry-go-round and I'm lost as to what is going on Sprigg. Dave comes home from work, has his dinner then picks up his sports bag and heads off out. He doesn't come back until late and he smells like he's been sleeping rough in one of the trawlers down at the harbour. He won't tell me or the kids where he's going and yet we all know that rugby practice is on a Tuesday and Thursday night.' Jane held up a hand to prevent Sophie butting in. 'And whatever you say on behalf of his defence, I think he's seeing another woman.'

Sophie however didn't believe that Dave was playing away.

'Let's look at this logically. All the trawler crews that I know are men, so unless he's seeing the fish shop lady and I doubt that because old Maud is knocking on for seventy, he has to be doing something else... something for you, Annabelle and Scott.'

Jane wasn't convinced. 'Like what? I've lay awake at night thinking through every scenario and coming up with nothing, except one. He's screwing around with the old trout from behind the club bar.' She lowered her voice aware that others could hear. 'There's a honey blonde that works evenings behind the club bar, all tits and teeth, it's gotta be her as nobody else would have him.'

Sophie scoffed. 'Dave doesn't know Sharon Tuddy, does he?' She was trying to make light of the conversation, but it didn't have the impact that she had hoped it would.

'Oh come on Sprigg, give my old man some credit. Sharon Tuddy is like the back end of a bus that been bashed against the bus garage wall too many times. No, if anybody its old brassy tits and teeth.'

Coming out of the kitchen the Saturday boy took one look at them both, saw Jane wink and did a quick about turn going went back in the kitchen again.

'What's wrong with you?' asked the manager.

'I can't go out front just yet Mr Fordham only there's that woman that I was telling you about. The one with enormous tits. She keeps heaving her breasts up and down knowing that it's difficult for me to look elsewhere. I'm not sure if she's after my body?'

William Fordham laughed and went to the spyglass window to look for himself.

'Christ,' he said 'she is stacked.' He continued to look. 'I doubt that she's after you Simon. I think she's just playing with you. Take a word of advice from one that knows. Look, enjoy and learn. The trouble comes later when you put all that into practice.'

Simon Slater wasn't quite sure what to make of the advice, but reluctantly he went back out front to clean the counter top and begin his education.

Jane winked again and this time he smiled, his eyes fixed on her chest. Jane smiled back then turned her attention back to Sophie. 'You need to remember something important Sprigg about men.

'At first they woo you with chocolates, bunches of flowers and regular trips to the cinema, meals at a nice restaurant and romantic walks along the harbour wall, however once they get their end away the change appears almost overnight. You're either pregnant or being proposed too. The change is like no other, expectation replaces the confectionary, you see more flowers in the cemetery and if he suggests a long walk then beware as something's wrong and he's thinking how best to tell you.'

'That makes it sound, like it's all doom and gloom Jane?'

Jane gave Sophie a shake of her head. 'Trust me Sprigg, there's no such thing as the honeymoon period. After a few weeks of wedded bliss you'll be waking up next to an unshaven, beer smelling over weight male who looks like he's been dragged through the cats litter tray during the night.

'You will complain and for the next few weeks they'll shave again, smell of roses and when they kiss you like they did in the back row of the cinema you'll forgive them for their minor mishaps. Soon you'll become putty in their hand all over again, only several nights later the snoring starts. Then they let their hair grow and tell the kids that they're a born again Christian and that god sent Adam down to earth to look after Eve.'

Jane wagged a solitary finger back and forth. Sophie was not to interrupt.

'So forget the marriage vows because you need to remember that they were written by a man. Forget it when the vicar tells you that everything hence forward is holy and sanctified by Christ. Love and war, remember that Sprigg because that's what marriage is all about, fighting your corner and winning. Whatever it takes. Only never forget that we women have a few tricks of our own.'

'Like what?' Sophie asked.

'Retail therapy, a girl's prerogative and whatever my old man can do, I can do better.'

Jane opened her purse and removed a bank credit card.

'I've got his bit of plastic, so the hairdressers, this breakfast, lunch later and shopping today will be on Dave. I'll teach that bugger to go sneaking about town with some brassy trollop. This is how we women go into battle and win the war Sprigg.'

Jane finished the last of her hot chocolate.

'Drink up Sprigg, only we have some shops to hit.' She looked across at Sophie who was silent with her mouth open, looking stunned.

'Oh and by the way your hair looks fabulous!'

 **Chapter Eight**

Anxiously the nurses checked the ward including the cleaner's cupboard, the medical stockroom, the laundry room and the bathroom finding no sign of Anna Van Janssen. It wasn't until the end of the search that to their dismay they discovered the damaged window in the day room.

'But, we're one floor up!' exclaimed the junior nurse.

'That's hardly going to deter somebody like Anna,' replied the older and more experienced nurse. 'We should have realised that something was brewing in the wind when she stopped rebelling against the regime that had been put into place. Come on, we had best let sister know what we've discovered.'

Evelyn Trubshaw trudged despondently behind her colleague knowing that this latest incident would not bode well on her student report. This was her second secondment to a ward where a patient had gone missing earning her a reputation of being a jinx.

*****

Snatching freshly laundered clothes from the storeroom Anna had found it relatively easy to slip past the only nurse left on the ward while her colleagues enjoyed their break. Using extra blankets from her the store she folded them and placed them under the bed sheet to give the impression that she was sleeping soundly. It wasn't until they checked for her early morning medication that they discovered that Anna was missing.

Placing a cushion against the glass she had managed to break the only unbarred window on the ward effortlessly climbing down the old cast iron rainwater pipe to the grassy knoll below. Sat in the security office the gate guard thought he saw a movement as something going fast leapt headlong into the shrubbery beneath the ward window. Seeing no movement in the grounds he dismissed the sighting as belonging to a muntjac deer, one of many found in the grounds foraging for food at night.

'Are you sure that it was a deer?' his companion asked as he reversed the tape.

'I'm almost positive that it was, it was small and certainly looked like a deer.'

They checked the tape. The creature was fast and running on all fours. Convinced that it was a deer they went back to watching the late night movie on the portable television. Neither guard saw the figure that crept past their hut and slipped out of the front gate. Anna Van Janssen was free.

'Which way?' she mused, remembering the hazy ride to the hospital where under heavy sedation everything on the journey had blurred into a passing green sheet. Anna kept walking until she came across a road sign.

Ashburton Grange to the west and six miles, to the east Cockleshell Cove seven. She remembered the sounds of the seagulls, but first she needed to check the house where the police had arrested her. Using the moonlight to make the way ahead easier she walked in a straight line following the road ducking behind a hedgerow anytime that she caught sight of a cars lights coming towards her. Throughout the escape she only saw one patrol car, but it was too far away for her to be concerned. Anna laughed mockingly when it was no longer in sight.

Two hours later she saw the chimney tops belonging to the houses of Ashburton Grange on the horizon. 'Soon Matthew,' she whispered, 'soon we will be together again and then we'll show the authorities just how wrong they were to take me away from you.'

*****

Matthew Van Janssen had been in a dream when his unconscious thoughts woke him with a start. It had been a fitful slumber, filled with anxious chases and shouts. The moment he had opened his eyes a vision of Anna had appeared, he imagined her walking. The vision was so clear that it had made him sit bolt upright.

In a cold sweat he was relieved to find himself alone although still in the lamp room. It was early and the old beacon room was without any heat. With the moon south east and moving around to the west the approach of a new dawn was breaking free of the horizon. Matt scanned about the room, but there was no sign of Rosie. Not as daft as he, she had probably found somewhere warmer to rest her head.

Below the cliff edge the tide had come in covering the rocky outcrop. Picking up his glass tumbler and the whiskey bottle he descended the two flights down to the kitchen where he filled and switched on the kettle. The whiskey had left his mouth numb and with an unusual taste. Pulling together coffee, sugar, milk and mug he watched the kettle boil. It annoyed him that Anna was still haunting his life. Without his tee-shirt he shivered.

Clawing his way back through an unsettled sea mist Matt pieced together the last remnants of the dream hoping to make some sense of why it had happened. The last thing he could recall was seeing Anna smile. It frustrated him that he had let her into his dream. Looking beyond the kitchen window at the blue, yellow horizon he guessed the time to be about four thirty.

62

Arching her back into a long curving stretch Rosie was waking too.

'Did she wake you also girl?' he asked as the cat jumped down from the boxes to circle his ankles reassuringly to have him know that all was okay.

Matt filled the mug and sat on a wooden chest.

'I've a foreboding feeling Rosie that a storms brewing and it's heading our way.'

He looked across at the empty chair. The last time that it had been occupied was by Sophie, how he wished that she was still sat there so that he could talk to her. She was easy to get along with and so understanding. Reading his mind Rosie jumped up on the empty chair and stared back at him. It summed up the impact that Sophie had made on the cat.

'You like her too don't you girl, so do I.'

From an opened box he found a blanket. Wrapping it around himself he watched the sun come up. As a young boy the sunrise had always held a fascination for him. Rosie settled down onto the chair cushion although she left one eye partially open sensing change was afoot. Matt was aware of her trepidation.

'She gets me like that as well.'

Damn his sister. Further along the shoreline where the sea was up to the beach a few lights were already glowing in the windows an indication that the town was coming to life again. Sipping the coffee, it was good and strong as the aroma filled his nostrils.

It had been a week since he had seen Sophie and in that time he had finished the last touches needed on the Stag and checked upon the others. Carlos had been informed and the shipment arranged. He was about to start the new commission, but Matt wondered if the offer to help still stood. He hoped that she was going to dance later, realising that he should have asked. Pushing a small pebble around on the floor with his bare feet, the cat watched.

'What do you reckon girl, should I risk everything and chance love or just go looking for friendship?'

Raising her head then letting it drop back down Rosie purred making her feelings known.

'Okay, love it is, only you know best. If it goes belly up, be it on your head this time though!'

Stretching out her paw Rosie touched the leg of his jeans. He returned the approving gesture stroking her neck.

The first week in their new home had been good and uninterrupted allowing him time to complete his work. Matt liked the peace and watching the tides go in and out twice a day. Other times when he made himself a drink, hot or cold, he would look back at Cockleshell Cove and wonder what Sophie was doing.

Several times he'd had to stop himself from getting in the Chevy and driving into town to visit the stationery shop. Looking down at the waves below, he was mesmerised by their rhythmic beauty.

'You never know girl, she might come back with Ollie.'

Rosie sniffed at the air then settled again as her sleep wasn't yet done. She would know if the dog that came to visit last week was about.

*****

Waking with a sudden jolt Sophie sat up in bed and took a sip of water to refresh her mouth. The time on the digital clock read three fifty two. Somebody unknown, a woman possibly had walked through her thoughts as she had slept, dreaming.

Feeling slightly uneasy, although she had no real reason why she turned on the light then turned it off knowing that she was being silly. If only she had given Matt her mobile number. Seven days had come and gone, seven days lost.

Chapter Nine

Somewhere around ten past five the inside of the lighthouse was infused with a wash of glorious sunshine pushing aside the magical show of astral stars and leaving behind just the feint trace of a ghostly moon. Across the width of the horizon the sky was tinged a cerulean blue, warm and inviting. In the agricultural fields and hedgerow behind the lighthouse the trees were preparing for winter, shedding their golden brown leaves.

Anna had managed to find sanctuary curled up in the safety of a large stack of recently baled hay, estimating that she was four miles clear of the mental hospital and only a couple left to cover before she reached Ashburton Grange. Going back there could be risky, but she had to see the house for herself just one last time and make sure. So far the road beyond the hedgerow surrounding the field had remained relatively quiet.

A little after six she arrived on the edge of the village keeping a look out for any patrolling police, but surprisingly there were none. The small house that she and her brother had shared looked empty and dismally uninviting. Pushing aside the metal gate Anna immediately noticed that the dahlias that Matthew had planted a month before she had been arrested were missing. Also gone were the potted plants that he insisted upon having beside the front door. She peered in the window at the living room which was empty, a hollow shell without furniture and his ornaments.

'The bastard wasn't lying,' she cursed to herself, her brother had definitely moved on.

She went around back to the rear garden where the grass was clearly uncut and much longer than she had remembered. Next to the wooden shed were lines of crushed grass and earth where Matthews's sheets of metal had stood weathering for effect. Fresh roots were beginning to push through again indicating that he had moved the metal some weeks back.

Sitting nearby under a bush a cat watched as Anna peer in through the window of the shed. The cat stood up and stretched hard getting ready to go home having spent the night outside. Anna saw the creature move, she scooped up a large stone and threw it at the feline narrowly missing the cat's head by inches.

'Fuck off,' she hissed *'you should know by now that I hate cats!'*

The mottle brown moggy raced across to the fence and scaled the wooden upright in two moves without looking back. The mad woman had returned. Anna picked up another stone of equal size, but she dropped it realising that the slightest noise might wake the neighbours.

'Damn the cats,' she snarled 'I hate them, hate them all. Always so bloody demanding of love and affection.' Had Anna found Rosie asleep under the bush, she would have throttled Matt's cat there and then.

Gently heaving aside the door of the workshop she was instantly greeted with a cloud of dust and undisturbed cobwebs another sign that her brother had not occupied the shed for a good two weeks. Retracing her steps through the long grass she found the kitchen door had been bolted on the inside and like the other downstairs room this also was devoid of furnishings except the cooker which belonged to the landlady.

Anna cursed with frustration returning to the road. She went next door carefully lifting the letterbox lid belonging to the old lady who had been a resident in the road longer than any other. Elderly people she surmised were always up and about early having gone to bed early the night before. Knowing the occupant only as Brenda she peered through the portal looking out for signs of movement inside. After a minute, maybe longer she let the flap down gently. Brenda must have gone to bed later than expected.

It had taken Anna most of the night with a couple of hours rest amongst the hay bales to walk the six miles to Ashburton Grange and now it had proved to have been a wasted journey. On the other side of the rented house was a young couple with a new baby. She knew that it wouldn't be worth calling to enquire if they knew anything, they'd hardly been around when she had lived with her brother.

Rummaging through the rubbish bins she looked for anything that might have been addressed to Matthew. A utility bill, an invoice, anything that would record his new address. The bin was only half full and mainly with somebody else's discarded rubbish, nothing to say where her brother had gone.

Annoyed that he had not entrusted her with the new address she left the gate open as she walked away from the property. There had to be another way and she would keep searching until she found out. Walking towards a copse of trees at the other end of the cul-de-sac, she needed the trees for cover as traffic in the distance suggested that people were beginning to stir.

'I bet this move had to do with another woman,' Anna snapped, punching a balled fist into her open palm, 'my brother is so gullible when it comes to loose women.'

She bent her fingers back cracking her knuckles and spitting venomously down at the pavement. 'Just like that bitch Helga, I will again have to deal with another slut!'

Approaching the corner where the road twisted left then right she ruminated over the last time that she and Matthew had been together, the night when she had surprised him by hitting him over the head, wanting and needing to have sex with him. He was so beautiful naked, just as she was. Anna could not understand why he continually refused her advances. She was willing to let him take her anytime that he wanted. Pulling forward her tee-shirt she admired the fullness of her breasts. It confused her as to why Matthew was so hostile whenever she suggested that they make love. As children they had chased one another in the meadows and promised to love one another, whatever the future had in store. Had Matthew lied to her even back then, Anna could not be sure, but she knew that it hurt to have her love spurned.

Fighting back her tears of rejection she recalled when they had gone skinny dipping in the river near their grandparents house, totally naked they had enjoyed the refreshing feel of the water on their bodies. Had not the sight of her hardened nipples and rounded breasts done nothing to arouse her brother's passion. Anna had spied on him once as he had examined himself producing an erection. It had fascinated her as she watched.

Walking towards the trees the inside of her mouth felt parched. Back at the ward the early turn nurses would be coming around with tea and her morning medication. Even though she despised taking the tablets they did give her a nice long sleep.

Without medication her moods were unpredictable. She thought of Helga, balling her fist once again. As Matthew's partner, Helga had stolen the sex that should have rightly been Anna's. Like the tart that had stopped Matthew from answering her calls during the night, Helga had ruined everything. It had taken weeks of planning, scheming and precision timing to get rid of Helga with Johan's naïve assistance, but it had worked and Anna would do it all again if she needed too. Willing herself towards the wood Anna felt tired needing sleep.

Suddenly from around the corner she caught sight of a postman coming her way. She ran across the road to where he was about to head down a side turning. If anybody could tell her about Matthew a postman was her best opportunity.

'Excuse me…' Anna cried, as she grabbed hold of his forearm.

The postman turned surprised to see anybody up so early. He was alarmed at having had his arm grabbed. He was equally startled when he saw that he had been stopped by a young woman who was scantily clothed and looking like she had been living rough for several days. She smelt as though she had been sleeping in a cow byre. Backing away she let go of his arm. As he steadied himself he caught sight of the laundry tag on her sleeve.

'Hello love, you're up early what's wrong?' he looked around to see if there were any witnesses about.

'Number forty seven, Hilltop Crescent,' Anna announced, as though it was urgent 'it's empty!'

Ernest Duggan knew of the address and occupant, nice young man, handsome and always polite. Well-built and a rugby player, just like Ernest had been once. He recalled sorting through the mail the day before and readdressing several letters to a new address in Cockleshell Cove.

'Yes, I think it is...' Ernest replied courteously, although cautiously.

'Do you know how long it's been vacant?' Anna asked.

Ernest did, but he wasn't prepared to tell. It was too early to start citing data protection, but the more that he looked at the young woman the more her expression seemed odd. Her eyes appeared to focus then loose interest as though she were on drugs.

'No, not really only this street isn't on my round any longer.'

Anna struggled to get her thoughts together. Any other time she could be cunning when the occasion demanded it, but without her medication to control her mind she was beginning to have problems with her equanimity.

'I called at number forty nine and spoke to Brenda, she told me that you would be along soon and would be the man to ask.'

Ernest knew of Brenda Robinson, a little deaf in one ear, but otherwise she had all her faculties.

Anna rotated her finger near to her temple. 'Brenda can be a little vague at times. She told me that Matthew had moved to the coast, only she couldn't remember exactly where.' It was a prompt and Anna hoped that it worked. 'It is important that I find Matthew Van Janssen only I have a very urgent message to give to him regarding his grandparents. It is imperative that I find him!'

Anna noticed the confusion in Ernest Duggan's eyes, doubt replacing his initial uncertainty.

'And you'd be a close relative?' he replied.

Anna nodded. 'Yes, a cousin.'

Ernest had been a postman before the woman had been born. He knew most of the tricks in the book regarding disclosure of information and he wasn't about to compromise his position, however serious the situation. There were rules and procedures to follow.

'Look love, I'd really like to help you, really I would, but my supervisor is a frightening man and he would have my guts and pension if I gave up any information about Mr Van Janssen. However, if you went down to the sorting office this morning they might be able to help.' If she did, it would give Ernest ample time to warn the depot and have the police standing by.

'Please,' Anna begged *'please, I really need to find him, it really is a matter of life and death.'*

Precisely whose life and whose death Anna had yet to determine as she didn't know the name of the slut that was sleeping in her brothers bed. Taking a tissue from her pocket she wiped her eyes of false tears.

'Matthew Van Janssen,' she bartered, 'I know that he rented the property from Jackson Meldrew the estate agents in the town. The landlady is a Miss Sandra Hemming and Matthew plays rugby when he's not bashing or bending metal. He's a sculptor.'

Anna hoped that it would prove she knew something private about the occupant, her cousin.

'You don't have to tell me the exact address, just the area that he's moved too then I can do the rest.' She again placed her hand on Ernest's forearm lowering her eyes. 'I promise, nobody will ever know who it was, who told me.' She zipped her lips together with the ends of her fingers.

When he had got up this morning Ernest had never dreamt the day would start so difficult. He knew something wasn't quite right, but if he didn't tell her something she might never let him go and her eyes were wandering all over the place. She might be violent and he didn't want to struggle with a scantily clad young female, not without witnesses. Ernest thought she looked desperate and very alone.

'Alright, just this once though,' he conceded. 'I can tell you that your cousin was last seen heading in the direction of Cockleshell Cove. Now please Miss, I really must go otherwise I am going to be late and I have not been late for my shift in over thirty four years.'

Anna suddenly stepped forward, grabbed both sides of his head, pulled him down so that she could plant a kiss on his cheek.

'Thank you, you have no idea how much you have helped me,' she let go of his head and stepped back. 'I promise, it'll be our secret!' With that she ran towards the woods where on the far side the road beyond would take her towards the coast.

Wiping the kiss from his cheek Ernest Duggan continued on his way to the sorting office. By rights he should tell the police of the strange encounter, but if he did, he could end up in trouble. He had recognised the tag on the sleeve of her tee-shirt knowing from which hospital it belonged. If she did tell where she had got the information about her cousin, Ernest would deny ever having met her, only who would believe a mad woman.

Rubbing his cheek where she had kissed him he hoped that she hadn't left any mark. His skin was becoming thin with age and was easily marked. If Nora saw anything suspicious, all hell would reign again. Only this spring she had accused him of having a fancy piece somewhere in Hilltop Crescent. As a postman and knocking on so many doors it was hard to disprove although as Ernest had stated in his defence, at sixty four he neither had the inclination nor the energy left to fulfil any woman's sexual desires let alone his own.

With a whoop of joy and rejuvenated determination Anna ran between the trees with her hands outstretched touching flaking bark and vegetation just like when she and Matthew had run down to the river back home. Arriving, early evening and with the river to themselves she would suggest that they bathed nude. Staying until dusk she had dreamed of him getting another erection, only this time just for her.

Anna remembered seeing a foreign movie where a couple had made love on the riverbank, rolling about the long grass, touching, exploring and kissing as they succumbed to passion. She lay down on the bed of fallen leaves and touched herself believing that it was Matthew. Soon she thought, soon he could touch her as much as he liked and whenever he wanted. Soon they would be together again.

Chapter Ten

Despite his best efforts Matthew Van Janssen found it difficult to shake the thoughts of Anna from his mind. However much he tried, a different distraction mainly thoughts surrounding Sophie and the dance that evening took precedence. Once again he was annoyed with himself for letting his sister get to him emotionally, especially when she was locked up in the hospital.

Maybe he considered the punishing hours that he had put in, in the workshop had made him tense and a little tired, his vulnerability letting down his guard. Hitting the shower he let the hot water wash away the tension as he lathered up the shower gel.

On the window cill in the bedroom Rosie heard the shower running. It had been a good week exploring the fields out back of the lighthouse and going down to look at the rock pools below when the tide was out. She had even caught a few small fish. Life, the cat believed was getting better.

Throwing on a clean tee-shirt and jeans. Matt slipped into his trainers tousling the towelled hair into an abandoned style, he would do it properly later. Right now though his stomach craved food. Dropping two thick slices of bread into the toaster he switched it on adding the kettle at the same time. Opening a new tin of tuna he scooped the contents into a bowl for Rosie.

'Breakfast time girl,' he called, but the cat was enjoying the sunshine too much to stir or jump down. As and when the need arose, she could eat then.

Waiting for the toast to brown Matt was astonished that his culinary equipment had found a niche in which to hide in the rounded kitchen. There was even space for other odds and ends, some never used, but kept just in case.

Beyond the window the day looked promising, blue skies, warm sunshine and a slightly salty air. Spanning east to west the gentle breeze was ideal for linen washing. He threw his dirty laundry into the machine, added washing powder and conditioner setting the programmer for an hour to include a spin.

Matt stretched feeling the invigoration of the exercise pull on his sinews. He was ready to enjoy the coming evening. Looking towards the town he felt that he should have formally asked Sophie to the dance especially as there was no guarantee that she would be going.

Buttering the toast he looked over at Rosie on the window cill.

'Time to change the stars girl.'

Rosie opened one eye long enough to check on things then lazily she shut it again. If he was happy then she was happy too.

Sipping the coffee he flicked through the local newspaper, glancing over the adverts that took up most the pages. He read down the sports page taking note of opposition results. On one page he found an ad for a card shop. Matt dialled the number, but the call was answered by an elderly woman. He apologised for the mistake and hung up.

'We'd best exchange numbers later,' he muttered over to Rosie, but she was dreaming of other things and not listening.

'Hey you,' he said, gently nudging the cats tail. 'I believe legend predicts that you and your kind are the kindred spirit that travels the universe offering guidance to lost souls.' The cat purred, but didn't open either eye. He stroked the back of her head. 'And as a protector is that why you came into my life Rosie, to protect me. Did I need protecting?'

It was an interesting argument. Matt let Rosie sleep as he drunk the coffee. Thinking about it, Rosie had always been there, his reliable confidant and ally. She had been witness to his moments of frustration, been around when he needed help with Anna and slept by his side at night, stirring if his sister stirred. He watched her sleep, she was like a protector and good for his soul. He believed Sophie was equally as good.

Matt sat back on the chair thinking. He would have given anything to know the future, but even as a boy looking too far ahead was dangerous. Whenever he had thrown up a prediction, it had come back to slap him in the face. Destiny was a mystery sometimes best left untouched.

He sensed that the lighthouse possessed something magical, but so far he had found nothing to suggest that it was a physical presence, more spiritual. Whatever it was, it had settled Rosie and to some extent he also.

Taking hold of a freshly laundered blue shirt he held it up to the sun, it was creased and would need ironing, but it was one of his preferred styles.

'This will do for tonight,' he showed Rosie, she opened an eye then closed it as quick. He was still deciding on what colour trousers to wear when the ringtone of his mobile distracted his thoughts. He felt the hairs on his neck rise as Rosie instinctively pricked her ears.

'Oh come on,' he replied, the irritation adding serious emphasis to his reply 'how and when?'

Rosie sensed a disquiet coming.

'I take it that the police been informed?' Matt asked.

A minute later the call ended. Matt splayed and stretched his fingers on the kitchen work surface pushing down hard until they began to hurt.

'That damn sister of mine and just when things were going so well.' It was unusual for Matt to be so angry. *'Fuck, doesn't she ever give up?'*

As though agreeing, Rosie arched her back and leapt down to the floor ignoring her food. She went to him, the supportive hand on his shoulder and his protector. Like him, Rosie splayed her claws in readiness for the battle ahead.

'Don't worry girl,' Matt assured her, stroking the back of her head 'she'll not get beyond the front door this time. This is our home girl, not hers.'

Setting up the ironing board he switched on the iron before making the call to the police. Matt needed to know what action they would be taking in searching for his missing sister. The sergeant told him that everything possible was being done to find Anna, but their resources were already stretched. Despite the lack of manpower the sergeant told Matt not to worry.

Gliding the iron over the sleeve of the shirt he injected a jet of steam along the crease as he thought. *'Not to worry,'* he thought to himself. The police sergeant really had no idea about Anna.

If Anna had escaped from the mental hospital and was roaming free, he had to somehow warn Sophie and have her know the whole story. It was something that he had hoped to avoid. Even by association of friendship Sophie could be in grave danger. Hanging the ironed shirt on the back of the door he looked down and along the beach at Cockleshell Cove. It looked so picturesque, so peaceful and yet unsuspecting.

Chapter Eleven

Selecting the multi sequined dress from the rack Sophie held it up for Jane to see.

'What do you think... too short, too long... tell me?'

'Well,' said Jane, licking her tongue across her upper lip. 'That all depends on the level of your expectation.'

'Meaning what?' Sophie responded.

'Meaning Sprigg buy the right dress and you send a message. A dress can say dance with me until the dawn or seduce me right here and now.'

Jane provocatively lay the dress that she was holding over her chest swaying the garment from side to side. 'Now this one sends out all the right vibes. Wear something as sexy as this and Matt would be putty in your hands and in your knickers!'

Fortunately the shop music system was louder than it should have been. Sophie glared across to where Jane was dancing with the dress that she had selected.

'It's definitely your size and colour Sprigg.'

'Keep your voice down,' Sophie mimed back. 'I'm not sure what signals I'm ready to send just yet, but wearing that would promote me as the town prostitute.'

Winking at the two assistants behind the counter Jane put the dress back, instantly selecting another where the neckline plunged deep and would leave little to the imagination. She smiled wickedly.

'Wear this,' Jane advised 'and you'll have to dance that much closer, if only to hide his erection!'

Sophie shook her head despondently picking a dress that Jane wouldn't be seen dead in.

'For god's sake Sprigg,' proclaimed Jane 'my mother wore a similar style of dress on her first date and although I have no idea why she'd choose such a garment, I would hazard a guess that the only reason she my father undo the buttons and take it off was because his family was financially loaded.'

Sophie put the dress back with a chuckle picking something more stylish and less conservative. Spinning around she held it up for approval.

'Now that's more like it and Matthew Van Janssen won't look so uncomfortable, although he'd need to dance just as close. I like the colour.'

Sophie went over to where Jane was going through another rack of clothes.

Whispering close, she offered advice. 'Remember, I'm going to a dance not to get undressed.'

'Have you ever heard of the spring tide?' asked Jane without batting an eyelid.

'Of course I have, why?' asked Sophie.

'Well, when the level of the water rises so high and with such force that it becomes impossible to stop the charge, it's like that with a woman Sprigg. When the time is right we readily accept what's coming. We hold back as long as we can from opening the flood gate, but then at the very last moment you relent and let everything go in pure wild abandonment. That's what you have got to imagine Matthew Van Janssen doing to you.'

Jane held up another potential dress which was more Sophie's style. It was a little more reserved although with hints of mystery, exquisitely colourful and cut away at the front just enough to show a little cleavage and the length above the knees, the was ideal for the occasion.

'Now that I like.' Sophie said, with a smile.

Jane passed the dress over. 'Go try it on,' she demanded, before Sophie had time to change her mind. 'You've got to be adventurous Sprigg before life passes you by.'

Sorting through the bargain box she added a black see through lacy bra and matching thong. 'Here and don't come back out until you tell me that you're buying all three items.'

Sophie felt the awkward pause as she took the items. She didn't need to look in the mirror to tell that her cheeks were burning. Rushing to the changing room she pulled across the curtain. Behind the counter the two young assistants joined Jane in laughing. Ten minutes later Sophie emerged carrying all three items of clothing. She asked one of the girls behind the counter to hold them for her.

'Well,' asked Jane 'are you buying them?'

'I like them, truly I do. The dress is ideal,' she came close so that she could whisper. 'The underwear is a little risqué for me Jane, I don't have anything like that at home.'

Jane put down a baby doll set with tassels that she had been admiring.

'I'm definitely not buying that!' Sophie insisted, her eyes blazing with indignation.

This time Jane was the one to whisper a reply. 'Actually Sprigg it wasn't for you, it was for me.'

'Oh, I'm sorry,' she replied. 'I thought things weren't good at the moment?'

Jane held up the two piece set. 'Maybe, this might just rekindle the fire again. I'm willing to give anything a go at the moment.' In the shop lights the bedtime set was almost transparent. 'Men get very excited about the bits that they can't see.' Jane put the set down on the counter and asked the girl to hold it for her as well.

Selecting another nightie as sexy Jane held it against Sophie to check for size.

'God gave you assets Sprigg so that they could be admired, caressed and kissed. You should be ready for any eventuality. Listen, when Matt finds out what you've got on underneath that dress he will carry you up the stairs of the lighthouse so fast that the old beacon lamp will positively glow again.'

Like schoolgirls they giggled, the thought amusing them both. Sophie conceded. 'Oaky, I'll buy all three, but that'll do for now. I'll consider the nightie for the next dance, let's see what happens at this one tonight before I start presuming too much. Anyway, you never know, I might not need one!'

Jane liked that. 'That's more like it Sprigg, live dangerously, worry about tomorrow when it arrives.' It wasn't really sound advice because Jane had found herself pregnant having not taken precautions.

Shopping with Sophie was never ever easy, but somehow Jane had persuaded Sophie to invest in a new dress and underwear. Jane did think about getting something new for herself, but she didn't want to tempt providence, her sensible side kicking in for once. Handing the spikey haired girl her husband's credit card she watched as the girl totalled the cost.

'Is that all madam?'

'That'll do for now,' replied Jane, 'although we could be back soon, it all depends.' She winked and received a smile in response.

Wrapping the dress first in tissue paper the assistant added small scented pellets to the box which was put aside for expensive purchases. 'These will help keep the dress fresh,' she explained. The girl was about to do the same with the underwear when Sophie suggested a bag instead.

Sophie watched as the girl popped the items into an accessories bag, there wasn't really enough lace on either garment to cover anything substantial and the price was hugely extortionate, but she

76

wasn't paying for it, Dave was. Punching in the pin number Jane watched as the girl wrapped her purchase.

'At my age, it helps hide the cellulite!' she said.

They left the shop arm in arm carrying their bags. Excited that the dance was only hours away.

'And Dave won't be upset, when he gets the bill?' Sophie asked.

Jane dismissed the cost with a dismissive flick of her wrist. 'It serves him right for being an arsehole lately. Anyway he will only add it to the petty cash expenses account like he always does.'

They were half way down the parade of shops when a nineteen forty nine battered blue Chevy suddenly drove past. The driver hit the brakes hard bringing the vehicle to a halt.

Chapter Twelve

Both Sophie and Jane sensed that something was wrong the moment that Matt stepped out of the truck. He looked apprehensive, albeit that he had a smile on his face.

'Retail therapy ladies?' he asked.

Sophie pulled the bags close in so that he couldn't see what was inside.

'Only girlie stuff,' replied Jane.

'Hi,' he said, with a smile looking at Jane. 'We've seen one another at the rugby club although never got the chance to talk, I'm generally Matt to my friends.'

Jane felt the light-headed sensation pass through her body as she stood next to him. Up close he was tall and broad. She liked the fact that he considered her a friend. Matt's eyes focused on the shopping bags.

'Have you bought anything nice?'

'Maybe,' Jane replied with slight reservation. 'Are you going tonight?'

'Yes and you?' He looked at Sophie.

'Oh yes, we're going,' responded Jane, butting in before Sophie could respond. 'And what's in the bag is a surprise for later. Make sure that you ask Sprigg for the first dance and you might just find out what the surprise is!'

Sophie looked at Jane with dagger in her eyes, Jane however was unrepentant.

Jane studied Matt, starting with his mass of hair, following the contours of his broad shoulders, muscle tone and honed physique. There wasn't a thing out of place. Hearing the word *'anytime' pass* through her mind. She suddenly sighed, following quickly with an apology.

'I'm sorry, it's just a ladies thing, probably the menopause!' Sophie looked at her quizzically.

'So what brings you into town,' Sophie asked. 'The expression on your face as you drove by suggested that you were out looking for somebody or something. Rosie's okay isn't she?'

It pleased him that she liked his cat. 'Yes, Rosie's fine,' he replied. 'I was actually out looking for you.'

Had he seen Anna instead it would have solved the problem and he could have left looking for Sophie and prevent a lengthy explanation.

'Damn it,' Jane thought, as she continued to study Matt, leaving Sophie and he to talk. Why didn't her husband come looking for her in the town with a bulge in his trousers.

'We should have exchanged numbers,' he continued, insisting that it had been a mistake on his part.

'You can have mine if you're looking to fill your dialling list.' It slipped out before Jane could stop herself causing Matt to laugh, although Sophie glared at her.

'Dave's had my number for some time now.' Matt replied. Jane stared in disbelief, one word out of place when she got home and that husband of hers was dead.

Matt noticed the new hairstyle. 'I like what you've done to your hair, although it's just as nice when it's wet!'

Jane nudged Sophie's arm. 'She had it styled especially to make her look irresistible!'

Sophie wondered what was wrong with Jane. She was acting like a schoolgirl with a crush. It was fortunate that Matt was accepting of her odd behaviour and had eyes only for her, although occasionally he did seem to be looking elsewhere.

'Well it was worth having done.' Matt replied, much to the amusement of Sophie.

'So does that secure a dance tonight?' she asked, pushing herself forward for an invite.

'The first, the middle and the last.' He said tactfully touching her arm.

'Listen up you two,' Jane suddenly interrupted. 'I still have a few things that I've got to get the kids for this evening, so why don't you both cut away and have some fun and let me get done what I've got to do. Only make sure that you leave some energy for the dance later.'

Matt looked awkwardly back at Jane. He had come into town to find Sophie, not spoil Jane and Sophie's time together. 'No, please,' he replied, 'I will go. I didn't mean to ruin your morning. I just came into town to give Sophie my mobile number.'

Sophie looked puzzled. Matt could have given the number to her later at the dance. Feminine intuition told her that there was another reason for his being there. She was apprehensive to suggest anything because Jane had booked a table for lunch for them both.

'You haven't ruined anything. We can do this anytime.' She kissed Sophie on the cheek then did the same to Matt. 'Remember the spring tide Sprigg.' She smiled at them both, saying that she would see them later at the dance.

Sophie watched Jane wave before she turned the corner and disappeared. Her friends had been so quick she wondered why Jane had virtually run away from their outing. Sophie was pleased to see Matt just a little surprised.

'Would you mind if we went for a drive rather than stick around town?' he asked.

Sophie nodded her agreement. 'This is all very mysterious Matt, is everything okay?' she asked, as they walked over to where he had parked the truck.

Matt pulled open the passenger door so that Sophie could settle herself in the seat before he took his. She discretely placed the shopping bags in the footwell between her feet, hidden from sight. She realised that Matt had not replied as he closed his door and inserted the key in the ignition. He was about to pull away from the kerb when as stick of lipstick fell from her handbag. It was the shade of deep red.

'Is that also for tonight?' he asked.

Sophie smiled. 'Perhaps, unless you've an aversion to lipstick?'

'Not at all, it's just that I didn't think you wore any.'

'Normally I don't unless the occasion is special. I chose this particular colour because it complements the dress that I'm going to wear.'

Matt approached the junction and stopped to let another vehicle pass before he headed out for the coast road. Sophie felt excited to be up front of the vehicle, it was larger than she expected, very comfy and had nice leather seats.

'So why the urgency to find me Matt,' she asked, you could have given me your number later at the dance?'

His attention was focused on the road ahead. When the opportunity presented itself he looked her way. 'I had a somewhat restless night and woke with a start having experienced a bad dream, my first thought was of you. Things had been good all week until I received a call just before I came into town. The news wasn't good.'

Sophie had a sudden sense the dread, sensing a disappointment looming and that he was going to say that couldn't attend the dance. She felt her stomach churn. Looking down at the shopping bags she wondered if they had been for nothing. When they reached the lighthouse Matt pulled up close to the front door and switched off the engine.

'The call was about my sister. Would you mind if we went straight in rather than go for a walk?'

Sophie agreed and moments later they were inside and the front door was locked. They went up to the kitchen where Matt made coffee as Rosie fussed pleased to see Sophie again.

'She likes you.' He suggested that they go up to the lamp room so that he could explain his behaviour. Rosie followed too. Passing the bedroom the bed looked like it had not been slept in all week. Matt saw her look.

'We've spent every night up here in the old beacon room. Under the stars, both Rosie and I find the atmosphere relaxing.' He stroked the cats head. 'We like it up here, don't we girl?' The black cat purred in response.

Sophie detected an underlying tone, although she did agree the circular room was rather special. 'You sound like you've got problems Matt?'

He gave her question a shake of the head. 'Only one and before you start thinking wild thoughts, you are not the problem. I wished that we had exchanged numbers only I've been wanting to call you all week.'

Sophie felt relaxed in the lamp room and it was just as Matt had said, it had good vibes. 'So the call about your sister, was it bad news?'

Matt nodded. 'Sometime during the night my sister escaped from Ashburton Hospital and anybody living around here will know that the old Victorian hospital houses patients with psychiatric problems. Anna is a big problem and she could be heading this way anytime soon.'

'So what's wrong with your sister Matt?'

Matt hung his head low as he described the condition. 'Anna suffers a delusional personality problem and she wants to have sex with me, whenever, wherever. Anna has an idiosyncratic belief that we are meant for one another. Obviously, I've rejected any suggestion or physical involvement, but that leads to acts of sudden aggression and violence.' He paused before going on. 'The last time Anna attacked me physically I ended up in hospital having treatment for a head wound. Anna was arrested, assessed at the police station then sectioned. She was supposed to be on a secure ward. She is several months in on her treatment programme. The problem is Anna is dangerous and without her medication, there's no telling what she might do.'

Sophie gently put down her coffee mug before she placed a supportive hand on his forearm. 'That's extremely sad to hear about your sister Matt, will she be alright?'

He shrugged. 'Anna is resourceful, she'll manage. What concerns me most Sophie is that Anna can be so very unpredictable. She followed me here from Holland virtually blackmailing me into helping and putting a roof over her head. When I came home from work I was wary of what I would find. Anna suffers mood swings, which can vary from hour to hour.'

She squeezed his arm a little tighter. 'A little bit like Jane.' Sophie tried to lighten the tension. 'And you think that she'll come here?' she asked.

Matt raised his head. 'That's a distinct possibility. I had to find you before we went to the dance tonight and explain about Anna.'

'And you think that would stop us being friends?' she asked.

Matt shook his head, suggesting it wouldn't. He told her about the relationship with Helga and how she had run off with Johan, with Anna's persistent intervention. He told Sophie about how their biological parents had not wanted them because having children interfered with their professional careers. He told her how without the love of their grandparents, neither he nor Anna would have survived their younger years.

'I feel that as the older sibling, I am responsible for Anna.'

Sophie however wasn't entirely in agreement.

'The weight of responsibility can only be carried so far along the blood line Matt and there comes a time when Anna must sort out her own life and problems.'

Surprisingly he laughed. 'That's what Rosie keeps telling me!'

The laugh had somehow broken through the tension in the air. Sophie was pleased that Matt had the confidence to confide in her. She joined in the laughter making Rosie lift her head. She stroked the cat affectionately and Rosie moved to sit on her lap.

'Do you still hear from your parents?' She asked. It made her sad that they had rejected both son and daughter for the sake of work. How could anybody abandon two small children? The thought made her shudder.

'No. My father is a teacher in a well-known Dutch school on the outskirts of Amsterdam and our mother is the Matron of a hospital near to where my father works.'

He stared into the mug looking at the murky colour of the coffee.

'Despite saying that neither Anna nor I were mistakes, they did not want us. As a very young boy I became as confused as Anna suffers now. As children our parents gave the impression to others in the village that we were a well-balanced family, that was until they gave us up for adoption and we were legally given over to our grandparents. No, I have not heard from either my mother or father in years.'

'What about holidays, Christmas, Easter or summertime, did you not see them then, as a young child I mean?'

'No,' Matt shook his head adamantly 'they were like ghosts. Like a spectral enigma they had simply vanished from our lives.' He looked at Sophie, his eyes filled with emotion. 'In some ways it would have been better had they been dead. I really believe that Anna would have coped better. The psychiatrist explained, it could be one of the reasons why she has this fixation on me. Other than our grandparents who were there for us both, I am the only other person with who she associates love and emotional ties.'

He paused to drink the remainder of his coffee.

'I suppose, as the older brother I should have seen the signs. As young teenagers we would go skinny-dipping, nude swimming in the river nearby during the summer evenings or early autumn. Holland is a very free thinking country. It never occurred to me that my sister saw our going naked as something else. I have never touched my sister Sophie, never.' She believed him.

'Later as we grew that much older I stopped going swimming and that is when the problems began. Anna would come to my room and tell me that she was frightened of the dark. We ended up sleeping in the same room, only I would let her have my bed as I slept on the floor. Anna has the distinct ability to disassociate and attach herself almost at will.'

Sophie was beginning to get the picture. Getting involved with Matt however could put her life in danger. With Rosie on her lap she wondered if it was best to call a halt to the friendship before it went too far.

'You've talked about it affected Anna, how did the abandonment affect you Matt?'

Matt looked startled. It was probably the first time anybody had ever considered asking, not even the doctors at the hospital had asked.

'If you are asking, am I about to be committed to Ashburton Grange for similar problems, then then answer would be no and you've nothing to worry about Sophie.'

Matt got up momentarily and walked over to the window.

'I think losing both parents emotionally so young made it possible for me to make the adjustment in my mind. In a way I mentally shut down and compartmentalised the detachment between reality and what might have been. I still have emotions, can still be hurt like any other person, but I'm more guarded now.'

Sophie wondered if he would do the same if she ended the friendship, there was a side to Matt that she didn't know. She studied him as he looked out at the waves below. The experience must have hurt him badly, but he was good at hiding it.

'And your ex-fiancé,' she asked, 'how did Anna help destroy the relationship?'

Sophie needed to know only to be forewarned was forearmed.

'To begin with, odd pieces of jewellery, pieces that I had got Hela started to disappear. Later I learnt that had been pawned away by Anna. Then on another occasion Helga would detect an unfamiliar scented perfume on my pillow, which was definitely not Helga's. Helga would begin an argument and let her imagination run wild, accusing me of all sort of clandestine affairs, wondering what I was doing in the bedroom and with whom whilst she was at work. The last big argument was when she found a pair of knickers in the laundry basket, a pair that didn't belong to her. Helga threw me out of the bedroom that we shared and I moved into the spare room despite my pleas of innocence.

'Distancing herself from me entirely Helga met Johan and they started to meet on a regular basis initially at lunchtimes. Soon after that however, her loyalty to me had waned and instead Helga had become close and trusting of Johan. Inevitably becoming his lover, Anna had secretly taken pictures of them together in the bedroom without their knowing. One day I returned home to find copies of the photographs plastered all over my studio wall. I knew then that the end had finally arrived.

'Johan came to see me towards the end because being who I am, a big man and strong he feared that I might hurt Helga.' He looked into Sophie's eyes. 'I have never hurt a living thing, human or animal and I most certainly would never hurt a woman. I moved out that night and two days later I found myself on the ferry sailing across the sea to England. That was the one part of my sister's plan that she had not banked on.'

With Rosie still on her lap Sophie sensed that the cat was tense listening to him describe his sister.

Matt continued. 'My journey took me to a place called Dundown Abbey, where I started all over again. The people were very friendly and happy to accept a stranger that was not of their shore and in England I discovered two things that I needed badly, peace and the promise of a better life.

'Ironically though, it's strange how a vision of contentment can quickly turn into an unexpected nightmare. At first everything was ideal, but soon small complications started to materialise in the shape of lonely women, dissatisfied housewives that came looking for a good time to reinvent their marriage. When their husbands were hard at work they would come calling at my workshop, not to admire the pieces that I had crafted, but to fill the void in their life. I found myself having to move on a regular basis. The lighthouse however is my last move. Should I encounter any similar problems then I will head back home to Holland.'

Sophie whistled low. 'Boy am I glad that I showed an interest in your work on our first meeting.'

Matt smiled. He was glad that she had taken the explanation in good heart.

'And Anna, I take it that she wasn't around when these lonely housewives came knocking.'

'Thankfully not, not least at Dundown Abbey.' He gave a shake of his head as the thoughts flowed through his mind. 'That would have been a complete disaster and especially for the women of the village. Evil becomes Anna. Following close on my heels she first appeared as I moved into Ashburton Grange. It didn't take her long before she was interfering again in my life.

'She would come along to rugby practice to make sure that there wasn't any interested females standing on the side-lines. The same went for reporters or scouts. They were fine if they were men, but women of a certain age, young and attractive women were in danger of crossing her path. Carlos, my art agent has told me countless times to get rid of her, but it is has never been easy getting rid of Anna.'

Looking down at his empty mug, he asked. 'Would you like another?'

Sophie politely refused stating that too much liquid swimming around inside would possibly mar the evening. He smiled and went on.

'The family doctor tried to help prescribing depression tablets, but they only made Anna's moods seemingly more unstable. One night she disappeared and went missing for two days. She was found by the police under a disused railway bridge having slashed her wrists and taken an overdose. At the hospital her wounds were stitched and bandaged and her stomach was pumped. When she regained consciousness she told the police that the reason that she had wanted to end her life was because I had sexually assaulted her. Subsequently, I was arrested and questioned overnight until the family doctor intervened and cleared my name.'

Sophie looked shocked. 'That wasn't in the least bit funny!'

Matt nodded in agreement.

'She attacked me when my back was turned. The police released me realising that her story was purely fabricated. It was after the attack that the psychiatrist had her sectioned under the mental health act. Anna was sent to Ashburton Mental Hospital for an indefinite period. The call earlier with news of her escape doesn't exactly fill me joy.'

Sophie moved closer to be next to Matt who had half expected her to get up and leave. 'Skeletons in the cupboard, I think you English say.'

Sophie scoffed. 'We each have them Matt and I've got my fair share, believe me. Maybe not as bad as yours, but they're still there and come back to haunt every so often.'

'That is why I came into town this afternoon to look for you before we went to the dance.' He didn't elaborate.

'If Anna turns up here, will you let her stay?'

Matt's eyes were set full of determination. 'Most definitely not. If she comes here, she's going straight back to the hospital with the police.'

'There's one question that I do need to ask Matt and it might seem a little insensitive, but I need to know, did you ever…?'

He gently placed a fingertip over her lips so that he could complete the sentence. 'No, we never had consensual sex and I have never made any such advances towards my sister. Does that put your mind at ease?'

Sophie placed her hand over the back of his. 'I wasn't judging you Matt, I just needed to ask.'

'I understand and I would have asked the same question had it been the other way round. So I haven't frightened you off then?'

'No, not unless you decide to dance with anyone else this evening.'

She leant over and kissed his cheek telling him that she needed to get back home as time was pressing on and that she needed a long soak in the bath. With time left to apply her makeup and slip into something special. Having seen his shirt hanging in the kitchen and the ironing board still up she guessed that he also had things left to do.

Sophie gently eased Rosie from her lap moving her into the sunshine. She kissed the back of the cats head adding. 'See you soon.' Rosie raised her head up in acknowledgement.

Sophie asked to be dropped near to where Matt had found her earlier so that she could finish collecting some bits before she went back home. She was about to get out of the Chevy when Matt suddenly reached across and took hold of her hand.

'Thanks Sophie, I somehow knew that you would understand. I promise later, at the dance I'll dance with nobody but you!'

Chapter Thirteen

The long soak in the bath should have been enjoyable, but after a while the water had lost its heat and appeal. Taking out the plug Sophie let the water drain away. Looking at the lone reflection in the mirror she was apprehensive about the dance despite Matt's assurance that nothing bad would take place.

Going over various possibilities in her mind she was not keen on having an encounter with somebody who was supposed to be on medication and had just escaped the mental hospital. In the safety of her bathroom the gloss of the occasion had become tarnished. Anna Van Janssen had become a complication that Sophie hadn't reckoned upon.

Using her fist she rubbed clear the condensation from the mirror.

'You sure can pick em' Sophie Sprigg,' she told herself, towelling her body dry. She did think about phoning Jane and asking her advice, but she dismissed the idea wanting to give Dave and Jane time to sort through their problems before they left the house.

Inspecting first the knickers and then the bra she gave both items one final check before removing the price tag. The black lace set was racy, although very classic. She found herself looking in the mirror and smiling. Perhaps this is what Jane had meant about her being living a little. There was also something mysteriously charismatic about the underwear that she found to be compelling. Slipping into the bra and pulling up the knickers she took a long admiring look at herself in the full-length mirror, making a minor adjustment to the bra strap. Looking again, she liked what she saw.

'I'm wearing these for you Matthew Van Janssen, you had better damn well appreciate them!' she muttered to herself.

Padding through to the bedroom she was eager to finish dressing and getting ready. Unzipping the back of the dress she stepped in and pulled the straps up and over her shoulders before reaching behind and securing the back. Jane was right it not only looked good on, but she felt good in it. With a sigh she was convinced. 'Time to put your fears to bed Sophie Sprigg and knock them dead.' She allowed herself a twirl of satisfaction. 'This had better work.' She said, punching the air.

Sophie smiled at herself, if only her mother could see her now, she would say how beautiful she was, gasping in awe at her daughter. Maybe, thought Sophie it was as well that she didn't know about the underwear. It had been a long time since Sophie had worn anything so new or exciting.

Applying just a hint of mascara she puckered a line of red rouge to her lips before painting on a thin veil of lip gloss. It would help prevent the lipstick from melting under the dance floor lights and add volume to her lips. Dreamily her thoughts were of Matt, later he could remove both if he so desired. Sitting herself at the white antique dressing table she chose her perfume, something subtle, slightly fragment although not anything overpowering. She was about done when Jane called.

'I've been pacing the floor all afternoon wondering if and when you would ring me Sprigg, only I need to know what happened after I left you.'

Sophie apologised. 'I'm sorry, I did intended calling, but time seemed to just run away in the opposite direction and before you knew it I still had to bath, dress and finish off.' She paused momentarily. 'Besides which, I really didn't want to interrupt you or Dave before you left for the clubhouse.'

'And what precisely would we have been doing,' Jane replied 'the kids are downstairs remember.'

'I meant that you might be talking things through or sorting your problems in the normal way!'

Jane chuckled. 'If we have sex Sprigg there's little ever conversation, we just... oh, look never mind about me, what happened with you when I left?'

'Nothing like what you think Jane.'

Sophie heard the sigh of exasperation from the other end of the line followed by silence.

'Go on, tell me why I picked up all the wrong signals?'

'Matt needed to tell me about some things that had happened in the past, to explain certain family matters and why he left Holland for England closely followed by his sister.'

'Oh... you mean the loony one!' Jane specified.

Sophie was almost floored by the revelation. 'You knew,' she replied, the vexation catching in her throat.

'Sure, she came up in conversation at the dinner table a few months back. Dave and Matt had been talking after a match about his sister. Matt told Dave that he went through a bad spell as a result of the scatty cow going ape-shit. She was arrested after assaulting Matt and a couple of police officers and she's now nicely banged up in a secure ward at Ashburton Manor.'

'Not any longer she isn't,' replied Sophie 'she escaped sometime during the night!'

'Fucking hell,' Jane muttered, letting out a low whistle 'then that is bad news.'

'Is she really as wild and dangerous as he describes her to be?' Sophie asked.

'That and some,' Jane responded. 'Dave told me that Matt's home was trashed before the police arrived and carted her off. During the arrest she attacked a policewoman then a male colleague. It took four of them to drag her away from Matt. He was unconscious at the time of the arrest. Apparently she has a personality problem with a serious aversion against women.'

Sophie sighed and nodded to herself, it was just as Matt had described.

'Do you want a gun?' Jane asked. Sophie believed that Jane was being serious. 'Only Dave has two locked away in the cabinet out back in the garage!'

'Whatever does he keep guns at the house for Jane?' Sophie was intrigued as Jane had never mentioned any firearms before.

'Shooting you daft mare, what do you think. Dave belongs to the Cockleshell Gun Club. He and some mates go out at weekends, normally early morning either Saturday or Sunday to bag some rabbit, pheasant or the odd fox, if a local farmer has a problem.'

'No, thank you, I definitely do not need a gun.' Sophie was horrified that anybody could shoot defenceless animals. 'I think that I could handle Anna if she turned up at my door.'

Jane however wasn't so sure. 'Tread carefully Sprigg, this is one sister of a boyfriend not to be messed with. Anna Van Janssen is like an untamed wildcat when she gets going.'

Jane sprayed perfume onto her neck and behind her ears. 'So did he mention the ex-fiancé?'

'Is there anything about Matt and his family that you don't know about?'

'Only that Matt was engaged before he landed on our shoreline, although it's old hat now Sprigg, but it still makes good listening when coming from the horse's mouth. So what about it,' Jane prompted 'is there anything new that I don't know?'

'Only that his fiancé did the dirty on him and went off with another man, on account of the involvement by his sister.' Sophie didn't want to go into too much detail becoming aware of the time.

'And that took all afternoon to discuss?' There was a hint of scepticism in Jane's tone.

'Family matters can be very private and painful as we both know. It probably hurt telling me!'

'Ouch - thirty all,' accepted Jane. 'Sorry Sprigg, I was just being nosey.'

'No, it's not you, it's me Jane.' Admitted Sophie. 'I'm all scrubbed up, ready and look glamorous, but I've serious reservations about going. Matt assures me that Anna is not going to turn up and yet I have this niggly sensation deep in the pit of my stomach which tells me that she's already there. The problem is I don't even know what she looks like.'

Jane was surprised to hear Sophie be so cautious. Her best friend was reserved and sometimes unchallenging, but there was something else. 'Matt, he's got to you hasn't he,' Jane asked 'and it doesn't really have anything to do with Anna, his sister, does it?

'Yes, I suppose he has got to me and in a way that I didn't expect. No, it's not really about Anna. I'm confused Jane. I just wanted a carefree relationship and once again I've walked into a minefield.'

'The important factor here Sprigg is where exactly do you want to go from here?' This was one of Jane's serious moments.

'I'm not really sure Jane. One minute I want him really bad and the next I have moments of doubt, only I can't figure out why.'

Jane laughed although it was almost a whisper.

'And you don't think that I didn't have the same thoughts before I went out with Dave. Men have this knack of doing things to your mind Sprigg, things that confuse us. It's what they do best. Women have moods depending on the time of the month, whereas men just swing back and forth between the known and unknown. That's what makes them infuriating at times. Why do you think god gave them a set of two testicles, not just to help with their balance when standing, but because without them they wouldn't be able to cope, think or make a decision.'

Sophie was still confused. 'And how does that help me?'

Jane laughed again. 'It doesn't and that's where the confusion arises. They hold us spellbound sometimes, whilst they swing indecisively between maybe and possibly not. Many's the time that I have had to push Dave into taking decisive action or have him take the lead. Men have different characteristic traits to us Sprigg. Why do you think a lot of them refer to a situation *as bollocks* it's because they are having difficulty arriving at a satisfactory conclusion?'

'I thought they had a set because it helped with their sperm count!'

Jane exhaled. 'That too, although why then do they spend so much time fiddling with them. It's not looking for inspiration. Biology taught me one thing and that was that it only takes one of those little buggers to swim upstream, latch onto us and produce a lifetime of hell and responsibility. Men could easily do without half of what they carry around. If they did their brains wouldn't keep hurting so much!'

Sophie chuckled. 'I don't think of Matt like that,' she replied, defending his manhood.

'Believe me Sprigg when I say that no man is any different to the next, muscles or no muscles. They might be handsome and have a gorgeously toned physique or be like my old man and have most of his body under his chest heading south. Underneath that exterior ego they're all the same.'

Sophie found Jane's expressive descriptions so amusing, she also had an answer for everything.

'Talking of heading south, how's the underwear?' asked Jane.

Sophie wriggled her backside on the chair of the dressing table. 'Stylish, but the knickers are flossing my backside!'

'Well there's a quick remedy. If they irritate that much don't wear any.' Jane suggested.

Sophie sensed the horror of anything happening and she being examined without underwear. She had this discerning vision of having her clothes cut away by a paramedic or doctor in casualty. 'We're not all like you Jane Aldridge, some of us still have some dignity left.'

Jane was quick to respond. 'To hell with dignity, sometimes a little of the unknown is what keeps a man interested.'

Sophie stood up to take another look at herself in the mirror. 'Do you know, I'm not sure that this dress isn't see through?'

Jane felt her sanity being stretched. 'For fucks sake Sprigg will you stop with the apprehension all the time - you're going to a bloody dance to lead a horse to water. Get Matt to the trough and he wouldn't care if you're wearing your grandma's best string corset or a silk thread.'

There was a silent pause before Jane continued. 'Even if the dress is see through who really cares as it will only be Matt that gets to touch the goods and think of the competition in the room Sprigg. Christ half them will be dashing to the bathroom to remove their underwear if they think it will help.' Jane shuddered at the thought. 'It wouldn't be a pretty sight neither, saggy tits and arses, they'd look a consignment of lumpy potatoes!'

Sophie took another look at herself, she was definitely nothing like a bag of King Edwards.

'I suppose you're right only stick close in case I need help.'

'Who from Matt or loony tunes?'

'The competition,' replied Sophie. 'Did you know that Anna accused Matt of assaulting her?'

'No, I didn't hear that.'

'Luckily the family doctor was there to help and clear Matt of any criminal charges.'

'I'll stick close, don't worry Sprigg.' Jane said reassuringly. 'The sister sounds like she fabricates a good story to get her own way. One thing, are you sure that after tonight you want to get involved?'

Sophie didn't rightly know. 'My head is saying one thing and my heart another.'

'Then you've got a decision to make before midnight.'

'You make it sound like I'll turn into a pumpkin if I don't.'

'I'm just saying that's all. Think about the future seriously Sprigg, only it's a long term commitment and so far your track record has limited experience. Shagged by a Frenchman who buggered off back to the arms of another woman and now we've a Dutchman on the horizon who has a not-all-together sister. What's wrong with a nice local lad?'

'The problem is that they've all been taken.' Replied Sophie.

Jane liked what she knew and had seen of Matt, but she was also wary that good looks could be deceiving.

'Okay, then I suggest that you let the evening sort itself and if it's meant to be then karma will intervene. Just remember Sprigg that half the room will be occupied by a pack of rugby players should Anna Van Janssen turn up. I'm sure that they can sort any trouble.'

From the floor below Dave called out and asked if Jane was nearly ready. She replied asking for another minute more then she would be down.

'At least it sounds like you're talking?'

'Yeah, I'm trying to give Dave the benefit of the doubt, but we'll see. I have a feeling that this dance is going to be full of surprises. Listen Sprigg I gotta go, are you going to be alright getting to the clubhouse?'

'Yes, I'm fine, it's not far from the shop so I can walk it.'

'Isn't Matt picking you up?'

'He didn't say that he would.'

Jane shook her head in dismay. 'I'll get Dave to come across and pick you up.'

Sophie again expressed that she would be alright to get to the clubhouse stating Matt could drop her back after the dance.

Jane eventually relented. 'Alright, only be careful and we'll see you there.'

Sophie ended the call stating she needed the bathroom and had to adjust her knickers which were cutting in, she didn't say how.

Ten minutes later there was an unexpected knock at the door. Sophie walked through the hallway armed with a wooden rolling pin. Tentatively pulling open the front door with her foot against the back panel she was confronted by an Arab standing in the porch.

'Are you Miss Spligg?' he enquired, his smile encrusted with tobacco stained teeth. 'I am Rakeesh your driver!' Idling behind and beyond the front gate was a silver coloured saloon with a magnetic printed logo stuck to the door panel.

Dropping the rolling pin drop discreetly behind the door Sophie looked puzzled. 'I haven't ordered a cab?'

'No, you not order Miss Spligg. Another lady, she call Asif in the office and say to pick you up at seven thirty.' He checked the time on his Mickey Mouse watch. 'It is time now, yes!' From his trouser pocket he took out a scrap of paper which he showed to Sophie. 'Look, you see, Rakeesh make no mistake. Asif take call from Mrs Allwitch.'

'Aldridge, its Mrs Aldridge.' Sophie corrected.

'Yes, that right - Allwitch. I wait in car for you to get things and when you ready we go to the rugby club, yes?'

Sophie smiled telling Rakeesh that she would be down in a minute. She closed the door and went back upstairs to collect a shawl and her handbag. She would accept the cab rather than stand at the door and have a pointless argument. If Jane had ordered the taxi in good heart it was the least that she could do to turn up safe.

Adding a final splash of perfume on her wrists Sophie dropped the crystal bottle into her clutch bag. She took a deep breath, looking out at the evening sky where the sun had almost disappeared leaving in its wake a new moon.

'Go change your destiny Sophie Sprigg,' she whispered, before descending the stairs.

In the back seat of the taxi she watched Rakeesh as he manoeuvred the vehicle between the narrow streets, the journey would take less than five minutes by car. Sophie could so easily have walked, but Jane was right and Anna could be lurking anywhere.

Parking the car as close as he could get to the clubhouse entrance Sophie noticed Matt's rusty blue Chevy. She thanked Rakeesh and offered to pay the fare, but he pointed to the clubhouse where Dave Aldridge was stood waiting. Rakeesh prophesised a good night ahead telling her that it was a very good night for romance.

Chapter Fourteen

Dave Aldridge kissed Sophie on the cheek smelling the scent of her perfume.

'You look amazing,' he declared, as he reached for his wallet. 'If things don't work out with Matt tonight, I'll leave Jane and run away with you, preferably to a desert island!'

Sophie smiled as he paid the taxi driver with a ten pound note telling him to keep the change. Rakeesh supplied a receipt and waved goodbye to Sophie as he put the car into reverse. She felt embarrassed knowing that apart from the shoes on her feet Dave had paid for everything else that she had on.

'I wish you would let me pay you for the cab,' she said, unclipping the catch of her clutch bag. He lay his hand over her wrist.

'No bother Sprigg, we use Rakeesh and his firm all the time. We have an agreement. They supply us with a blank receipt and we fill in the details. It leaves Rakeesh happy because he gets a good tip and the tax man is none the wiser.'

Sophie thanked him. Dave and Jane were good friends, but like two peas in a pod they were ideally suited to one another. Sophie hated to think of them at loggerheads with one another.

'Matt's already here,' Dave said, pointing at the entrance 'although I think he needs rescuing soon, only the peroxide bottle brigade are crowding his space.'

'Then I had best get inside before the fight starts.' Sophie kissed his cheek again and gave him a quick hug for good measure. 'You know Dave, Jane loves you like crazy, she always has.'

'I know,' he solemnly replied, 'and I feel the same about Jane. It's just that I've had to do something for myself recently Sophie, something that involved a search for self-respect. I promise you that I am not over the side as Jane thinks. When she finds out what I've been doing, it will come as a big surprise.'

Sophie wasn't amused to think that Jane had been fretting for nothing.

'Well, what the hell was the thing with the marriage guidance councillor then?'

Dave Aldridge raised his palms in his defence. 'I didn't think it would get to that,' he sighed, 'that part, I hadn't banked on happening.'

'Take some advice Dave and tell Jane the truth tonight, otherwise the hole that you've dug for yourself could take some serious filling!'

Sophie looked for a reaction, pleased to see that what she had advised had sunk in. Dave looked seriously worried. Whatever he had been up too had obviously backfired and not gone quite to plan. Sophie felt obliged as a friend to help.

'You have to admit that you've been acting really odd Dave and not coming home until late?'

'I had too Sophie and it was part of what I've been doing. Believe me when I tell you that I've done it for Jane and the kids.'

Sophie bit her bottom lip. 'Jane needs an explanation this evening Dave and whole heap of reassurance. I have never seen or heard her so low. It's not fair to put her or the kids through this torment!'

Dave Aldridge nodded, his head was hung low.

'I am innocent Sophie, please believe it, you know me. Sometimes, I just go about things in the wrong manner. I would never hurt Jane or our children, they are my life.'

Sophie squeezed his arm to show that she cared.

'Okay, only no more secrets, not now or ever after tonight. Jane's my best friend and a faithful wife. You would have a hard job finding another like her Dave.'

'Always the peacemaker,' he smiled, 'do us a favour Sprigg and never change.' The expression on his face suggested that he could explode if he didn't tell his secret soon.

'Maybe,' she nodded in response, 'although it all depends on the man.' She turned to head over to the door. 'Now I had best go and rescue my knight from the fair haired maidens inside.'

Dave Aldridge watched her walk towards the door. Sophie was stunningly beautiful, gentle and kind. The kind of woman any man would be proud to introduce to his mother and father as a prospective daughter-in-law. Matthew Van Janssen was indeed a lucky man. Suddenly remembering that he was due behind the bar he called out after Sophie.

'Hey Sprigg, hang about. I'm working the bar tonight and it's strictly a tee-total session for me so in case Matt can't take you home. Jane and I will, okay?'

Sophie waved back indicating that she had understood. 'Thanks, I'll keep you posted!'

She disappeared through the clubhouse door where a bulb had blown in the lobby. Emerging from the shadows Jane stepped forward.

'So what did he have to say for himself?' she asked, dragging Sophie into the ladies toilet where the illumination was better. Stood against the sink basins and applying an extra layer of lipstick were three bottle blondes. They left a moment later after adjusting the straps of their dresses and heaving up their silicone false chests. Jane and Sophie watched them leave.

'Dave assures me that he's not over the side and that whatever he's been up too, he'll come clean tonight!'

Jane would have been suspicious had she not heard it from Sophie.

'Right, I won't keep you long, not now that they've applied more war paint. They'll be heading back to the bar where Matt is keeping audience!'

'Dave told me that you'll be surprised when he tells you!'

Jane unclenched her hands feeling the tension ebb for a moment. 'Well the explanation had better be *fucking* good and physical because we hardly spoke on the way here.' She suddenly took a step back. 'By the way Sprigg you look absolutely stunning. It's no wonder that my husband was spluttering around you like a lemon.'

Jane wiped the anxious moisture from under her chin.

Sophie gave her best friend a hug. 'Give him a little more time and he'll come up trumps Jane, we both know Dave of old.'

'He has until midnight otherwise I turn into the devil and take the kids to live with my mother. He might not be involved with somebody, but I need to know what he's been doing Sprigg. The not knowing is knotting my insides like a *fucking* octopus caught in a dizzy underwater fit.'

'Trust me Jane.' Sophie replied, adjusting the back of her knickers between her cheeks. 'He'll spill all later.'

Jane walked over to the sinks where she dabbed some cold water down her front and let the cooling effect disappear between her cleavage.

'If you do snag Matt this evening Sprigg, get that hook in deep and good. The old trout's at the bar are hovering around him like raw bait just waiting for him to drop his guard. Sex alone is bait enough to woman like that. They don't want any commitment, just a good time.'

'Don't you ever think of anything else?' Sophie nodded.

'What else is there as interesting to occupy a girls mind,' Jane replied. She actually smiled, the first since she had arrived.

'The tedium of changing beds, washing the laundry and preparing the dinner each and every day is hardly the highlight of a woman's life. We either fantasise or go window shopping. You've a lot to learn girl.' Jane turned back to the sinks. 'Don't worry Sprigg, whatever the reason, be it good or bad, my old man's gonna pay for his secrecy. Come on let's go,' she said, pulling on Sophie's arm 'let's go and rescue Matt.'

The room with the dance floor and bar was far larger than Sophie had expected and the lights had been dimmed low. On the outer edge of the wooden parquet floor the tables had been arranged with fresh linen and candles. It was nothing like a rugby clubhouse.

'Goodness Jane, Matt's knee deep in admirers.' Sophie held onto Jane's arm, stopping her from walking forward. 'What should I do?'

'Get in there Sprigg and box clever.' Jane advised. 'That lot are nothing compared to you. They're only botox, peroxide, silicone implants and sagging arses where gravity has taken over. The only thing that keeps them together is catalogue ordered stretched Lycra.' She yanked Sophie's arm. 'Come on fun time!'

Weaving their way through the crowd Sophie was pushed ahead of Jane and with one final thrust she arrived to stand in front of Matt. Instantly, he pushed himself away from the bar and the women clambering at his side. He let forth a low meaningful whistle. 'Wow, the star of the evening has arrived!'

On either side there were grunts of envy and ungracious insinuations, but a single glare from Jane put an instant halt to anything else from taking place. Standing before Matt, Sophie turned on the spot so that he could see all.

Smiling and ignoring the women at the bar Sophie sensed the hostility, but Jane was as promised at her side. She also had Matt's fullest attention. Approvingly he kissed her on the cheek. 'You look absolutely fabulous, amazing Sophie!'

She wanted to punch the air, but she resisted.

With a gnash of teeth, jaws set hard and defeated before the battle had even begun the women began to disperse looking for other prey propping up the bar, a lot less attractive and possibly with not as much to offer as Matthew Van Janssen, but anything was better than nothing.

Coming in close so that she could whisper in his ear, she said. 'The dress was bought with you in mind.'

Matt had not looked left, right or ahead as the women surrounding him had departed, his focus was solely on Sophie.

'You're really beautiful.' He said as he took her hand.

Sophie chuckled. 'Was that not the case the day that I fell head first into the rock pool?' she asked.

'Different,' he replied 'but just as stunning.'

It was the right response and made Jane smile. Matt kissed her on the cheek. 'And that's for earlier!'

'Earlier what?' Jane asked.

'For taking Sophie shopping with you and being discreet when I turned up.'

Jane felt a trickle of perspiration disappear between her breasts. Matt was certainly hot property and under the dim lighting his eyes were like that of a wolf, hungry and inviting. 'Perhaps one day I'll recall a favour in return!'

'Mark it up on your calendar and I'll do whatever!' he replied.

Sophie grinned as she looked into Jane's mind. Matt had no idea what the favour was that was going through Jane's thoughts.

Spotting Dave loitering near the entrance Jane made an excuse to leave them alone as she headed across the dance floor. At the table nearest the door was a woman, young and attractive. She had engaged Dave in conversation. Approaching Jane was instantly aware of the woman's low cut dress which left nothing to the imagination. Like a red rag to a bull the female saw Jane coming.

Next to the bar Sophie and Matt had followed Jane with their eyes. They too saw the woman.

'Now the war is about to start,' Sophie whispered to Matt. Perhaps we should be close by just in case we're needed?'

Guiding her discretely across the dance floor Matt made sure that Sophie wasn't jostled especially by some of the women who had found partners and were up and dancing. They took up a clear space near where they could offer assistance should it become necessary.

Matt pulled Sophie in close and slowly they moved together to the beat of the music, their eyes glued to Jane's back.

Sophie felt the upsurge of physical heat as it slowly began to ascend her body. The more that Matt moved her around the edge of the dance floor the more the shimmer of light from the disco made Sophie's dress transparent. She was unaware of the attention that it was causing as Jane made her move.

Chapter Fifteen

Grabbing Dave by the arm Jane smiled superciliously at the woman sitting at the table near the door. In the next moment she yanked Dave away *'come on you we need to talk!'*

Sandra Wareham looked slightly bemused as they left the room.

'Should we follow?' Matt asked.

'No, I think giving them some time alone will help sort their differences in a manner only they can.'

Sophie looked across at the table occupied by the attractive brunette who had been talking to Dave. She thought she recognised the woman only she couldn't think where she had seen her last.

In the carpark outside the stars were now out in force. Knowing what was about to take place Dave Aldridge got in first before Jane could launch herself into a verbal tirade. He wanted to begin by saying how beautiful she looked in the moonlight, but he had the good sense to realise that she wasn't in the right mood to be complemented.

'Before you even ask, the woman at the table is a friend and nothing more.' He held up his hands to placate the onslaught. 'Give me a moment Jane and I'll explain everything.'

'You've got two minutes Dave Aldridge and it had better be *fucking* good otherwise your nuts will be a trophy on the club gate!'

He did think of going closer, but Jane wasn't sending out the right vibes for anything intimate, not just yet, maybe later.

'Everything that I have ever done in our marriage Jane has been for you and the kids, don't you realise that?'

'What like sneaking off after dinner and not coming home until late, a little suspicious wouldn't you think. Even the kids have started asking where daddy is going and then when you do come home you smell like a bloody haddock. If the old girl at the fish shop wasn't knocking on I would swear blind that you were having it off with her in the stock room.'

Releasing the knot of his tie he unbuttoned the top of his shirt. 'Christ almighty Jane give me some credit for choice, Barbara Dunton is knocking on twice my age. The brunette that you saw me having a conversation with is Sandra Wareham, the clinician nurse from the Heedham Surgery.

Sandra is a registered trainer for the emergency responder unit in Heedham and because of her specialist knowledge she helps out at the lifeboat station. There have been no clandestine liaisons behind the sheds unless you consider mouth-to-mouth with a rubber dummy intimate. Sandra has been helping me get up to speed as a lifeboatman. I would have thought after all these years together you would know that I would never consider kissing any other woman except you.'

Jane's eyes widened the same time as she puffed out her cheeks. 'You a volunteer crewman for the lifeboat.' Dave had for once managed to take the wind out of her sails.

'I love you and the kids Jane more than I love my own life. My midlife crisis that dragged us to a marriage guidance councillor was because I suddenly saw myself as a couch potato. I needed to improve my health, regain my fitness levels and prove to you, Annabelle and Scott that I was worth having around for a few more years.

'When you get to my age a man suddenly sits back, takes stock of his life and what the future has to hold. Being healthy, fit and being around for his family becomes a major priority. Sandra has been putting me through my paces and given me a new lease of life. Now, I'm all those things again.

'Yes, we are co-owners of a successful engineering company, but sometimes there are other interests that need to be achieved in a man's life, like being part of a coastal lifeboat crew.'

Stepping forward he took his chance gently covering her hand with his. Jane didn't resist.

'Throwing a peculiar shaped ball around a pitch every Saturday afternoon with a group of men more interested in being in the bar after the match and high on testosterone was never going to float my boat forever and fulfil the ambitions that I had.

'Do you remember several months back you accused me of putting on weight and not looking after myself?' he asked, but Jane only replied by nodding. 'You told me that I owed it you and the kids to get myself fighting fit again. Perhaps you've not noticed lately, mainly because you've been asleep when I've come home, but I have toned up and lost weight.'

Jane pushed her fist gently into his solar plexus, coming against a wall of toned muscle. Dave was like he had been when they had first got married. She liked it.

'It wasn't until I took the kids to the beach one Sunday morning that I saw the solution. When the lifeboat hit the water I suddenly realised what I had to do. Sandra Wareham was the last stage of my training to tick all the boxes. The other night I was signed fit to join the crew by the coxswain and ready to do battle with the sea.'

Jane Aldridge stood before her husband with tears streaming down her cheeks, the weeks of uncertainty finally opening up the floodgates of emotion. She crashed against him throwing her arms around his back finding his mouth with hers. Dave responded by pulling her in tight feeling her breasts mould against his chest, they were good together. Had always been good together. Lower down his erection was already pushing against her groin.

'Fuck Aldridge this night can't go soon enough, when we get home I'm gonna fuck your brains out. I'll give you put me through hell like that.'

She suddenly pulled away sufficient to hit left arm. 'Look at what you've done. My mascara has streaked, my hearts racing and I'm as horny as hell, how am I supposed to go back into the club looking and feeling like this?'

Slipping her hand into his he took her around back of the clubhouse where the storeroom was always left unlocked. Inside there was just sufficient light to see the stacks of rubber matting, crash mats, tackling bars and nets containing practice balls.

Dropping the straps of her dress down over her chest he kissed, sucked and licked her body making his way down to where there was no turning back. With Jane begging him not to stop Dave swept Jane from her feet, gently laying her down on top of the rubber matting. Under the stars they made love like they had never done before. When it was over Jane lay naked caressing her husband, admiring his new body. 'Next time you big dope just tell me what you're doing. I can't stand it being without you!'

'I wanted to be part of something that would make you proud of me again!'

Jane raised her head up from his chest. She thought she caught him crying.

'You bloody fool, you of all people should know by now that the kids and myself are grateful for everything that you have ever done for us. It goes without saying that we are immensely proud of you. Ordinary you are not Dave Aldridge and you never will be.' She kissed him hard. 'I would never have gone round back of the coastguard station had I thought that you were otherwise.'

Jane gently held the last of his erection as it lost impetus. She smiled to herself, he was all hers and always would be.

'But, a member of the lifeboat crew, *fuck* me Dave that's amazing. You wait till the kids hear about it, they'll be over the moon.'

'So now I have two mistresses,' he smiled, 'you and the sea.'

She hit him once again before they embraced holding one another until neither had any air left in their lungs. 'Do you think we should go back inside,' Jane asked, 'only you're supposed to be helping out behind the bar?'

'In a minute,' he replied, 'I'm sure they can manage without me and there's enough of the boys around to help in my absence.'

*****

From inside the darkened lobby Matt and Sophie had watched Jane and Dave talk before kissing then head off between the parked cars going around back where the storeroom was sited.

'I guess we're not needed now,' Matt implied.

With the moon masking her face Sophie put her arms around the small of his back.

'They have previous for going around the back of places. They'll be back when they're done, maybe an hour from now!'

Matt grinned holding onto Sophie. Placing her hands either side of his head she gently pulled him down until their lips collided. Kissing one another she felt his hand slip down the crease of her back and rest upon her right buttock. Feeling the intensity of his desire surging through her own body she held onto his mouth as long as possible.

'You feel really good,' he said, wanting, needing air.

'I'm really pleased that you're satisfied Matt.'

Seeking out her mouth again he kissed her hoping the night would never end.

Chapter Sixteen

The moments alone spent in the lobby were private, passionate and had long been coming. In the shadows they had been missed or ignored by others using the facilities of the cloakroom. Eventually when Sophie and Matt re-joined the dance they looked around, but neither could see Jane or Dave anywhere. When they did eventually join the room there was a tumultuous cheer from the group of men at the bar.

'How do they know?' asked Sophie.

Matt smiled. 'Instinct perhaps.'

Sophie wasn't convinced, but she thought it best left rather than pursue a needless conversation. She watched as Jane spoke with Sandra Wareham and moments later kissed her cheek inviting her over to the bar, signalling to Matt and Sophie that they should also join in.

'You look happy,' Sophie whispered in Jane's ear.

'I am, the result of a fresh breeze passing through the Aldridge household Sprigg. Everything's sorted.'

'Everything?' asked Sophie, noticing the black streaks left by the mascara where Jane had been crying.

'My knickers are in my bag, so everything's sorted and Jesus was it good!'

Jane introduced Sandra Wickham and explained what Sandra had done for Dave. For making her go without sex, sending her to hell and back she made him buy a bottle of champagne so that they could celebrate.

'Do you want to sort your face?' Sophie asked, as they waited for a set of champagne flutes. Jane exhaled long and forcibly.

'No, I'll leave it as it is. Let the old trout's further along the bar wonder why I've crying.' She smiled at Dave as he stood at the bar settling the order. 'If my old man can cry, then so will I.'

It was good to see Jane happy again and her smile, the real genuine Jane smile was back pushing aside the tension lines. From the other side of the dance floor Trudy wanted to know that everything was good by putting up a thumb. Sophie returned the gesture to say that it was.

Jane saw and smiled over at Trudy. 'That dress really is too small for her, if she does the tango with Ben everything will fall out!'

Sophie nodded shaking her head. It was sorted and Jane was back to her normal self. A crisis had somehow been averted again. *'Matt likes what I've got on,'* she whispered in Jane's ear, *'you was right!'*

Jane grinned, 'I told you so. The only one that ever doubts you Sprigg, is you yourself. Have a bit more confidence and push the boat out once in a while. The results can be surprising.' Jane thumbed towards the back of the clubhouse wall. 'Only take my advice, the stockroom out back is okay when you've an urgent need, but in competition with the cobwebs and rubber matting, I would chose a comfortable bed anytime!'

Standing nearby Sandra Wareham nodded and waved as her date arrived, a doctor from the surgery. She excused herself from the group and went over to where he was waiting.

'She heard that,' Sophie chided.

'Sandra's a nurse isn't she,' Jane replied, 'I bet she's seen some action in her time!'

Sophie fanned her hand up and down in front of her face, it was hot in the room. By the bar Dave and Matt heard the two of them laughing. 'What's amusing them?' asked Matt.

'Take a piece of advice Matt, never ask, just look innocent and wonder in silence. It's safer to be ignorant than know!'

'That good eh...?'

Dave smiled. 'As a group we've all known each other a long time, we went to school together. Some time back I learnt my lesson the hard way and since then I stopped asking and according to Jane it's an unwritten law, being a woman's prerogative to ask, only not necessarily the man right.'

'Thanks for the advice.' Matt smiled. 'And Sophie, what would say were her best qualities?'

'Besides having a body to die for and natural good looks. Our Sprigg is a sensitive soul, she loves animals and is the kindest person I know.'

Matt agreed infinitely with everything that Dave had said, knowing how Rosie had instantly taken to Sophie.

When the DJ introduced another slow number Matt slipped his hand into Sophie's. 'Are you enjoying yourself?'

'More than I have for a long time and you?' He kissed her unashamedly full on the lips pulling away only when he knew others were watching.

Excused from bar duties having paid somebody else to stand in for him, Dave pulled Jane onto the dance floor. 'This is to prove that my stamina levels are up again.' She nuzzled in close laying her head on his shoulder with her mouth close to his ear, 'well Tonto don't go burning it all here, because I'm not finished with you and there's more to come when we get home.'

'They look happy now,' Matt observed, returning from having talked with the DJ. Sophie also seemed happy as she grinned, watching Dave and Jane dance together.

'Yes, things are going to be different now. It's funny how a twist of fate can turn around your life.'

'Like taking a friend's dog for a walk along the beach!' he mused.

She playfully dug his ribs. 'That was entirely Ollie's fault and you know that I had no control over where he was heading that day.'

'I'm not complaining, I believe in fate and destiny. Therein lies the mystery of our chosen future.'

'Like the yellow brick road!' Sophie suggested.

'Something like that, I suppose.' He replied.

They joined the dance slowly moving amongst the sway of couples in the centre of the room, bumping against some they knew and others they didn't, not that it mattered. The idea was to have a good time. Around eleven thirty people began to drift away in a waiting convoy of taxis. Dave didn't ask, nodding at Matt, instinctively knowing that he would be taking Sophie home and that she was in safe hands.

The last dance arrived and the DJ announced his next record - *Foreigner - 'I Want to Know What Love Is'* as requested by Matt. Taking Sophie in his arms he held her close with one hand behind her back, slipping his free hand into hers.

'The last dance, as promised,' he said, looking into her eyes.

Chapter Seventeen

With the engine of the Chevy ticking over Matt suddenly turned to Sophie, his eyes appearing darker than normal in the moonlight. He appeared serious.

'This was a really good evening and better than I thought it might be. I would like to invite you back to the lighthouse, but my instinct tells me that that could be tempting fate. With Anna roaming the area, I would never forgive myself if she attacked you and anything happened to you Sophie.'

Sophie felt the knot in her stomach tightening. How could he do this she wondered? He had danced with her, kissed her passionately hinting that more was to come, then at the last stroke before midnight Matt had let her down, not gently, but hard landing with an almighty bump. The landing hurt her pride.

'I thought you wanted me Matt,' she asked, 'that you really wanted me?' She felt the stinging tears welling at the sides of her eyes.

'You've no idea how much,' he replied, 'it's just that I want to give you everything and for it to be a memorable moment, but I can't not with Anna on the prowl. When the time is right, I want to show you just how much you mean to me Sophie. I don't want this to look like it's just about sex.'

He noticed the shiver as it invaded her body beneath her shawl. Slipping off his jacket she let him to put it around her shoulders.

'It's important to us both that you see me for who I really am and not some musclebound, testosterone fuelled rugby player who just picks up a beautiful girl at a dance and takes her home to share breakfast with the next morning. I want a relationship to mean much more!'

Sophie felt her head beginning to spin. The disappointment was so unexpected that she just wanted to get out and run. The evening had been so wonderful, but because of his wayward sister everything had come to a grinding halt. Sophie felt cheated, only she could think clear enough to know by whom, Matt or Anna. All evening she had mentally, physically and even spiritually prepared herself for the night ahead, wanting him to make love to her, to tear the clothes from her body and take her. Suddenly all the doubts that she had experienced in the bathroom that afternoon came flooding back.

She turned to face him.

'If I had considered for one moment Matt that you just wanted me for sex, I would not have turned up tonight, but it's not like that. I have known since that afternoon at the headland when we first met what kind of man you are. As for going back to the lighthouse tonight, I really thought that we would and yes I would have willingly stayed over to share breakfast, but because I chose too.' She looked out of the passenger window to hide her tears. 'Right now, I'm confused, I'm hurting and I would like it very much, if you would please take me home!'

The Chevy rolled slowly forward towards the club gate. Sophie looked up at the stars and scoffed silently to herself. Change her destiny, it had become nothing but a farce. She had a vision in her mind of Dave tearing Jane's clothes from her body and she did the same to him. Together they would have their wild night of passion, but not she, not Sophie Sprigg. Her tears were warm and charged with anger.

Driving through the unlit streets her confusion was mounting and Sophie was ready to call it a day. She resisted the urge to believe that she had been used. 'I'll tell you when to turn left and right, but for the moment just head to the centre of town!' There was no softness to her voice.

Matt sensed the difference in her mood. He had ruined a great evening and shattered her dreams. Manoeuvring the truck through the back streets he didn't quite know what to say to make amends. Once again Anna had managed to interfere and destroy everything that he held precious.

It turned out to be a short journey and when they turned into Sophie's road she pointed out the terraced property that belonged to her. She was about to open the passenger door without kissing him goodnight, when Matt gently put his hand across and placed it on her wrist.

'Could I come inside for a minute?' he asked.

Sophie looked at him, the incredulity of his asking as surprise. This was not the passionate lasting moment that she had been expecting. For a moment the tears chocked her reply. He was asking for a minute when she had been expecting a night of love making. Removing his hand from hers she slipped from the seat and down onto the pavement.

'Maybe another time Matt, but not tonight!'

Matt felt her drifting away from him. He tried one last ditch plea.

'You should know by now Sophie, that I like you a lot and much more than that. Going anywhere near the lighthouse after the dance would be unsafe tonight. I am only trying to protect you.'

She turned around to face him, wondering what he would do if she did allow him in.

'I like you too Matt. I thought that was obvious, but I feel that I am getting mixed messages here. I understand about Anna, I do, although I thought tonight I came first. I think it's best that we just forgot what happened this evening!'

He placed both hands on the steering wheel accepting defeat was staring back at him. Up high in the sky the stars watched on. Sophie looked at Matt as he continued to stare straight ahead. Once again she had been foolish to let fantasy rule her heart. Maybe it was noble of Matt to protect her, but she was a big girl now and she could look after herself.

Sophie wasn't going inside, not until she had made him understand how hurt she was.

'Sooner or later. we would have reached the point in our relationship where nothing else would have mattered or taken precedence, not your sister or any other outside influence. Being together would have strengthened that moment. Goodnight Matt.'

She gently shut the passenger door so that it didn't wake the neighbours. Sophie wanted to cry out loud, but she would wait until she was inside then she could let it all go. However much she tried not to feel used, she did and that she was cheap.

Matt suddenly jumped from the driver's seat and pushed shut his door. He ran around the bonnet to where Sophie had the key in the door lock.

'You're right, I did come to Cockleshell Cove to start all over again because I needed to sort my life, my future and realise at last that for far too long Anna had been a thorn in my side. I needed tonight as much as you, but I've seen Anna in a violent, uncontrollable rage and it's not something that I would want you to witness. Anna can kill as easy as she takes in breath.

'I admit that she and I have ruined the evening and it did not end as I imagined it would. In different circumstances, I would not have hesitated in taking you back to the lighthouse and making breakfast in the morning, but...' Sophie didn't give him chance to finish.

'And about that Matt, about your love life, tell me honestly is Anna going to be there every time we kiss, every time we hold one another close or we go to get into bed together?' Matt opened his mouth to respond, but Sophie was on a roll. Jane would have been proud of her.

'I wanted this night as much as you Matt, not just the sex, but the love, the companionship and maybe a lot more. I felt that if we were going to make this work, then there had to be a mutual trust. As for your sister, I've dealt with girls like her all my life. In London, I had similar problems with a girl who was chasing Antoine, but I dealt with it in my own way. Together we could have sorted Anna if she'd been waiting at the lighthouse, but you've not given me the opportunity to prove that I can be there by your side. Oh yes, men have all the brawn when it comes to physical confrontation, but sometimes it takes a woman and clear thinking to see through a problem and find a resolve.'

Matt, who normally had a reply for any eventuality was left dumbstruck. Sophie's eyes, even in the moonlight were blazing mad. He had never expected a tongue lashing, not from Sophie. This was the Sophie that Dave Aldridge had never seen.

'You would be taking on an unpredictable tempest.' He replied meekly.

'Every storm has its weakness Matt, a point in which the eye loses strength and dies!'

Sophie suddenly became aware of a movement at her side, in the next house a curtain moved.

'Oh shit,' she muttered under breath, 'look if we're going to argue, let's do it inside. I don't want Edith telling the residents up and down the street about my love life.'

'Edith…' Matt reacted, 'who is Edith?'

Sophie pointed and waved at the ghostly face that was peering through the small gap between the curtains. 'My next door neighbour. Edith is also our neighbourhood watch co-ordinator and she takes her role very seriously. Your Chevy alone is bound to have her triggered her interest.'

A white bony hand waved back, gesturing that everything was alright. Sophie smiled and mimed that it was pulling Matt through the front door.

'See what you've done now. With Edith on the case, I will be the gossip of the town come lunchtime tomorrow.'

'Edith,' Matt asked smiling, not ready just yet to give up. 'Is she likely to happen every time I come visiting?'

'Touché, why do you think there'll be a next time Matt? This was a beautiful night, one of my best until the haunting of Anna appeared and ruined everything. I have to tell you the truth. At this moment in time, I feel cheap and like I've been used.'

Matt went to step forward, but Sophie had her hand outstretched to prevent him advancing.

'I would like very much for there to be a next time. I've wanted nothing else all week and to be with you. I would never see you as cheap Sophie nor would I ever use you. I am truly sorry for ruining the evening. I am however stuck in the middle, not that that excuses my explanation in the Chevy.'

Sophie felt suddenly tired as the last of her energy drained from her body. She stood in the hallway shaking her head not really knowing what to do.

'I never fight Matt, verbally or physically unless I'm cornered. However, like any animal I will come out fighting. Edith next door looks out for me and she means well and is a very dear soul, but I can look after myself. I might look all demure and helpless, but be under no illusion that cornered, I cannot scratch, kick, punch and bite as good as the next person.'

Taking a chance he stepped forward and caressed the side of her cheek.

'And I have never liked arguments or fights. I've had my fair share over the years and vowed recently to put them all behind me. Your next door neighbour Edith, she reminds me of my grandmother. She would watch when I was courting, banging on the window when it was time to come in. I would be forced to wave and watch as my girlfriend walked back home.'

'You mean to say that you went inside and let you girlfriend walk home alone?'

'Why yes,' he replied, 'we did things differently in my village and besides my girlfriend was older than me.'

'And precisely how old was you when you had this girlfriend?'

'Ten maybe and I think she was twelve, perhaps thirteen. I have always been tall for my age.'

Sophie shook her head in disbelief, maybe Jane was right and she did need to explore the world and not be so blinkered. Feeling a spark of understanding, although not quite sure from where, she sighed.

'Alright, let's forget Edith and your grandmother, kiss me and show me how much I really do mean to you!'

Letting everything go, the past, Helga and Anna he kissed her like he meant it. Sophie closed her eyes to be transported elsewhere. Not wanting to break the spell she led him into the front room where she pulled him down onto the settee.

'Did you bring precautions?' she whispered, as Matt was about to throw aside his shirt.

'No,' the devastation of his reply echoing in his eyes, 'I didn't think that the evening would end like this.'

'Me neither,' she replied, 'and I live here!'

Laughing, she in her bra and knickers and he with his shirt and trousers off they held one another accepting fate had played a cruel hand again. Somewhere on a nearby chimney an owl hooted.

Kissing her forehead then her lips he looked into her eyes, she was really beautiful.

'One day we'll get this right.' Kissing him tenderly on the lips, she murmured in response, 'one day, we'll abandon all caution and let nature takes its course.'

'One day, that will be our best day.' He replied.

Whispering in his ear he removed her bra and began sucking, kissing and licking at her rounded breasts before finding the darkened mounds that were her excited nipples. Willing himself to be controlled he failed feeling his erection straining against the cotton of his underwear. Sophie suggested that he remove them so that she could caress and take care of his swollen member.

Matt sighed as he continued exploring, kissing and caressing her exquisite nakedness. It would be so easy to be together, but both accepted that the time wasn't right, soon however it would come. Lying in one another's arms sometime after Sophie raised the subject before he did. 'We should at least talk about children Matt before we plan on having them!'

He smiled, 'that's a huge commitment, but I would be happy to discuss the future as long as we had lots of practice.'

Sophie rested her head on his chest hearing his heart beat. 'That's good because I want a family one day.'

Going to the bathroom she suggested that Matt took a look in the back bedroom where she had her paintings. When she came back out dressed in jeans and a tee-shirt he went in to do the same.

'They're very good!'

'I use the room because the light is best in the afternoon. Most summer evenings I tend to work late painting for as long as I can see the end of the garden. Do you want a coffee?'

'Yes please.' He closed the bathroom door and retuned joining her in the kitchen.

'These old houses are solid and have history, that's what I find fascinating about England. You have so many stories in your folklore, I bet this house could tell a tale or two.'

'You mean like being stripped naked and near ravaged under my own roof.'

He grinned, 'something like that,' he said, kissing the back of her neck, 'and next time I'll have precautions handy and we'll make love in the lamp room under the stars.'

114

'Is that a promise?' she asked.

He crossed his chest and heart twice, 'yes, it's a promise and soon!'

Taking his hand in hers she traced the lines on his palm. 'What are you doing?' he asked quizzically.

'I'm checking to see how many children, you will father.'

'And you can do that just by looking at my hand,' he watched attempting to follow, but her fingertips were moving too fast.

'Yes, I can. Last year Jane and I went to a spiritual evening because we had nothing else to do. Surprisingly enough it turned out to be fun. I especially I found it incredibly fascinating, so much so that I went back another night for a palm reading, where a clairvoyant told me my future.'

'What did she say?' he was fascinated to know.

'I can't tell you that, otherwise it would be like the betrayal of a confidence.' She followed the lines again on his hands just to make sure. 'Avoiding the cracks, the cuts and scars you're going to father two children, a boy and a girl.'

He pulled his hand away studying the palm, coursing the lines on his hand none of which were identical or singularly important. 'How can you define the gender so exactly?'

She kissed him, 'I can't, but that's what I would like when I have children!'

'Dave warned me that women have hidden agendas and that men, like fools jump in head first into a traps.'

'Did he now, I think I will let Jane know about that little confidence.' She smiled and winked to let him know that his secret was safe. 'And that is what makes us the stronger sex. What we lack in physical prowess, we make up in resourcefulness.'

He looked at her over the top of his coffee mug wondering if in the future he would fall into any of her traps. 'This clairvoyant that you went to see, did she give any predictions about us?'

'Again I can't say.' Sophie placed her hand over his heart. 'If it feels right Matt then anything's possible. That's all I can say.'

She watched him pull away from the kerbside and wave at Edith as he went down the road to the junction. With so many thoughts now going around inside her head she wanted nothing else except her bed.

Sophie remembered everything from the meeting with the clairvoyant, it was however too early to say whether any of the predictions would come true. Waving goodnight to Edith she shut and bolted the door, double checking all the other doors and windows.

Slipping out of her clothes she looked at the party dress on the back of the wardrobe door, it was beautiful and had been a good choice.

She checked her mobile, but there were no messages not that she expected any from Jane. Removing her makeup she looked out at the night sky wondering how far she would have to travel to meet with her destiny. Throwing a woollen pad into the wastebin she jumped when her mobile ringtone announced that she had a text.

'I had to stop and say goodnight. You looked stunning tonight, so beautiful in your dress and when I wake in the morning, I will kick myself that you are not lying beside me. Rosie will hate me for not bringing you back to the lighthouse. Matt xx'

Sophie went over to bedroom window and waited until she saw the lamp room flicker into life. Whispering *'goodnight Matt'* she didn't send a reply.

Chapter Eighteen

'He went back to the lighthouse on his own, are you mad?' Jane could hardly believe what she was hearing.

'It wasn't like you imagine it to be Jane. We're trying to take things slow and give the relationship time to develop.'

'By the time you two get it together, you'll both be too old to do it. Are you sure that he's not gay?'

Sophie giggled, there was no denying that Matt wasn't a true blue heterosexual. 'No, of course he's not. Destiny will eventually intervene and take its course all in good time.'

Jane, who still recovering from a night of unbridled passion was slightly vexed. 'There's a time for talking Sprigg and a time when you throw inhibition out of the window, last night was the latter.'

Desperate to steer Jane away from the subject Sophie remembered that Jane's mother had stayed over to look after Annabelle and Scott. 'You shouldn't be talking like that, your mum will hear.'

'She's heard worse,' Jane replied 'and stop trying to avoid the issue. What I'm trying to say Sprigg is that if you don't stoke the fire and keep the embers burning, the bloody thing will go out eventually. Matt might be the handsome hunk now, but in time everything changes.' Jane straightened out the corner of the pillow as she made the bed.

Sophie sighed. 'I hear what you're saying. You're all fired up this morning so I guess the flames of passion scorched your insides last night and as we're on the subject you were gone a long time at the dance?'

'We needed to make up for lost time,' replied Jane, pinching her knees together, god she ached.

'With your mother there!'

'No problem, she's partially deaf.'

'And were the children excited about Dave being part of the lifeboat crew?' Sophie asked.

'Annabelle was a little apprehensive, but Scott thinks it's brilliant.'

In the privacy of her own bedroom Jane lay back on the bed realising just how much she had missed her husband. They had made love until three in the morning.

'I hope also, that you apologised to Sandra Wareham?'

'Yes. I'll get to see her soon and have a coffee to make amends. I can't believe that she taught Dave first-aid. When the kids were little, they'd only have to scrape a knee to have him go green.'

'Well I think he's brave!'

Jane caught on how Sophie had cleverly steered the conversation away from her and Matt. 'So this talk that you had last night, did you mention children?'

'Yes, the subject came up.'

'And…' Jane asked, pushing for more detail. 'Good, only talking won't get you started!'

Sophie was quick to reply. 'I remember your experience going around back of the coastguard station. That's as good as any contraceptive.'

Jane laughed. 'So the reason you didn't have sex was because he forget to bring them along. No wonder you didn't get beyond first base.'

'Second base and he liked the underwear.'

'So you at least got naked together!'

'You forget that you're a Roman Catholic Jane Aldridge, intimacy should be private.'

Jane laughed out loud. 'And you think the Vatican is full of virgins. Come on Sprigg get real. Men are like wishing wells, drop a coin down the well and they wish for all manner of things. Men confuse the hell out of life. If Matt gets you in the sack, it'll be like finding the Holy Grail. Christ, my Irish priest has six kids and they weren't conceived by miraculous conception!'

'For that blasphemy Jane you will definitely go to hell.'

Jane chuckled back. 'If the lord almighty had been around back of the clubhouse last night looking in the stockroom then I'm already booked in.' She ran her free hand down over the smooth skin of her abdomen, feeling around and remembering how Dave had made her feel even better saying how good she looked, even after producing two beautiful children.

'You are impossible,' replied Sophie, 'I dread to think what poor Annabelle and Scott will turn out like, with a mother like you!'

118

Jane giggled, 'like a saint and an angel.'

Sophie thought she heard a voice in the background only she didn't quite catch what was said. 'Was that your mum?'

'Yes, she's just told me to stop cursing and blaspheming. She also believes that I am destined for hell.'

'I cannot believe that you had sex last night with your mum there, have you no shame!'

'I told you, she's partially deaf.'

'Not so deaf that I didn't hear what was going on last night Jane Aldridge!' Sophie heard a door click shut presuming it was the bedroom or bathroom.

'Oh hell!' Jane exclaimed, almost a whisper.

'Now what's wrong?' Sophie asked, thinking Jane had hurt herself.

'She did hear. I'd forgot that she slept downstairs last night because she'd hurt her back gardening. When we got home Dave carried me straight up the stairs and threw me on the bed.'

Sophie closed her eyes stopping her imagination from running wild.

'You mean she heard everything. Jane I would be so embarrassed if that was my mum.'

The laughter was uncontrollable as Jane rolled about the bed naked.

'What's so funny?' asked Sophie.

'Well when I tell Dave, he'll be dumbstruck. Ever since our courting days he's been wary of my mum. It's the reason we had to go sneaking off around back of the old coastguard shack. She had eyes and ears everywhere.'

Sophie thought about Edith and how she'd watched when she and Matt had arrived at her place.

Quite expectantly the door to the bedroom opened. *'And don't you think young lady, that I didn't know what was going on before you needed to get married. You forget that I married your father!'*

Abigail Meredith looked at her daughter lying naked on the bed.

'It's hardly surprising you can't get yourself up this morning considering what went on last night.'

Sophie heard a gasp believing that it came from Jane.

'And after I've finished doing what I've got to do, you get yourself in the bathroom and shower before your children come home. And as for you Sophie Sprigg, I would keep hold of that man up at the lighthouse. From what I hear, he's worth knowing.'

Jane was quicker than Sophie to respond. 'And how do you know about Matthew Van Janssen?' she asked.

'Eyes and ears everywhere,' Abigail Meredith diligently tapped the side of her nose, 'remember that my girl. Now get your naked arse off that bed and be ready to hit that shower very soon. You've been moping about these past few weeks and it's time you cleaned this house!'

She shut the door and went back to the bathroom.

'There,' said Jane with a whisper, 'now you know why Dave is so wary, when she's around. I suppose that I had best get in the shower.' Jane breathed in, 'still, if she did hear anything last night, it's her fault for sleeping downstairs. If anything, she jealous.'

'Jane,' Sophie remarked, 'that's not a nice thing to say. She's probably still getting over the death of your dad. Two years can be a long time without somebody. I expect she misses him. She's bound to be lonely.'

Walking across to the dresser Jane selected a fresh pair of knickers to wear.

'Yeah, I suppose you're right, next time I'll make sure that she sleeps in Annabelle's room if I want to bonk my old man. So when are you seeing Matt again?' she asked.

'I'm not sure, I'll contact him later!'

'Do you remember when we went to see that spiritualist you was told that destiny would run its course, well I think it did for me and Dave last night.'

'But, you don't believe in it?' Sophie questioned.

'Maybe there is something in what they say after all. As a Catholic we're taught not to believe, there again the bible doesn't advise on what to do if you think your old man is over the side. That wasn't etched into the stones that Moses brought down from the mountain. Maybe Sprigg, I tuned in to my inner self.'

'So now you're doubting your god?'

'I didn't say that, only he doesn't have all the answers, that's what I'm saying!'

'You'll be saying Hail Mary's till eternity if you don't stop Jane Meredith.' The voice came from the landing.

Jane whispered into the phone.

'I am never gonna be a saint, only a sinner. It's a bloody darn sight more fun. Stuff the Holy Ghost and why should he have all the fun!'

Sophie cleverly steered the conversation away from Jane's religious interpretation.

 'What did your mum think of Dave being part of the lifeboat crew?'

'She's worried that he might find the going a bit tough, although I know my Dave and he'll rise to the occasion. He's not the fool that he makes himself out to be.'

'And you're not apprehensive, as and when the siren sounds?'

'I'll worry about that when the time comes.'

The door suddenly burst open again.

'Have you got any moisturiser that I can use please?'

'I'd better go Sprigg, I'll give you a call later when I have the bedroom to myself again.'

The echo of a derisory cough was all that Sophie could hear before Jane pulled open a wardrobe door where she had bathroom supplies.

'Thank you, I'll go now. Goodbye Sophie!'

'Later Sprigg, when I've got rid of my mother.'

The line went dead.

Sophie was hesitant as to what to do next. Should she text Matt, wait for him to call her or leave communication a day and let the dust settle. Their coming together had been like a kettle boiling over and in the cold light of day Sophie was still confused. Musing over the text that Matt had sent she wished she had replied.

 **Chapter Nineteen**

Using the hand hammer to mould a piece of metal, Matt missed the incoming call from Sophie. He had to work fast with the glowing metal so that the molecules would twist and bend to whatever shape was required. It was extremely noisy and hot work. Dropping the finished product into a bucket of water, it fizzed and spat back at him where the cooling process would quickly temper and harden. Later he would weld the pieces together.

Early morning had been surprisingly warm for the time of the year, but with Anna out and about Matt was reluctant to throw open the workshop doors. Again she was interfering in his life. Using the back of his forearm he wiped the sweat from his brow. Around mid-morning he checked his mobile phone annoyed that he had missed the call.

Similarly around the same time Sophie was awash in baking flour with a streak down one side of her nose and under an eye where she had scratched an itch. Following the recipe from a book was not her ideal way to spend a Sunday morning cooking, but she felt the need to occupy her mind and discard the negativity that kept rearing its ugly head every so often.

She had considered taking Ollie for another walk along the beach, but had decided against it. With the shelves of her fridge stacked with pre-packed dinners, she wondered why she was bothering to bake a cake. Closing the door of the fridge her mobile rang.

'Hi, I'm sorry that I missed your call. I'm in the workshop hot bending metal for the new commission. With the noise of the furnace it's almost impossible to hear anything else. Is everything alright?'

'Yes, I'm fine. I was just calling to check that you were okay. I didn't mean to interrupt you if you're working.'

Wiping his brow again Matt prevented the sweat from running in and stinging his eyes. 'You didn't and it's about time that I took a break. What are you doing?' he asked.

'Not a lot, only amusing myself baking and putting a pastry top on a meat pie. My mother keeps making comment that I eat too many take-aways and pre-packed meals. At present, I'm covered in flour!'

'I'd really like to see you, only I been thinking about you all night!' Sophie didn't want to admit that she had been thinking about him too.

She sounded more sympathetic to the events of the evening before.

'My grandad, who I loved very much, once told to go with my instincts and never look back. It was good advice and I have always forged ahead, not just with buying the house, but part-owing a shop too.'

'So are you saying that I should have turned the Chevy around and come back last night?'

'It didn't happen Matt so it wasn't meant to be.'

There was a sudden *whoosh* from the bellows behind as air belched through the hot coals.

'Do you have plans for today?' he asked.

'Only to clear the mess away in the kitchen and cook my pie and cake, why?'

'I could really do with some help on this new commission, if you've nothing else planned. I could pick you up and you could cook here?'

She laughed. Not only would Matt get free help and labour, but a hot meal into the bargain with perhaps a slice of cake with tea. 'And I wouldn't be in the way?' she replied.

'Definitely not and it would give us more time together, to get to know one another. You would need some old clothes though.'

'How old?' Sophie asked.

'Anything, an old tee-shirt - worn jeans and trainers, anything that you don't mind getting covered in dust and that would protect you from the odd spark from the furnace. Bending hot metal in a workshop is no place for fashion.'

Sophie turned out the gas on the oven.

'I'll cycle taking the coastal path,' she replied, 'the bike has a sturdy basket on the front which will carry the food.'

'Thank you,' she heard him sigh, probably an emotion of relief, 'obviously, I would pay you for helping.' He wanted to make sure that she knew, he was wasn't just using her.

Sophie however wasn't happy.

'If you do that Matt I won't come. I want to come because I want to see you and I did promise that I would help. We're friends remember. Would it be okay if I brought a change of clothes and take a shower after?'

'That would be a good idea as the workshop gets very hot and sticky. It might look adventurous under the spotlights, but it can be a dirty place to work.'

'How do I get in, as I gather you're in lock down mode?'

He smiled to himself, she did understand.

'Bang hard on the workshop doors, I'll know that it's you.'

Running upstairs Sophie rummaged through the bottom of the wardrobe looking for a particular item of clothing, something that she hadn't worn in years. Holding up the bib n' brace to the sunlight, it looked as good as the last time that she had worn it. She folded an old tee-shirt that she kept for her art, adding a pair of old socks and sturdy pair of shoes. From the dresser, she took clean underwear and additional extra clothes.

Pumping extra air into the tyres, she'd wrapped the food in clean kitchen towels laying them carefully in the basket before putting the rucksack on top to stop everything from leaping about. She did consider taking wine, but she guessed Matt would probably have some chilling in the fridge. Pulling the gate shut Sophie used the service alley to avoid being caught by Edith. Cycling to the Sunday bakery she purchased a French stick.

Going past the church where she had attended the spiritual meeting with Jane, she waved at the vicar knowing that her mother was probably already inside. The bike ride was refreshingly pleasant as the sunshine shone down on her face and shoulders. It had been a long time since she had taken the coast path, but it was sturdy and without any unsuspecting ruts.

Banging on the door of the workshop as advised she heard Matt lift the heavy bar away. She stood clear as he pushed the door open. Taking the items from her basket she propped the bike up against the wall.

'You can leave it in the workshop,' he offered, 'rather than leave it outside, I assure you that it won't be in the way.'

'No, thanks,' replied Sophie, 'it's old and not worth a lot. Quite often it sits around back of the shop where the salt air helps clean the framework. Pulling shut the heavy door, he slipped the iron bar back into place.

'That's an impressive fortification,' Sophie acknowledged. Instantly the heat from the furnace was very noticeable.

'Before the lighthouse, I've had various pieces go missing from workshops and missing metal does cause me problems. Metal is expensive and a delay in delivering a commission on time can damage my reputation. The heavy bar across the workshop door makes me feel safer.'

'Aren't you insured against loss?' Sophie asked.

'I was at Ashburton Grange, but not here. The assessor is coming sometime this week to help me complete the forms. It's not that they're complicated, you just have to know how to word the sections properly and not every insurance company wants insure an unusual place like a lighthouse.'

He wiped dry his hands with a towel so that he could kiss her. Sophie responded to the kiss ignoring the salty taste on his lips. It wasn't until he let go that he realised as she wiped the salt from her mouth. 'I'm sorry, I tend to forget just how hot it can be in here!'

'It's not a problem Matt. I'd expect as such working in here.' She picked up the rucksack, pie and cake. Shall I put the pie and cake in the oven,' she asked heading for the inner door, 'we can eat later.'

Matt agreed and told her to use the bedroom or bathroom to change. When she reappeared he stopped what he was doing, grinned, crossing his arms over his chest as he leant back against the work bench.

'You remind me of a puppet character that I once knew, called *Flopsy Anouk,* she was a cloth puppet that I would watch on television when I was very young.'

Sophie turned around to proudly to show off her workwear. Then walking over to where he was stood admiring her, she unlocked his arms. 'Now you don't have to worry about how mucky I get!'

Matt showed how to work the metal in the brazier, how to turn the ends when it was white hot before cooling the metal in the water. Using a pair of his gauntlets Sophie was soon wiping her brow, it was hot, sticky and dirty work. She enjoyed being in the workshop and helping, but more than that they were together. If only her mother could see her now she thought, she would have a fit.

Soon most of the pieces that needed shaping were twisted and bent to size and pattern. Laying down his tools Matt had been dismissive of the time.

'The cake,' he cried, 'it'll be burnt to a cinder!'

Sophie laughed as she removed the gauntlets, 'it'll be fine Matt, as I put it on timer. We probably need to check with the pie though and make sure that the meat is thoroughly cooked through.'

'This is what happens most days,' he said, letting the furnace flame die a little 'I get so engrossed that I forget to eat. I didn't realise that it's almost gone three.'

Sophie smiled. 'It's good that you occupy your time like that Matt.' She looked around the workshop. 'I love being here, it's so thrilling to see a piece come together.' She wiped her brow of perspiration. 'This is so much more intense than painting.'

The basic shape of the welded structure had started to resemble a bird. Sophie was in awe of how good it looked. 'I so want to see the finished article.' She went in closer. 'The bird looks as though it's about to fly away.'

Matt angled the spotlights down and instantly the wings took on a different shade of colour throwing long shadows across the stone floor. Walking around the metal structure the colours were representative of some Caribbean Island, somewhere exotic. Standing beside Matt he pointed down to a small plaque which he had just welded to the base.

'You should read this,' he insisted. The long thin piece of metal had been skilfully etched and read 'Bird of Peace' by Sophie & Matt.

'Matt,' Sophie exclaimed, open mouthed, 'this is your piece, your work. I can't take any of the credit for the small effort that I've put in today.'

Encouragingly he put his arm around her shoulder. 'You've helped a lot. You heated the metal for the body, you bent the feathers for the wings and cooled the legs in the water. Carlos would say that you created a hell of a lot.'

'Is that your agent?' she asked.

'A friend and my agent.' He pulled a rough sketch over from the workbench that he had been working from. 'The customer gets the idea, either they or I put it down on paper and then Carlos gives me the okay to go ahead. We work well together.'

Sophie lightly touched the welds where the bird had slowly been pieced together. Along the curve of the wing Matt had added strips of flat copper to give the ends of the feathers a realistic look.

'Eventually, most if the metal will turn green with oxidisation, then it will look more natural than it does now.'

Sophie sighed. 'I wish that you didn't have to sell it Matt, I really love it!'

He smiled as he ran his fingertips over the copper strips.

'That's the thing with metal, you cannot afford to get too attached otherwise you'd be a pauper the rest of your life. Like an artist who creates a masterpiece, you have to remain detached in order to sell the end product.'

Dipping the lights down low he walked up behind her unclipping the clasps of her bib pulling down the straps from her shoulders. Sophie watched as they fell to her waist. Matt put his lips on the side of her neck and sent her senses to paradise. Sophie gasped as his hands went around of her ribs and cupped her breasts. Gently fondling and caressing her, she let him do whatever he wanted as her head arched back coming to rest on his shoulder. *'Oh Matt,'* she murmured, *'I need you so badly, I don't care anymore.'*

Turning her around, he tugged her tee-shirt up from her waist band pulling it over her head before hurriedly unclasping her bra. Sophie virtually tore the tee-shirt from his body wanting to be naked. Unclasping the belt she slipped his jeans down over his hips, moments later they were as she wanted. Lifting her from the ground he supported her holding onto her buttocks. Sophie found his mouth, kissing his long and hard. Feeling his erection pushing against her, she gasped.

She let go a cry of pleasure and relief as Matt entered her, pushing gently he increased the intensity as they made love. With each thrust Sophie wanted more, all inhibition lost to the moment and any reticence about being safe cast aside in wild abandon. Digging deep with her fingers she racked his back encouraging his movement as she kissed him and he responded as only he could. Sophie wanted Matt to know that she wanted every ounce of him.

In the background the flame of the brazier was still glowing, throwing a bright orange, blue and yellow hue about the workshop. Looking into her eyes Matt saw the reflection of the fire.

When the moment came Sophie felt herself tense before she let go throwing her head back. She dug deep into the flesh of his buttock urging him in even deeper. *'Now Matt, now,'* she cried as the flames of their passion exploded. Sophie felt the tears trickling down her cheeks. Bucking gently neither wanted the moment to end.

They stayed locked together in mutual embrace for what seemed an eternity as Sophie continued to sob, the years of wanting finally over. Inhaling long and hard she didn't care about the consequences. She had gone with her instinct, knowing her grandfather would have been proud of her. Letting her down gently Matt went across to where he had a stack of clean dust sheets.

Laying them over the bales of hay that were used for packing he plucked Sophie from the stone and lay her down, lying beside her. With the lights dimmed very low allowing the flames of the dying brazier to dance over their bodies neither spoke. Making love once again only this time much slower, no less intense, but with more feeling, they made the bond stronger. This time there were no tears only smiles, kisses, caresses and soft sighs.

'I'm glad that we waited,' Sophie said, as she lay with her head on his chest sweeping her fingertips up and down his muscular arms.

'You mean we waited for the right moment!' he replied.

She kissed him, before embracing his heart. *'It was the right moment Matt.'*

Suddenly, with the dying of the flames the temperature in the workshop dipped dramatically. Matt suggested that they go upstairs where it was much warmer.

'Are you okay?' Sophie asked, as he released his hold on her.

'I've never been happier,' he replied. He brought his mouth close to her ear where he whispered. 'Although, I am experiencing a slight problem!'

Sophie shot her head up from where she had been lying beside him. 'What's wrong Matt?'

He laughed, 'I have a strand of hay stuck between the cheeks of my butt!'

The echo of their laughter reverberated around the workshop as she reached behind and extracted the offending strand, breaking it away from the bale she tossed it in the dying fire.

'It wasn't there when we were... you know?' she asked.

He shook his head laughing. 'No, I don't need that kind of encouragement, only you!'

Sophie suddenly shivered rashing all over in goose pimples. 'I think it's time that we went upstairs.'

Matt threw the lid over the dying embers as she gathered together their clothes. Locking the workshop she went ahead of Matt passing through the kitchen, giving Rosie a knowing look before heading for the bathroom dropping the dirty clothes on the floor.

They showered together washing the dust and the dirt from their bodies, regretting that they had to wash away everything. Matt had already made it clear that he wanted her to stay the night. Grabbing two bath towels he wrapped the first around Sophie kissing her gently on the lips.

'I should invite you to help with creations more often!'

'And I would gladly accept, only first we'd best find something softer for you to lay on, rather than a hay bale.'

They put on clean clothes, jeans with fresh tee-shirts and socks although Sophie left her clean underwear in the rucksack. Jane had advised her to live dangerously and she was at last.

Checking the oven which was surprisingly warm the cake was nicely baked, moist and soft and only the meat pie needed another half an hour. Matt opened a bottle of white wine and found two clean glasses.

'Shall we take this upstairs?' he asked.

'That would be really nice,' Sophie turned to Rosie 'are you coming too girl?' Without waiting the black cat was down from the window cill and climbing the stairs ahead of them both.

'Will the pie be okay?' Matt asked.

'I put in on timer again. We'll hear when the countdown sequence when it finishes.'

Sophie grinned to herself, she was in need of nourishment to replace some of the lost energy that she'd used. It was obvious that Matt was famished. She remembered Jane telling her that Dave was always hungry after sex.

'I could cut us some of the French stick if you're that hungry?' she asked.

'That would be good.' Sophie was back up in a couple of minutes armed with two lengths of buttered bread stick. Sitting with the cushions at their back they sipped the wine and watched the waves coming up against the headland, spilling over the rocks and filling the gullies below the cliff edge.

'This is so relaxing up here Matt. As soon as you climb the stairs to the old beacon room, it's like entering a fantasy world. You could be stepping through the pages of a story book where nothing bad happens and where dreams come true.'

Matt held her close, he liked the way that she described the old beacon room.

'The sun will fall away to the western horizon later. If you like, after dinner we could spend the evening up here and wait for the stars to appear, although I can't guarantee that Rosie will stay with us.' He looked over at the black cat which was sleeping. 'I think she likes it as much as we do.' Matt refilled their glasses. 'Up here you can let your imagination wander and not be afraid of where it ends up.'

Sophie nestled herself into his contours sensing everything was right with the world and more importantly with them. 'What do you mean, where it ends up?'

'Dreams get invaded by strangers, people that we don't always know, whereas our conscious imagination we can control. We can shut the door on people we don't want to let in and open to those we do. That's why I like the lamp room. It has a three sixty outlook, as though it was meant to let in just the sunshine, moon and stars.' He pointed to the outside. 'Stepping beyond the viewing balcony we go wherever we like in our imagination.'

Sophie looked at Matt as he watched the waves. He had a sensitive side which she liked. 'Up here Matt, you're right, nobody can get to us.' He chinked the side of her glass agreeing.

Neither mentioned the unprotected sex. Lying against his chest sipping wine Sophie felt the change wash through her mind. Below in the kitchen the oven timer hit zero announcing that the meat pie was done. Sophie suggested leaving the bottle in the lamp room for later descending the wooden staircase.

Running ahead Rosie was surprisingly hungry as well. Matt added fresh food to her bowl. When she was done Rosie jumped up onto the window cill. Moments later she hissed at something outside. Matt went to the window, but saw nothing that concerned him. Sophie stroked the cats head sensing the tension in her neck.

'Probably just another cat in the territory,' Matt suggested 'Rosie can be quite territorial at times!'

They had their pie and bread, but decided to leave the cake. Sitting on the cill Rosie kept an uneasy watch on the outside. Matt had said that he'd go and take a look, but Sophie had persuaded him to leave whatever was outside, outside.

'This has been an amazing day Matt, please just stay with me. In fact stay beside me all night long, where together we can step beyond the viewing balcony.'

*****

Protected from sight by the thick undergrowth outside, where very soon it would be dark Anna Van Janssen watched the cat as she peered across to where Anna was crouched low, watching.

Matthews Chevy had been easy to find, being the only model this side of the town and there was no mistaking the cat, black as the night and just as deadly as Anna was.

Baring her teeth Anna snarled up at the cat vowing that revenge, when it arrived would be swift, yet without mercy.

130

So far she had not seen any signs of movement inside, but soon it would be dark and the lights would need to be switched on. Anna sensed that there was a woman inside. Her grandmother had called it a women's intuition, a gift that only women possessed.

Anna hissed once more seeing the cat claw at the window before she turned and crawled away along the bush line. She could wait until the right moment to strike.

 **Chapter Twenty**

Sophie wasn't sure if it had been the last fleeting moments of a dream that had woken her or whether the sound coming from below the bedroom was real. Whatever it was she slipped from the bed slowly, careful not to disturb Matt who was sound asleep.

Unaccustomed to the lighthouse, the loose boards and natural movement of the building, Sophie went across to the window closely followed by Rosie who had also heard something move. Stroking the cats back, Sophie whispered, *'you heard it too girl?'*

Instinctively sensing that she was no longer in the bed, Matt also stirred. Still needing sleep, he asked. 'What's wrong?'

'Nothing, we were just curious, Sophie replied, 'and Rosie thought she heard a noise outside.' Sophie made light of the incident, although it had concerned her. 'It was probably just the waves hitting the rocky headland.'

Beyond the window the visibility was virtually zero as a thick sea mist continued to roll inland.

'It doesn't look very inviting,' Matt remarked, as he pulled back the duvet. Forgetting the sound that had woken her Sophie jumped back in beside him. 'That's better!' he said, settling back down.

The red coloured illumination on the clock face registered that it was twenty five minutes to four, still very early.

'We should really set the alarm,' Sophie suggested, reaching across and over his chest, 'I'm sorry, but I clean forgot that it's my turn to open the shop this morning.'

'Won't your business partner do it?' Matt asked, hoping she could.

Sophie chuckled and kissed his shoulder.

'You don't know Vanessa, she's much worse than I am for getting out of bed.' Begrudgingly, she set the alarm for seven. 'It still gives us time to share breakfast together.'

Snuggling back down where the crease of the mattress was still warm, surprisingly neither felt like sleep so instead they talked. With Rosie keeping watch on the window cill. The fog had come in early and blanketed the coast in an impenetrable grey shroud, leaving everywhere damp and gloomy.

Around six thirty Sophie decided to hit the shower leaving Matt to add fresh coffee beans to the coffee machine. Slicing the remainder of the bread stick he set up the toaster. Looking down at Rosie's bowl he was surprised to see that she hadn't touched the pilchards.

Just shy of seven Sophie emerged showered and dressed. Matt sighed, the working day was about to begin. He switched on the toaster and popped the bread slices into the warming grooves. Seconds later Rosie appeared.

'She goes wherever you go, have you noticed that,' he said, as the cat made her way over to the pilchards. 'She likes you being here!'

'I like being here,' Sophie replied, as she stroked the cats head before picking her up and giving her a cuddle, 'we're friends aren't we Rosie.' The cat purred emitting a deep throated motor sound and affectionately rubbing her head against Sophie's chest.

Looking out of the window where everything beyond was grey she put Rosie down beside the food bowl again. 'This is rather unusual,' she said, 'only we don't normally get a mist this bad.'

'Maybe it was sent to prevent you from leaving!' Matt laughed.

'Fog or no fog, regrettably I still have to get to the shop, only we get a delivery every Monday morning.'

Matt placed the toast slices onto two plates adding butter and jam accompanied by a mug each of hot fresh ground coffee.

'This is nice,' Sophie smiled, 'I don't normally get time to enjoy breakfast at home. Most weekdays, Vanessa pops along to the local bakery where she buys a couple of bacon rolls. Extremely lazy, but so scrummy!'

'I very rarely have bacon in the house, although I'd best add some to my shopping list!'

Sophie swallowed the toast in her mouth. 'Please don't do that on my behalf Matt, we only get them because we both miss breakfast.' She patted her stomach, 'besides, we could do without the added calories. I've noticed also that my jeans are beginning to get tight around my hips.' She gave her thigh a slap to emphasise the point.

Matt reached over and held her leg. 'Everything fits just fine from where I am sitting.' He thumbed his finger at Rosie, 'unlike this lardy lump, who appears to be putting on weight.'

Rosie's tongue was actively engaged licking the remainder of the bowl. 'Maybe that's because she is content being here Matt. What do you have planned for today?' she asked.

'I have to finish burring down the rough edges on the bird's wings. Recoat the bits that I have missed and give everything a final check. The client wants the sculpture to have that antique, dour look as though it was created last century, with an expensive price tag.'

'And what about you, what do you think it should look like?' Sophie asked.

He gave a shrug. 'I'm not really fussed, as long as the customer pays.' He suddenly stopped talking, having heard something unusual from down below. Sophie had heard it too, but it was just the once. 'Perhaps it's the fog making the brickwork of the lighthouse move.'

Sophie looked at him, not entirely convinced.

'Will I see you later, after work?' he enquired.

She finished munching the last of her toasted slice. 'I have to drop something into my mum's after work, but I can come after that, if that's okay with you?'

Rosie fussed approvingly around Sophie's ankles making them both smile.

'Rosie say's that'll be good.'

'And you, do you say the same?' she asked toying with him.

Leaning forward, he kissed her. 'I'm in agreement with Rosie.' He took the plates over to the sink. 'I could collect you from the shop, then get the chance to meet your mother and father?'

Sophie's eyes sparkled. 'My mother already knows about you Matt. I spoke to her in the week and she's friends with Abigail Meredith, Jane's mum. Believe me, you've a lot to live up too!'

'All the more reason then, why I should meet them.'

'On your head be it,' warned Sophie. 'Mother's extremely wily and she can see through me.'

'So is she psychic like you?' he asked.

Sophie gave a definite shake of her head. 'No, only perceptive like any mother should be.'

Drinking the coffee Sophie told him more about the shop, Vanessa, Penny and Ollie. Anna did not enter into the conversation although Rosie appeared very restless and not just because of the fog. The black cat sensed something else was lurking around outside.

Leaning on the table top with his forearms the table almost gave way. Sophie hurriedly collected up the breakfast things and took whatever was left across to the worktop. 'That was close,' she said.

Matt kicked the table leg nearest him back into place.

'I should really get around to building stronger legs. The top is made from good strong oak, but the legs are probably too weak to support the top.'

Sophie saw the opportunity for a suggestion. Why not fashion a set from metal Matt, keeping the oak top. It's a lovely table otherwise, big enough to fit a lot of people around.'

He nodded agreeing, seeing that metal legs would make sense. 'I'll get the bird finished first then put together a design. That should fill my day nicely.'

Before either knew it, the wooden bird inset into the Swiss clock on the wall had made an appearance striking the bell, telling Sophie that it was time to leave. Matt wasn't keen on her going, but reluctantly he picked the keys to the Chevy.

'You're not biking along the coast path in this mist, one slip and you'll be over the edge. I'm sure that the roads inland will be a lot clearer so we'll put your bike in the rear of the truck and I'll drive to back to the shop.' Sophie could see that he was determined so instead she smiled and thanked him.

'It doesn't matter about the bike Matt, it's old and I hardly ever use it. It's not worth a lot!'

Gathering together her rucksack, Sophie suggested that it might be an idea to leave her old clothes at the lighthouse, where they would be available and handy for future projects. Matt was happy that she wanted to be involved.

Without either of them seeing, Rosie who needed to go outside urgently, slipped past when neither were looking. In the mist she soon disappeared. Moments later Matt secured the front door.

As Matt got ready the Chevy, Sophie went around back to fetch her bike, only it wasn't there. She looked around, but it was nowhere to be seen. She came back round front to inform Matt.

'I hardly think that it's been stolen,' she implied, 'not with a shopping basket on the front and attached to the handlebar, it's hardly going to improve anybody's street cred.'

Matt switched off the engine and together they searched for the missing bike. Going close to the cliff edge Sophie looked down. Way down below on the rocky outcrop her bike was a crumpled mess. 'Somebody must have thrown it down there,' she suggested.

Matt wanted to get her to the shop and away from the lighthouse as soon as possible. He promised to recover the bicycle when he returned. Driving down the leafy lane towards town, neither he nor Sophie realised that Rosie was still out.

****

In town the sea mist was high above the chimney tops as he had thought with the sun beginning to burn through casting aside great swathes of cloud. Somewhere in the distance a fog horn was intermittently sending out a warning to shipping of the hidden rocks along the coastline. The Chevy was turning left from the high street when Sophie's mobile rang.

'Are you ok Sprigg, only I've been trying you for ages?'

Sophie looked over at Matt and mimed *Jane,* causing him to grin and say hello.

'I'm really good. It's just that the signal is non-existent at the lighthouse and the sea mist is really thick there this morning!'

Jane was silent as she punched the air victoriously.

'I was so worried about you yesterday that come eleven thirty I sent Dave out to make sure.'

'Morning or night time, eleven thirty?' Sophie asked.

'Night time of course. He was doing okay, until that daft old bat that lives next door to you called the police.'

Sophie tried to stifle her laugh. 'Why, what happened?'

Matt pulled up outside the shop applying the brake.

Jane explained. 'She saw him peer through your downstairs window, moments before he stepped back to look up at the bedroom. I think it was that, that made her call the police. Apparently, she described him as a peeping tom.'

Sophie had changed the mobile to speaker mode so that Matt could hear the conversation.

'Edith probably meant well Jane,' Sophie explained, 'she really is quite harmless and was probably only thinking of my safety.'

Jane who thought the circumstances as funny continued, 'doesn't that daffy old tart ever go to bed?'

'Edith suffers from insomnia.' Replied Sophie.

'If Dave had got hold of her last night, she wouldn't have had a problem sleeping.' She stopped chuckling. 'The police pulled him over at the end of the road, where dressed in just his pyjamas and a long coat, his explanation took some convincing. Worse still, he had forgotten to take his mobile so he couldn't call me to verify that it was me who had asked him to check on your address.'

'Did Edith tell the police anything else?' Sophie asked.

'Only that the man outside looking up at your bedroom was a perverted ugly looking brute who was obviously up to no good!'

'I would have to agree with that,' Matt butted in.

'Good morning handsome,' said Jane. 'I don't need to ask where you two spent the night. At least it was warmer than the coastguard station!'

Matt looked quizzically at Sophie, who whispered that she would explain later.

'So did the police eventually let Dave go?' Sophie asked.

'Only after they had called the house phone and I confirmed his story. Had it been a week earlier, I would have denied all knowledge of ever knowing him. Annabelle and Scott found it highly amusing this morning and they can't wait to tell their classmates that their father got a tug by the police because he was out in his pyjama's looking through Auntie Sophie's window.' Jane paused to sniff and sigh, 'you're a tart Sprigg!'

Matt tapped the glass shield on his watch indicting the shop needed to be open. She leant across and kissed him before Matt called out goodbye to Jane. Sophie took her rucksack from the seat and closed the door waving as he drove away.

'Right,' asked Jane, 'now that lover boy has gone, was it good?'

'Absolutely amazing, you should see the wings on the bird and under the spotlights it stands almost as high as me. It gives you the impression that the bird will fly away any moment soon.'

'Not the bloody bird you dippy mare,' chided Jane, *'the sex, was the sex good!'*

'Everything that I imagined it would be and more.'

Inserting the key in the shop door Sophie opened up, turning around the 'Open' sign. She put the rucksack out back in the storeroom.

Jane scoffed. 'It didn't take you long to break loose from the starting blocks Sprigg and so much for taking things slow!' There was a hint of envy in her voice.

'You're always accusing me of not grabbing the bull by the horns, well last night I did.'

'It's a wonder you've any energy left to open the shop. Has Vanessa arrived?'

'No, not yet because today was my turn to open up.'

There was little point in asking why Jane had wanted to know about Vanessa, within minutes of cancelling the call, Jane would either text or call Vanessa, contacting Penny later.

'So now you've become an item at last!'

'I think it's safe to say that we are.'

'And loony tunes, was she around?' Jane asked, the seriousness in her tone stern like that of Mrs Meredith.

'I don't think so, although somebody threw my bike over the headland during the night and down onto the rocks below. Probably teenagers larking about like they do!'

Jane wasn't convinced and neither was Sophie, although without evidence or seeing Anna do it, it was wrong to accuse.

'Will you apologise to Dave for me and tell him that his bad experience was for a good cause. I had better go Jane only the delivery man has just pulled up outside.'

'Love you Sprigg, keep me posted.'

The line went dead and the fog which was no more than a thin veil of damp droplets was almost gone. Sophie checked her mobile, but there was no messages. She pulled open the door of the shop the same moment that Jane hit Vanessa's contact number and had the dialling tone make the call.

Chapter Twenty One

As soon as Matt returned, he went down to the rocks below the headland to retrieve Sophie's bike. He found both wheels buckled beyond repair, although he could do something with the handlebars, forks and frame. Hoisting it onto his shoulders he took the sweeping climb back up getting the feeling that he was being watched, looking around though he saw nobody about.

Working through the morning in the workshop Matt was surprised not to have been joined by Rosie who normally took up her position by the warm brazier. He called up the stairs, but received no response believing that she had probably found somewhere nice and warm to sleep. When another hour passed without any sign again of Rosie he sent a text to Sophie.

'Do you remember seeing Rosie leave the lighthouse this morning?'

A minute later the reply came back.

'No. She probably snuck out when we were looking around for my bike. Have you checked down amongst the rock pools, only I've seen her down there before, exploring x'

Matt nodded in agreement, he's also seen Rosie down amongst the rocks. The tightening in his stomach however, told him that trouble was brewing. He knew that Rosie would go to ground if Anna was about. He sent a reply.

'You're probably right. I'll check soon. Looking forward to later x'

Although he'd missed it earlier, Matt noticed that the strengthening bar securing the delivery doors had been lifted away from its mounting and put to one side. It was odd, because he recalled specifically housing the bar after Sophie had arrived the day before. Looking up, it was then that he saw that the only window in the workshop had been forced from the outside.

'Anna...' the name stuck in his throat. It would also account for why Sophie's bike had ended up down on the rocks.

*****

Matt called the police where soon after a patrol car was seen heading up the lane at speed, kicking up a trail of dust and stone in its wake the closer that it got to the lighthouse. Since her escape from the hospital the police had been extra vigilant looking for Anna, with some officers believing she was making her way back to Holland.

'*Are you sure that it was your sister?*' asked the driver, as he got out of the car.

'Come with me please and perhaps when you see what I recovered from the beach, it will help convince you.'

He took both officers into the workshop where he showed them Sophie's damaged bike, the forced window and the security bar.

'This is a heavy bar,' said the female officer, as her colleague checked the bike. 'Local youths have been responsible for a lot of theft and damage throughout the summer, although we've no reports of bikes being taken.' There would be no point in checking for forensic evidence as the sea and salt had washed away any distinguishing marks.

'I'm not necessarily concerned for myself, but I am for others.' Matt replied, as they began recording their report.

'And the missing cat, would your sister harm or hurt the animal?' asked the female officer.

'Rosie was never comfortable around Anna. She would hide herself away if my sister went anywhere near her. Yes, I do believe that's why she's missing!'

The police conducted a cursory search in and around the lighthouse, although finding nothing to suggest that Anna had been responsible for the damaged window, the removal of the security bar or the bike. With a promise to keep searching they left, leaving Matt alone and wondering where his sister was hiding. He double checked every room, although as expected found nothing missing or moved. If indeed, it was Anna then she had not got beyond the workshop. He spent the next hour adding extra bolts to the front door and workshop window and doors.

He was about to start work on the commission piece, when he received a call from an unknown source. Apprehensively he accepted it. '*Hello?*'

'Matt, it's me Sophie. Are you okay?' she asked.

'I'm fine, why aren't you using your mobile, I didn't recognise the number?'

'Of course, yes I'm sorry my mobile battery is dead. It's charging in the storeroom and won't be ready for another good hour, so I had to use the shop phone. Are you sure that you're alright, only you sounded slightly apprehensive when you answered?'

He told her about the police and why he had called them, leaving the damage to the bike until last.

'It doesn't matter Matt, it was old and rarely sees the light of day. I am however, worried about you if Anna did come to the lighthouse, you could be in danger.'

'I can fix the bike?'

'No, don't bother. Maybe sometime in the future, you'll use the frame for a piece that you create. I called to see if you wanted me to buy more wine?'

'No, we've got more stored under the stair cupboard. 'I'll let you know when we get low!'

'So how's the bird coming along?'

'Good. I finished the wings, shortly after the police conducted their search and I'm about to start on the table legs.'

'Wow, that's good Matt, then maybe I should go and let you do what you do best!'

He laughed. 'Is that all, I do best?'

Sophie put her hand over the mouthpiece so that she whisper. *'I can't answer that here, not with customers in the shop, maybe later you can show me what you consider to be best.'*

She told the elderly ladies to browse around and call her if they needed help.

'I've got to go Matt, am I still seeing you later?' she asked, her fingers crossed.

'Yes. The lighthouse is locked down better than a castle.'

Sophie said goodbye, telling Matt that she would be ready at five. Turning to see two curious sets of eyes looking her way, she feigned innocence and sighed. 'An old aunt, adorably loving, but she still thinks of me as a young girl. She worries about me!'

Accepting her explanation with knowing nods, they both smiled at Sophie. 'We have nieces your age, we understand. Now can you please tell us where you keep your parchments of ancient scrolls on Dorset?'

*****

Pulling the darkened goggles down over his eyes, to shield his vision from the glare, Matt agitated the yellow flame at the end of the oxy-acetylene torch in readiness to weld together the first table leg to the metal support.

Chapter Twenty Two

Vanessa walked through the shop door to smiles from Sophie and the two customers, the ideal way to begin the week she thought.

'You look as though enjoyed the weekend!' she enquired.

'I did and you?' Sophie replied.

'I enjoyed the rugby club dance Saturday, finding it rather entertaining.'

The expression on Sophie's face changed, first shock then horror. 'I didn't see you there!'

Vanessa's eyes lit up. 'Obviously not. I was there though and with a group of my friends that had come up from Exeter. I would have come across and introduced myself, but hunk of the century had you firmly in his grip.'

The two elderly ladies stopped browsing so that they could listen.

'You mean Matthew Van Janssen.' She felt herself blush. 'Did you know that he'd moved into the old lighthouse?'

'I know.' Vanessa replied, the grin creasing her cheeks.

It seemed to Sophie that every female for miles around knew. Vanessa took the brown paper bag through to the kitchen where she tore aside the seal to reveal two thick cut bread, bacon and egg sandwiches. Much to her surprise Sophie felt hungry.

'He plays rugby with Dave,' Sophie revealed.

'As does Jonathon. They're all in the same team.'

Sophie wished that she had paid better attention to the partners sporting habits instead of spending every waking hour either in the shop or in her back bedroom painting.

'And I suppose you know about his sister?' she asked.

The two ladies who had come to a decision about their purchases, laid them down on the counter.

'This is a really lovely shop,' one of them said, 'much more interesting than some of the malls our Women's Guild takes us too, back home.' The woman leant forward over the counter so that she could whisper, getting Sophie's full attention. 'And whoever your friend is talking about, he does sound rather dishy!'

Sophie glared at Vanessa who was looking back out through the kitchen door. It was going to be an interesting with lots to catch up on. Vanessa had already spoken to Jane and knew most, if not everything, but hearing it from Sophie was going to be much better.

'I can assure you, that he is handsome,' Sophie replied, scanning the items through the till, 'although keeping things secret in this town can be quite challenging at times!' She was looking directly at Vanessa, who punching the air disappeared quickly to make the coffees.

The other lady also leant forward, only she didn't whisper.

'My Harold was once a handsome man and turned a lot of women's heads about the Dales. I sympathise with you young lady, only I had similar problems dear. I found the best way to handle such things was to puff up my chest, smile gracefully and show everybody concerned that Harold belonged to me and nobody else. Soon after the competition melted into the sunset and never materialised ever again!'

Standing at her side with her purse open, her friend quickly added.

'Of course once it were known that it were Harold that had put Mavis in the family way, the competition completely disappeared!'

Sophie managed to keep a straight face, although out back Vanessa couldn't help herself. Calling out she had her own advice. 'Take heed Sprigg and think how handy that would be if such a thing happened to you.'

Bagging their purchases the elderly women said goodbye, promising to call again before they left Dorset at the end of their holiday. As soon as the bell over the door had stopped ringing Sophie went to the kitchen.

'You're as bad as Jane, sex mad!'

Vanessa felt her sides hurt, having laughed so much.

'Well, if that dress Saturday wasn't a come on, then tell me what isn't?'

'What do you mean?' Sophie asked.

'And you don't know,' Vanessa asked, noticing the doubt in Sophie's expression. 'Christ Sprigg, the dress was nearly transparent. You could see everything under the lights coming from the disco.'

Sophie stood open mouthed, the horror of the occasion dawning upon her. No wonder the men at the bar had been watching her dance. Mortified she took a mouthful of her sandwich.

'Was it really that bad?'

Vanessa nodded, 'I had to avert Jonathon's attention before he got aroused.'

'Oh my god. It was Jane who told me that the dress would be ideal for the occasion.'

Vanessa chuckled almost chocking. 'Of course she would, it's the style that Jane would wear, but she's always been a tart!'

Sophie thought of Matt, what had he thought, when she'd walked up to him. Reading her mind Vanessa took another mouthful of her coffee.

'So did you get it Saturday night, only it looked like you would?'

Sheepishly Sophie replied. 'Not Saturday, Sunday.'

Vanessa punched the air in triumph.

'At last Sprigg, perhaps now you won't come in on a Monday morning wearing such a long face.' She put her coffee mug down on the side. 'I hear loony tunes is on the loose again. You need to tread carefully there Sophie, only she's a nasty piece of work. Jonathon was telling me how Matt turned up at one training session with his head bandaged and cuts on the back of his hands where she'd cut him with the meat cleaver. I did try calling you earlier, before you left for work this morning.'

'Why, was something wrong?'

'No, I was going to volunteer and open the shop today. I thought you'd be exhausted from the weekend!'

'Is that why we have egg and bacon sandwiches this morning?' The reply was simply a grin from Vanessa.

Cockleshell Cove was living up to its reputation for not being able to keep secrets, any secrets. Sophie, Vanessa, Penny and Jane had been friends since meeting at school when they were just five. They had grown together, supported one another through good and bad times eventually maturing into grown women. From her shoulder bag Vanessa took out a long roll of paper.

'What's that?' Sophie asked.

'The advertisement for the annual Cockleshell Cove Children's Home fete and auction.'

Sophie watched as Vanessa unrolled the poster. 'I was only thinking the other day that it must be due.'

'The committee have pencilled it in for Sunday the 25th of the month. Jonathon's been roped in to help the committee and raise the marketing initiative. We've got Jane and Dave down for a stall, so there's an opportunity for you and Matt to do something as well. Penny has promised to do her usual baking and even Trudy is dragging Ben along, although I'm not quite sure in what capacity yet.'

'As long as I'm not going to be scrutinised every time we hold hands, kiss or link arms!'

Vanessa sellotaped the poster to the front window where it would get maximum coverage.

'The consequences of love Sprigg. Didn't you listen to anything that, that daffy old bat Harman taught us in biology?'

Taking down one of the two paintings that Sophie had advertised for sale on the shop wall she laid them down on the counter.

'We could use these to raise some money for the children. We've had them here a long time and they've had little interest, they'd be better off at an auction than sitting here just gathering dust. Would these count as my contribution?' Vanessa agreed, although she would be sorry to see them leave the shop.

'You know Sprigg, if you sold a few more locally you could get your name out there. Sell a dozen or so and you'd be on the road to becoming a known celebrity.'

Sophie scoffed. 'I wish that I had your optimism Vanessa.'

'Have faith in your ability Sprigg. Finding love is a damn good start in making other dreams come true.'

Sophie smiled. 'Yes, you could be right, perhaps I need to be expanding my horizons more!'

'And about that dress, who really gives a damn. Christ Sprigg, if I had a body like yours Jonathon would go to work exhausted every day and the men at the bar are always high on something or other. You just made Saturday night more bearable for them having been there, rather than the women who were trying to muscle in on their one muscle.'

'I've never been to a rugby match, what's a *scrum*?' Sophie naively asked.

Vanessa explained as best that she understood. 'A bunch of grunting, sweaty men who huddle down low to the ground. They lock on, holding one another by whatever means they can grab hold of, which consists of mud laden shorts, thighs and crotches, locking shoulders and buttocks. I've never understood it, but they get a thrill from all that touching and holding on tight. I grimace when Jonathon does it, only one sudden move in the wrong direction and it could seriously affect his tackle for the rest of his life. Interfering with his blood flow and the like.'

'Jane say's that it's where men keep their brains.'

'Yeah, something like that. Somehow Jonathon has managed to come out unscathed.'

'So a fly-half, isn't part of the scum then?'

'No, they loiter on the edge of play waiting for the chance to get the ball before sprinting away like a demented gazelle running from a lion. Generally they're fast on their feet, why?'

'Matt told me that he plays fly-half.'

'Fast or not he still gets in the bath with the rest of the team after the game. When you see him next, I'd check his tackle and make sure that everything looks like it should.'

'They have a bath together?' Sophie asked, shocked.

'Sure, it's traditional. Swapping mud, dirty jokes and sizing one another's dick. Mud, blood and bath-time frolics I think it's called. After which, clean and dressed, they're wired ready for an after-match meal of pie and mash, sausage and mash or anything with mash washed down with copious tankards of ale.'

'And that's what makes them different from other men?' Sophie was curious, eager to know.

'Most of the women that follow Cockleshell Rovers call the team the *'grunt and groan bunch.'*

'How's that?' Sophie pursued.

'Whether they're having sex or scoring a try, there's little difference.'

Sophie looked bemused so Vanessa helped out.

'Sex Sprigg, knickers off, scrum down and when you reach the touch line you've scored. Rugby is full of grunting and groaning men with a few rules added!'

'Oh,' replied Sophie, thinking back to how Matt had unleashed his needs in the workshop. Fortunately there had been little grunting or groaning, mostly just passion. 'And a try is a goal, yes?'

'Five points in the bag Sprigg.'

Sophie wondered if she would ever understand the dynamics of the game.

Pulling at Sophie's old top and jeans Vanessa told her that she could do with buying some trendy outfits.

'Why,' Sophie remonstrated, 'they're comfortable and I like them.'

Pushing her breasts together Vanessa demonstrated what men wanted, 'they like to see the goods on display in the shop window. It keeps them interested!'

'Matt likes me just fine the way that I am. I wouldn't feel comfortable having any other man looking at my breasts.'

'I'm talking about fashion Sprigg, not when you're naked between the sheets. Look at Jane, she always looks fashionable.'

'She's always got them on show you mean. Anyway, I'm not sure that I want to look like Jane, half the time she's more out of her clothes than she is in. That poor Saturday boy at the coffee shop doesn't know what to do with himself when Jane's around!'

'Rubbish,' replied Vanessa, heaving volume into her own bust. 'Flashing a bit of flesh around is healthy and you see, Matt will forever be putty in your hands. Men can't think of two things at once and immediately desire comes into the equation, their dicks beings to fight for air.'

Sophie felt herself flushing, Vanessa was as bad as Penny and both were following in Jane's footsteps.

'I don't go around looking at men's trousers,' she replied indignantly.

'And there lies the problem Sprigg. You've been living in the dark ages since you came back from that stint up in London. Moving with the times demands an interaction.'

To demonstrate what she was getting at Vanessa unbuttoned Sophie's blouse to show some cleavage.

'With this and your paintings on show we'd have men flocking through the door. Think of it as a marketing incentive, without having to pay for the privilege of a consultant.'

Sophie felt sorry for Jonathon.

'I am not flashing my natural assets to anybody except Matt, business prospects or not. My art yes, but not my breasts!'

Vanessa laughed. 'Pity, we could have had a tee-shirt printed up, *'running in, please pass.'*

Vanessa took the other painting down and brought it over to the counter where she compared the two.

'Right, if you're not willing to promote your god given wares, we'd best rearrange the shop window and reinvent change. Maybe later you can get naked with rugby's pin-up of the year and see if he's got anything in his workshop, that he'd like to donate to the auction. Remember Sprigg five points when he scores!'

Chapter Twenty Three

Anna observed closely as the police vehicle reversed swinging around to face the opposite way before going back down the dusty track gradually vanishing from sight. Holding on tight to Rosie the cat twisted and squirmed frantically in an effort to escape the mad woman's clutches, but she was stronger than she had imagined she would be.

'Keep still… damn you,' Anna warned, as she watched her brother go back inside the lighthouse. She followed his shadow across the lobby wall before it disappeared. Leaving it another few seconds she stood up.

'You see, I said that you wouldn't be missed you miserable wretch.' Anna held Rosie by the scruff of the neck bringing the cats face around so that she could look directly into the creatures eyes. 'I've had to wait a long time to settle an old score with you!'

With a loud clunk she heard the locking bar drop back into place inside the workshop.

Anna kept on talking believing Rosie could understand. 'I didn't think that my brother would find the tart's bike so fast.' She laughed hysterically, 'still that'll teach the cheap whore to come calling on Matthew. He should have the courage to tell these women that he belongs to me and nobody else. Helga was easy prey and willing to play along with the game, but I have a feeling that this little slut from the town might be harder to dispatch. Still it will be fun watching her squirm, when I lay my hands on her pretty little face and body.'

Sensing the imminent danger that Rosie found herself in, she suddenly lashed out viciously with her claws outspread, sinking her sharp teeth into the fleshy part of Anna's hand between forefinger and thumb. Anna screamed out in pain as the claws tore through her forearm. Unable to maintain her grip any longer, she let go of the black cat. Rosie sprang down to the grass, turned and hissed before she ran off towards a nearby hawthorn bush.

'Come here, you evil bastard,' Anna spat, as she raced across to the bush, but Rosie was long gone and hardly likely to return. Licking her wounds she watched the cat dart away across the field. *'When I catch up with you again, I will tear you limb from limb and cut out your heart. I'll show you what happens when you defy me!'*

Rosie continued to leap between the long grass running as fast as her legs would carry her daring not to look back in case the mad woman had found a way through the hawthorn. She heard the echo of the threat, realising that if she was caught there would not be a second chance of survival.

With the cat gone the damage to the bike seemed less triumphant. Anna crouched back down, reconsidering her options, whether to walk boldly up to the front door and demand that Matthew let her in or wait and seize the opportunity later. She chose the latter. In the meantime, she needed to deal with her injuries.

Taking herself down to the rock pools where the numbing cold water would help, she vowed. *'Soon, I will make each one of them pay for the misery that they have caused me!'*

Chapter Twenty Four

Having closed the shop at a quarter to five, earlier than normal, they stepped back from the wood façade and linked arms admiring their efforts. The window display looked convincingly different, as though it had just received a new lick of paint. Combining ideas they had discussed and arranged, then rearranged until the result pleased them both. As an added bonus on either side of the display was Sophie's paintings, looking remarkably effective.

'They will definitely attract interest, plus some tourists.'

Vanessa was keen to encourage Sophie, hoping that she would paint more and perhaps sort some for the auction.

Sophie looked pensive, 'do you think it needs just a bit more,' she implied, 'something else, maybe a centre-piece?' Lying on a bed of coloured shells, empty crab carcasses and small pieces of driftwood they both nodded, something was missing. 'Although quite what, I'm not sure?' Sophie added.

Vanessa shrugged her shoulders. 'Maybe something bold to promote the subject in your paintings. You've captured the headland in one, with the lighthouse and trees in the background. In the other the sweeping arc of the cove, including the harbour. We need something nautical, like an anchor?'

'It would certainly be eye-catching,' Sophie agreed. 'Only where would we get an anchor that small?'

Vanessa grinned, raising her eyebrows, 'how about from a talented metal worker?'

'Of course,' Sophie said, snapping the ends of her fingers together. 'We would have to pay for the metal and maybe his time!'

'Okay, we can afford it and it would take centre-stage. You never know, it might also attract some local commissions.'

'He's pretty busy at the moment, but I will ask.' Sophie looked at the wall clock, it was just gone ten to five. 'Matt will be here in a minute, we can ask him what he thinks.'

'Good, sweet talking a vulnerable man whose testosterone is peaking is bound to have him say yes. Jane told me that Matt's work is highly sought after around the world, is that true?'

'As far away as the Middle East, New York and Africa and probably places, I don't know about.'

Vanessa let out a low whistle of admiration, 'that is impressive, Jonathon's only ever given me the impression that Matt plays around with his metal. Is he rich Sprigg?'

Sophie shrugged, 'I don't think so. He has a mortgage the same as you and me. I'm really not sure what he charges for a piece.'

'And he had you help him finish a commission yesterday?'

'I only dealt with the mundane bits, Matt put all the main elements together. I think the buyer lives in Paris.' Vanessa's eyes went wider still.

Having stepped across from the quiet junction Jonathon was striding out eager to see Vanessa. He tapped her on the shoulder and waited for her to turn. She squealed when she realised it was him. Six years they had been together and pleasingly nothing had changed.

'What do you think?' Vanessa asked, kissing his cheek.

'It's good, but it needs something central, something special!'

'That's in hand,' said Sophie, planting a kiss on his other cheek.

'Something nautical to compliment your paintings,' Jonathon remarked and like Vanessa he was forever trying to encourage Sophie to paint and sell her paintings further afield.

Sophie smiled, Jonathon had always struck her as the quiet, intelligent type, unlike Vanessa who was bubbly and sometimes a little wild.

'Okay beast, time that you took me home!' Vanessa suggested.

Sophie chuckled, as Jonathon winked. Vanessa grabbed her shoulder bag, kissed Sophie goodbye going up the road arm in arm with the man she loved. They were ideally suited, chalk and cheese, but the match worked.

Sophie pondered, wondering what the children would be like if Vanessa ever had any. Hopefully, like Jonathon she thought.

She heard a vehicle horn then saw Matt's Chevy pass between the parked cars as he waved at Jonathon and Vanessa. Sophie took him straight to the window display, asking his opinion.

'It's attractive, but do you think it needs something focal?'

'That's just what we were thinking. We were wondering if you had any good ideas.'

'Maybe,' he was non-committal, although seemingly thoughtful. She would ask again later.

'Would you mind if I popped home first and changed into a dress. I feel like I've worn these clothes for the past two days?' she remembered what Vanessa had said about her being fashionably, unfashionable.

'Yes, sure.'

He helped her shut the shop and drove back the short distance to the house where she had a quick shower to wash away the dust from changing the window display. Matt in the meantime took himself off to the back bedroom to re-evaluate her art again, only this time in the sunshine. When Sophie stood in the doorway of her studio she was wearing a long summer dress with a cutaway front. Matt grinned as he came forward to take her in his arms.

'You're not only incredibly beautiful, but very talented. You capture the light in a landscape as though you were just walking through the picture,' he pointed, indicating to the where he meant, 'there,' he said 'walking through the trees!'

She kissed him long and passionately. 'I thought that I'd save that until we were inside. Edith was on the prowl next door and it's not good for her blood pressure to witness such acts of intimacy.'

'I'll remember that whenever we come round here.'

'Any signs of Rosie yet?' she asked.

'No, but she'll come back when she's hungry. Rosie has gone missing before, but she always finds her way home eventually.'

He stood back and admired her once again. 'I like you in that dress, although there was something in the workshop, that I thought you might want see. Would it still be okay for you to see, wearing a dress?'

In under five minutes Sophie was changed back into jeans and a casual top. If Matt had noticed any show of cleavage in the dress he had not said. She sighed feeling more relaxed.

'Does the sculptor approve?' she asked.

'You look great, whatever you wear. It will always meet with my approval.'

'Does that include my lace underwear?'

'That as well,' he said grinning, 'although without you are a dream come true.' He grabbed her hand, 'now I think we best go see your mother before this gets out of hand.'

As the Chevy pulled away from the kerb they waved at Edith and she returned the gesture smiling at them both. 'She likes you Matt.' He gave the elderly neighbour an extra wave.

'What did she do before she retired?' he asked.

'Edith was a social worker, or so I believe.'

'A caring person then?' replied Matt.

Because of Anna, he had come into contact with a number of social workers finding them very understanding and supportive, although none as yet had found the answer to his sister's problems.

Sophie settled back into the seat, it was always so soft and comfortable. Living next door to Edith she could be relied upon to solve any issue and was also good for surplus supplies of forgotten tea, coffee or sugar.

Quite out of the blue Sophie had a question, 'Matt do you gamble?'

It made him smile. 'Not unless I'm certain of a winner. Why do you ask?'

Sophie grinned indicating with her finger that he should go next left.

'No particular reason, only that mother likes the occasional flutter. She's going to adore you!'

*****

When it was time to leave Sophie's mother made them promise that they would call again, only next time give her prior warning, so that they could stay for tea. Driving back to the lighthouse Matt asked why they had changed the shop window.

'Vanessa had an impulsive moment. It's a feminine thing!'

'Is that why your mother asked me if I was divorced?'

Sophie chuckled. 'She wants grandchildren Matt. She's always been on at me to find the right man to make that happen. She's wanted little children to fuss over for a long time, only don't pay any heed to her whims. At the moment her dreams are on hold and she'll have to wait her turn in the queue. The question was just another tick in the box.'

The Chevy turned into the leafy country lane heading down towards the dusty track leading to the lighthouse. Matt suddenly laughed, 'I've never been asked that before.'

Pulling up just beyond the front door Matt left nothing to chance. The quicker that they were inside the safer Sophie would be. He called out for Rosie, but she didn't appear.

In the lobby he produced the key for the workshop.

'I had a chat with Carlos today and in the conversation I mentioned your art. He told me that if it was as good as I describe, he would like to see a piece.'

Sophie felt her jaw drop. 'You're teasing with me?'

Matt shook his head indicating that he was serious. 'Carlos is a good man to have on your side Sophie because he makes things happen. How I am not quite sure, but he does get results.'

He turned the key and pushed open the workshop door. For the second time in less than a minute she felt her jaw drop.

'The bird, it's finished and looks amazing.'

Pulling back a dust sheet he produced the table legs attached to the support. They were rounded at floor level, but ascended upward like the trunk of a tree, containing shaped leaves and small branches. Sophie thought it was perfect.

'You've created something Matt that could only exist here in the lighthouse. You've brought the oak table to life.'

Sitting ready on the workbench he had two empty glasses and a bottle of wine.

'We should toast our new table!'

'Our table?'

'It was your idea that I create something special, so why not 'our table.' After the police went this morning, I threw myself into what I had to do. Bending the hot metal an idea suddenly materialised before my very eyes. This lighthouse is full of good, inspirational vibes.'

Switching on the spotlights she walked around the bird again, 'Carlos will be pleased.'

'I hope so. I saw the poster in the shop window for the children's auction, are the paintings included?'

'They are now, only I promised Vanessa that I would include them and with Jonathon being on the promotion committee, it felt the right thing to do. It's for a good cause Matt.'

It was the right moment to broach the subject of a centre piece.

'Vanessa was wondering. No, we were wondering if you would create our centre piece for the shop window. We would pay you for your time and materials.'

'Like what,' he asked, 'have you anything in mind?'

'A small anchor perhaps.'

He pursed his lips together in thought. A miniature anchor would be good in the window.

'I'll do the centre-piece and also throw in something else for the children's auction, but I do not want paying for your shop window display!' The tone of his voice left no room for argument.

'Thank you Matt, I'll make it up to you.'

He smiled as they chinked glasses.

'I will hold you to that and will you in return think about a painting for Carlos, he is seriously interested.'

'Alright, but perhaps you'd best judge which one to send. That way the painting stands some chance having been seen by somebody other than the artist. Carlos, does he come from Spain?' she asked.

Matt laughed. 'Goodness No. Carlos is from Los Angeles. I was taking a break in Amsterdam looking around some galleries when I walked into the shop that he owns. He had me send him an image of a piece that I had created. We talked and the rest as they say is history. He has another gallery in Milan.' He sipped his wine. 'All it would take Sophie is a twist of fate to change your stars.'

'Cockleshell Cove falls a long way short of Los Angeles and Amsterdam. Matt. This is a small holiday town on the Dorset coast, not London. The only bright lights that I've ever seen, happen around the fifth of November. I'm a realist Matt, not an idealist. You on the other hand have raw talent that I don't possess. Please don't get your hopes up about my art or about me making big in the art world. I am just plain, simple Sophie Sprigg.'

'Just give it a try, that's all I ask.'

Sophie agreed. Somewhere floating around inside her head, she saw Jane saying, *'nothing ventured, nothing gained Sprigg.'*

'You're wasted if you don't at least try.'

She admitted that his argument had purpose, a strength that she admired in him. Sophie checked the craftsmanship on the table legs. It was exceptionally good.

'You know Matt, you could sell a great many tables like this one. People around here would like furniture made to a high standard, rather than all the prepacked stuff that is available.'

Rubbing the underside of his chin he considered her suggestion. 'The metal is fairly easy to source, but my problem would be the timber. The oak being so large was difficult to source.'

His nose suddenly detected a burning smell from the floor above, Matt rushed from the workshop ascending the stairs two at a time, calling back at a startled Sophie. 'The chicken, I clean forgot that I had left it in the oven before I came to meet you!'

Sophie laughed, picked up the wine bottle and collected together the two empty glasses. She switched off the workshop lights, securing the door. Ascending to the kitchen she found Matt placing a well done chicken on a wooden cutting board. Despite the over cooking, it smelt good and somehow it was still edible.

'That was a close call,' he admitted.

'It looks and smells divine, once we dispose of the skin.'

Matt apologised, 'cooking has never been my forte. Normally, when I'm working late, I end up with a glass of wine and a cheese sandwich. We could strip the chicken of meat and take it upstairs to eat, rather than eat off the chairs?'

Sophie hugged him tight. 'Matt, I don't care where we eat as long as we eat together. The lamp room is perfect and with some bread and more wine the chicken will go down a treat.'

'When I get the table together and up into the kitchen we'll eat a proper dinner, I promise.' Sophie didn't let on that most nights like he, she eat late producing a quick meal in the microwave or a convenient cheese sandwich with a cup of tea or coffee.

'Come over here to the window Matt.'

He did as asked. 'Over there,' Sophie pointed where there was a farm in the distance. 'That's Perry's Farm, it was once a thriving dairy farm until old man Perry retired leaving everything to his two sons. With rising prices and competition from other farms in the county the Perry boys set about making drastic changes. Keeping only a small herd for their own use, mainly dairy and meat they changed some of the outbuildings into lumbar storage, realising that there would always be a market for good seasoned oak, beech and elm.'

Matt looked at the farm in the distance making the distance roughly five miles away. 'And they cut and size timber?' he asked.

'Yes and a lot goes to property developers, building good high end houses, but they've always got surplus offcuts that would make good table tops, bits for furniture, coffee tables etcetera. I'm sure that you could strike up a fair deal with Robin and Richard, only they're reasonable men and very enterprising. As teenagers we all used to play around the headland.'

Matt raised his eyebrows, 'and when you were older?' he added, grinning wryly.

'About that, you had best ask Jane. The Perry boys were always keen on her rather than me and they happened, just before Dave showed any interest.'

'They must have sawdust for brains.'

They sat in the lamp room eating supper washed down with wine. Once again the evening was a beautiful peaceful occasion, although there were still no signs of Rosie which still concerned them both. Resting her head against his shoulder they watched the sunset disappear beyond the tree line. Soon the stars would appear taking their rightful place around the moon. Sophie felt very relaxed and protected.

Chapter Twenty Five

Beyond the bedroom window the only sound that could be heard was that of the waves, gently lapping against the rocky headland below as the magnetic pull of the moon sucked back the water bringing about a tidal change. Contently lying next to Matt, Sophie listened to his heartbeat, it was strong and rhythmic.

'Am I alive?' Matt asked, exhaling.

'Just about,' she murmured.

'Good.' His reply seemed vacant as though his thoughts were wandering.

'What are you thinking about?' Sophie asked.

'The earlier conversation about children.'

Sophie raised her head concerned that the prospect might have appeared daunting. 'Is the thought troubling you?'

'No, not at all.' The reply was decisive and his thoughts were with her again 'I was just thinking that our sex is wonderful, great in fact, but I'm not taking precautions.' There was a short pause, 'are you?'

Sophie feigned disbelief, letting her jaw drop.

'Matthew Van Janssen, you have the nerve to ask that of me after you ravish my body endlessly morning, noon and night.' She dug him in the ribs with her elbow. 'I'll have you know that I am a girl of virtue!'

He attempted to backtrack, realising his mistake, 'I was only trying to...'

She nuzzled where the pace of his heart had increased.

'I know what you was trying to do and if I didn't know better, I'd say that you've been talking to Jane.' She moved higher meeting his lips crushing his abdomen. 'Just so that it sets your mind at rest, I am always prepared.'

In the moonlight she recognised the smile and the look in his eyes which were white with dark middles.

'I brought the subject up Sophie, because I lose all self-control with you.'

His expression was one of sincerity. She kissed him. Matthew Van Janssen ticked all her boxes.

'My mother would lecture me when I was a teenager telling me about the birds and the bees, it was a wonder that I never became an animal scientist. She was worse, when she found that I was going to London to study. She would say. *'make one mistake and it will come back to haunt in time, only time is no friend when you could so easily have avoided the moment.'* I never told her about Antoine. She would have flipped.'

'You were a planned baby then?'

Sophie grinned, 'so I believe although I don't think any child is ever a mistake, at some point there has to be interaction. Tell me Matt, did you ever discuss the subject with Helga?'

'Not really, Helga was not the maternal type, she had a career and like my parents children didn't figure in her life or her long term plans.' His voice trailed off as though there was nothing else left to say about Helga.

'This moment in time Matt, right here, right now this is what we have going for us. I am of the opinion that what takes place was meant to be. It might sound wild and perhaps uncontrolled, even mystical, but until I met you my life had been extremely unadventurous. It was time that I took risks, made changes and re-routed the course on my eternal sat-nav.'

Matt didn't reply which surprised her, but Sophie wasn't ready to be silent. 'I am also a firm believer in honesty. What we have now is great, but if you've plans that doesn't involve a long term relationship, a family or marriage, now would be a good time to be up front before we both get hurt!'

Matt adjusted his position in the bed so that he could support her weight better.

'I was thinking about us and yes I am serious. You said children were the result of love, I believe that to be true. The one time that I confronted Helga about her infidelity, she retaliated angrily telling me that she was pregnant. She refused to say who the father was, but after having established that she had been seeing Johan behind my back, I accused her of hurting only one individual and that was the unborn baby. Soon after that she and Johan took themselves off to a private clinic near to the German border, where she had the pregnancy terminated.'

Sophie held him tight having him know that she would never do anything so terrible. Matt went on. 'I felt crushed, worthless as though my insides had been torn from my body and cast into a never-ending abyss of darkness. What hurt the most, was that I never did find out the gender of the baby. Unless medically necessary, I am not in favour of such extreme measures.'

She felt Matt sigh.

'The memory of that unborn child still haunts me. You however are a very different person Sophie.' He put his hand under her chin and gently lifted her head so that she had no option, but to stare at him.

'If, as a result of our love you found yourself pregnant, I would be there every step of the way with you and it would be our baby!' He kissed her tenderly sending a message.

Withdrawing her lips from his so that she breathe, she nuzzled the side of his neck, 'and I promise Matt, that you'd be the first to know.'

*****

Was the noise in her dream, Sophie wasn't sure. Instantly, she had opened her eyes scanning the bedroom and the sky beyond the window. Had her subconscious heard the scratching, a familiar and yet pleasing sound. *'Rosie'* she whispered, as she slipped from beneath the duvet. At her side Matt was still asleep, the fluttering of his eyelids suggesting that he was still dreaming.

She went over to the bedroom window, unable to see anything significant that resembled the black cat. Again, moments later the scratching started again, first clawing wood, then glass before returning to the wood. It was Rosie trying to get in, Sophie was sure of it. Taking her jeans from the back of the chair, Matt sensed that something was amiss and woke.

'What's wrong and where are you going?' he yawned, sitting up.

'Can't you hear it Matt?' she asked, placing her finger to his lips so that silence enveloped the bedroom. Slipping naked from the bed he stood beside her. Moments later the scratching resumed.

'Rosie has done this before electing to come home in the middle of the night.'

He jumped into his jeans as Sophie slipped a tee-shirt over her head.

'I'll wager anything that she's hungry,' he sighed.

Together they went downstairs heading for the kitchen and the front door. Matt switched on the kitchen and stairwell lights sending bright beams of light to the outside. Suddenly he turned and gestured that Sophie should stay back until he checked that it was Rosie. Looking around the kitchen worktops Sophie searched for something that might offer some protection.

Pulling aside the heavy oak door Matt was instantly aware that Rosie was nowhere to be seen. Had she been there Rosie would have announced her return noisily before darting up the stairs.

Feeling the hairs on the back of his neck rise he was aware of a figure approaching, coming out of the darkness. He knew before he saw her face that it was Anna. Also noticeable was the knife that she held in her right hand. In just his jeans he felt very vulnerable.

'Where's Rosie, Anna,' his voice was tinged with anger, 'and what have you done with my cat?'

A blood curdling laugh echoed through the night. *'Always the bloody cat,'* she replied, her teeth clenched together like that of a wild animal, 'when are you going to be concerned about me Matthew. I am your sister after all and for once shouldn't you be thinking of me and not some flea ridden bag of fur.'

He saw the look of vengeful intention in her eyes as she came closer, her pupils set hard and set insane with jealousy. He had seen that look before, the night that she attacked him in the hallway at Ashburton Grange. Anna raised her forearm to show where Rosie had scratched her.

'This is what I got for trying to be friendly.'

She walked forward to approach him, but Matt raised his hand firmly in front of her. Anna stopped walking, confused, realising that her brother was without doubt indeed strong, much taller and powerful, although she had the advantage of the weapon.

'Stay right there Anna,' he warned. 'What are you doing here, when you should be in the hospital?'

Illuminated by the lights the red welt on her forearm looked angry and sore. Whatever the fate of Rosie's fate, she had not gone down without a fight.

Anna Van Janssen tutted loudly peering over his shoulder at the lobby behind. *'So where are you hiding the whore my big brother and how much does she charge? Such a waste when you could have me anytime and for free.'*

Matt shook his head despondently, Anna was far from being healed and the anger inside of her was increasing with each second that she stood before him. So far she had not tried to approach again.

'Let me get you help Anna,' he pleaded, 'you look as though you are in need of food, a good shower and some sleep.'

He reached behind to retrieve his mobile from his back pocket, but it wasn't there, realising that he had left it on charge in the kitchen. Silently listening to the conversation between sister and brother, Sophie descended the stair treads, taking a step at a time fearing for Matt's safety.

Anna Van Janssen spat aggressively down at the ground, she was not in the mood to be pacified.

'I am never going back there. I left the hospital to be with you. Think about it brother, kick out the whore and I promise that I'll turn my back as she leaves. When she's gone we can start all over again just like when we were children. Just like when we went swimming naked in the river.' She grinned, not a happy smile, but more a lustful leer. *'I knew how much you wanted to touch me, even then brother!'*

Matt looked at the pitiful sight of his younger sister, her tortured mind held together in a bad place, where she had never run from the darkness of her despair. Inside his chest, he felt an immeasurable pain that she had ended up like this. Anna was his little sister. He wanted to reach out and hold her, comfort her and tell her that everything would be okay, but he knew that he dare not. Anna would use the knife the second that she got the chance.

'Please Anna, return to the hospital for me this night and when the doctors say that it is time to leave we can sort out the future.'

There were no promises or vows, simply that he would be there to help shape the next stage of her life. Anna looked at him unflinching, unblinking as a dog would set itself, ready to launch an attack. Slowly she turned the angle of the knife in her right hand.

'This is where I belong Matthew with you. Last chance, get rid of the whore hiding on the stairs inside and we can start again tonight, in your bed.'

'No...!'

The cry came loud and resonant, coming from her brother. Anna was momentarily distracted by his response.

'Sophie is no whore and this lighthouse is not your home Anna. Damerscoot Hoorn is where you belong, not here with me!'

His words were without emotion, coldly hitting hard where they were meant to be understood. Anna narrowed her eyes as she arched her head low, growling like an animal that stalked wounded prey. She stopped twisting the knife.

'I watched as you went down to the beach to fetch the whore's bike, twisted metal just as I had intended. When I get my hands on that ugly bitch I will bend and twist her body, moments before I cut her badly. When I've finished, you won't recognise her Matthew. Do you not realise brother that she only wants one thing from you, just as Helga did. Look how I had to get rid of her for you. Nobody loves you like I do, nobody.'

'Bringing a knife with you is a funny way of showing your love for me Anna. Is that how you intend to love me forever, with violence and threats?' he replied.

Suddenly from inside the lighthouse a face appeared. Sophie had had enough of the mad women's rants and it was time that she faced Matt's wild and crazy sister. Anna laughed hysterically seeing her appear.

'At last the scheming bitch has the balls to show herself.'

Feigning an act of clemency, she lowered the knife letting the blade drop down against her thigh. Anna gestured for Sophie to come forward. She stepped aside where she had a clear vision speaking more calmly.

'Step outside little whore where I can get a real good look at you or are you too afraid hiding behind my big brother.'

Sophie walked defiantly beyond the front door and slipped her hand into Matt's much to the annoyance of Anna. Matt felt her squeeze his hand. Derisively Anna laughed loud and long with the moon overhead to witness all.

'Hardly a worthy catch is she brother. Look at her, a pasty faced cheap tart and she lacks what I have, what you can have.'

Anna heaved up her breasts up to demonstrate what he could have.

'Say the word and I'll cut her throat here and now and be done with it.' She spat out defiantly at Sophie, but the phlegm never reached its mark. *'Nothing, but a cheap trick from the seaside town. You have lowered your standards brother.'*

Keeping his eyes trained on the knife Matt responded strongly.

'You will never be anything like the woman standing beside me Anna. She is loving and kind, gentle and has friends. Real friends Anna, not the pretend friends you imagine inside your head. We're going back inside now and I am going to call the police. You can run, but sooner or later they will pick you up. The police thought that you had gone back to Damerscoot Hoorn, you should have gone.'

Again Anna laughed.

'You scraped the barrel low, very low this time Matthew. This cheap trick from Cockleshell Cove is ten times worse than the whore that you bedded in Damerscoot Hoorn. At least Helga had the sense

to get rid of the child that was yours!' Her response was full of spite and hatred, anger and revenge for what she could not have.

The moment Matt and Sophie took a step back towards the front door Anna launched her attack. Matt was a rugby player, a swift fly-half and attacking opposition on the field was not uncommon, but Anna was different.

Like a mad, out of control wildcat she rushed at him waving the blade left and right. With his left hand he pushed Sophie back and out of the way, defensively using his right forearm to protect himself. Screaming like a banshee Anna brought the edge of the blade sweeping down where she connected with his arm. Instantly Matt slapped her hard across the face sending her stumbling backwards with the force. Anna lost her footing as she fell grasping the knife.

With the agility of a cat she was up again in seconds and coming again just as fast. Matt pushed shut the front door engaging the heavy duty bolts, grateful that he had added them to the door the day before. Anna slammed her body hard into the panelling, beating the heavy door with her clenched fists and kicking out with the soles of her feet. Realising that it was useless she turned the knife around and stabbed the end of the hilt against the double glazed viewing panel at the side of the door causing a small indentation, but it did not shatter.

'Can she get through?' Sophie asked, nervously watching the madwoman charge time and time again.

'No, it's too narrow even for Anna. She knows also that if she gets trapped, the police will be here soon and they'll take her back to the mental hospital.'

Sophie gripped Matt's arm adding pressure to the injury where the cut was bleeding profusely. He stroked her cheek with his free hand, 'don't worry, I've had worse on the rugby pitch, but it will probably need a couple of stitches. I think I'd best call the police.'

In the kitchen Sophie tied a tea towel around the wound as he dialled the number.

The abuse and shouts were relentless as Anna described in awful detail what she intended to do to Sophie when she got inside, banging out each threat upon the door panel, but the bolts held firm and proved the lighthouse was impenetrable.

Telling the police what had taken place, the control room assured him that patrols were already on route. Surprisingly the threats and the banging stopped as Anna vanished into the night leaving only the sound of the waves behind.

Matt pulled Sophie to him and held her for a very long time, neither spoke.

'Did I do wrong coming out?' she whispered, when she had stopped shaking.

'No, it showed Anna that we are serious. It had to happen sometime and tonight was as good a time as any.'

'I wouldn't want to meet Anna in a darkened alley, Matt.'

He smiled. 'No, and neither would I.'

Kissing her he was concerned that she had taken to heart the things that Anna had said.

'I'm sorry that she verbally abused you!'

'I've heard a lot worse, teenage girls can be quite nasty at school. They were nothing except the rants of a sick woman.'

Matt seemed pensively disturbed.

'I thought she might be getting better with the doctors help, this definitely proves that she is beyond help.'

Several minutes later the strobed blue lights from the police cars and ambulance flooded the façade of the lighthouse. Matt waited until they were exiting from the vehicles before he slipped the bolts, opening the door. Once inside he secured the door suggesting that they all went up to the kitchen where Sophie was making coffee. The paramedic checked his injury and cleaned the wound as the police listened to what they had to say. Minutes later an officer asked control for extra backup to begin the search.

'The wound is not as deep as I would have expected,' said the paramedic, 'maybe a few steri-strips and a bandage will do for now, although you should visit the surgery in the morning just to be sure.'

Matt was happy to do that and not leave the lighthouse or Sophie alone.

'Have you had a tetanus?' the paramedic asked.

'I can't remember, I play rugby so maybe?'

Sophie grinned, 'then best you pull down one side of your jeans Matt because you're just about to get a booster.'

As the female police officer discreetly looked the other way he undid his belt and dropped his jeans to his knees. The paramedic administered the booster. 'That'll prevent any infection, only there's no telling what infections your sister might have come into contact with.' The ambulance crew filled out the necessary paperwork and left.

The police sergeant accompanying the younger officer took a small device from the box that she brought in with her. He explained.

'A personal attack alarm, once activated the pulse sends a signal straight through to the station where we can mobilise a patrol without the need for you to call us.'

Sophie was all for Matt having the alarm, 'It's a good idea Matt, only there's no telling if Anna will come back!'

'I don't think so not now, not after tonight.' He seemed sure, looking across at the police sergeant. 'She can't have gone far.'

The sergeant was hesitant in giving any assurance.

'We'll do our best to find your sister although there are dozens of places in and around the headland where she can hide. Earlier this evening a patrol took a report from a local farmer of somebody living rough in his hay barn, the likelihood is that it was Anna.'

'She can be resourceful. Anna was a member of the guiding movement when we were children.' He looked at the bandage on his arm, 'and she knows how to use a knife!'

The police sergeant removed his cap.

'Anna escaped the hospital ward by giving her medication to another patient, the poor woman nearly died. The medical staff believe that she'd been planning her escape a good week before she executed it.'

Matt sighed, his sister would go to any lengths to get to him. 'The other patient is she alright?'

'Yes, she slept most of the next day because of the additional medication, but it could have been much worse.'

When other night-time patrols arrived the sergeant and his colleague left to organise the search. It would prove futile even with the moon to help, Anna was already well hidden. Later she would make her way along the headland and head into town.

It was almost an hour before the cars outside departed leaving the night to settle once again. Returning to the bedroom they undressed and got back into bed.

'Are you still interested in children?' Matt asked tentatively.

'Even more than I was before,' why?' she asked, murmuring and nuzzling her nose into his neck.

He didn't reply, instead he kissed her softly, his hands caressing and cupping her breasts. Lower down his erection was hard and ready. Sophie gently climbed on top and guided him in between her legs, giving out a sigh of pleasure as he held her hips pulling her down gently.

*****

Unseen, although safely concealed in the dark space under the dense hedgerow Rosie looked up at the bedroom where the light had suddenly gone out. She had observed the attack and seen the mad woman run off down to the beach below. Happy to remain where she was, Rosie would make herself known providing that the coast was clear and that there was no imminent threat of danger.

Chapter Twenty Six

Tuesday was Vanessa's turn to open up the shop allowing Sophie an additional hour with Matt, time enough to appreciate breakfast. They took it up to the lamp room where they could both relax letting the sunshine wash through their bodies, casting aside the disturbed night.

'Would she have really hurt Rosie? Sophie asked, nibbling the edges of her toast.

'Anything's possible with Anna.' He brushed the fallen crumbs from his sweater. 'She never did like the cat or appreciate the fact that I preferred Rosie's company in preference to hers. Anna ridiculously saw Rosie as not just a threat, but competition!'

'That's absolutely ludicrous Rosie's a cat, a pet!'

He gave a shake of his head, 'you had a first row seat on what reasoning did last night, when I tried to be reasonable. Anna has reached the level where she is beyond help!'

Despite being called a whore and pasty faced, Sophie felt a sympathetic cry for Matt's sister. 'She's very ill Matt that much is evident!'

'Her mind is a dark tunnel of tormented hatred Sophie. Anna can twist and turn her moods at will. Anna runs wherever the voices tell her to go.'

Sophie was taken aback by Matt's lack of compassion. She understood how much it hurt him to turn his back on his sister, but it was obvious that Anna badly needed help. 'It's like a demon has manifested within her soul.' He concluded.

Sophie had suggested that Matt see Sandra Wareham at the surgery and have his arm checked, if only to check for signs of an infection.

'That'll delay my preparing the metal for your centre piece.'

'You're more important to me than a bit of metal Matt, please go along to the surgery for me and have the arm checked.'

'What do you think Jane will say when she finds out?'

'I'd best not tell,' Sophie replied, raising her eyebrows, 'Jane can be unstoppable once she gets going. Promise me that you'll see the nurse and I'll make supper tonight!'

He grinned. 'Okay I'll go. Tell me is everyday going to be set with compromises?'

'Only until we don't have too, then there'll come a time when everything settles Matt.'

'Don't you feel settled?'

'I do with you, but there's a lot going on at the moment and until Anna is back under medical supervision, we need to talk and tell each how we feel.'

He agreed with what she was saying. 'So how does the auction at the children's home work?' he asked.

'Ralph Jackson, the auctioneer collects the items for the auction. He places a value on each lot that he thinks will sell well at market value. Ralph is in the business, so he knows how to price a product. He always makes a profit and makes sure that all proceeds go to the children's home.'

Matt nodded that he understood, he had only put a single piece in an auction many years back, but it had failed to sell. He still had it. 'I've a few oddments down in the workshop that Ralph could have, that could go to auction. They're nothing special, but they have been following me around for years.'

She followed him down to the workshop where together they sorted one corner that had not been touched since he'd moved into the lighthouse. Pulling back the dust sheets he revealed three pieces that had created before he had met Sophie.

Sophie gasped putting her hand over her mouth, 'Matt these are amazing!'

The first she found engaging. Lying beneath the overhanging branch of a tree with its claws across its swollen belly was a sleeping dragon. Sophie was instantly attracted to the dragon. The next depicted a dancer pirouetting in her own space and the last a galloping horse. 'I have to admit that my favourite is the dragon.'

'He's been asleep for a very long time, maybe the time has come for him to see the outside world.'

She stroked the sleeping mythical creature following the contours of his metal snout down to his long tail which was curved around his upturned feet.

'I would bid for him at the auction!'

'That's ridiculous,' Matt replied. 'If you really like him, then he's yours.'

'I'd rather buy him at the auction than have the children lose out!'

It was obvious that she was going to be unyielding on the matter and that the children's home had a special place in her heart.

Kneeling beside her he compromised, 'you can have this dragon and I'll do another, just for the auction!'

'Oh Matt, thank you,' she hugged and kissed him.

'There's something so magical about this dragon. It reminds me of when I was a little girl. When fairy tales began with a beautiful princess, a castle and a dragon. The dragon would pace back and forth outside until the handsome prince came charging up on a white horse.'

She looked to where he was studying the dragon. 'This lighthouse reminds me of that castle and you are my knight, especially now because of what happened during the night. You protected not just my honour Matt, but my life. Magical things happen here!'

'I was always reluctant to get rid of him because I always thought that he would ward off evil spirits, unfortunately, it didn't work with Anna.'

'Maybe it did work last night. Anna didn't succeed and she didn't get in. We could put the dragon in the old beacon room where it will watch over the lighthouse and protect you, perhaps also it will work its magic again and bring Rosie home safe and sound.'

Matt carried the dragon up to the top of the lighthouse where they decided that the best place to put him was on the ledge looking out down the leafy lane, where if anything unwanted was going to come it would be from town and not the sea.

'There, you've been reprieved,' Matt said, as he stepped back to stand alongside Sophie. 'I doubt he'll see much being asleep!'

'That's where the magic come in,' she stated. 'It looks like he's sleeping, but Dragons can sense danger. It's what the dragon sees with his heart that matters.'

She polished his nose with the hem of her tee-shirt.

'When we were re-organising the shop window Vanessa found an old newspaper under the display timbers. Inside was an article written on the lighthouse. It had to be partially rebuilt in eighteen fifty four after a very bad storm and renamed 'Smeaton's Beacon' after the man who designed the original lighthouse.'

'Maybe, there was reason why you found that old newspaper.'

'Perhaps, it's telling us that we should restore the lamp Matt and get it working once again. I'm sure that the fishermen of today would appreciate it.'

Matt seemed to ponder over the prospect. Getting the light to work and keeping it maintained would be demanding and eat into his other plans.

'I would be around to help!' Sophie offered.

'A good many things changed last night, making things better. Let's get the auction out of the way and then I'll have a look at the lamp.'

*****

Matt delivered Sophie to the shop several minutes late, but nobody would have believed that it was a dragon who was responsible. When Vanessa heard the shop bell ring she came running out from the kitchen.

'You cut that fine, wouldn't he let you get out of bed?'

Sophie yawned. 'We had a bit of a traumatic night!'

Vanessa made coffee and heard all about Anna and how Matt had his arm cut again. How the police were still looking, but found nothing. Sophie sent Jane a text and said that if she was in town to call in the shop, ten minutes later Jane walked through the door.

*****

'Had I been there with psycho, I would have whacked the loony into next week.' It was typical Jane, blunt and unsympathetic, her tone indifferent to anyone with a mental problem. 'A whore indeed.'

'She's not in control on her mind,' Sophie replied, in an attempt to lighten the mood.

'Not in control,' Jane came back, 'she needs a *fucking* frontal lobotomy and cement injected into the empty cavities, that girl is downright dangerous. She could have killed Matt and then come after you Sprigg. We did try to warn you!'

Sophie understood why Jane was agitated, both Annabelle and Scott attended schools near to the edge of town on the lighthouse road.

'I know, but it sorted out a few other things.'

'Like what?' Jane asked, as Vanessa put down the coffee at her side.

172

'That together Matt and myself are a formidable team.'

'So do the police have any idea where she might be heading?'

Sophie shook her head. 'She was at Kinslade farm having slept rough in the hay barn, only I doubt that she'd go back there. The police have tracker dogs out trying to pick up her scent.'

Pushing the last of the pastry into her mouth Vanessa interrupted. 'Christ, at any rate they're likely to arrest old man Kinslade, that dirty old bugger has always been involved with immoral practices.'

Both Jane and Sophie looked at Vanessa. 'And how would you know what old man Kinslade gets up too?' Jane asked.

'I worked there one summer helping out in the milking sheds. What I saw going on in some of the other sheds with the older girls was a real shocker, pervy old git that Kinslade is.' She shuddered recalling the experience of having watched.

'So much for sleepy old Cockleshell Cove. We have a psychotic nutter prowling the land and a perverted old farmer in whose barn the madwoman has been sleeping. You couldn't write a story about such stuff.'

'Matt's ex-girlfriend, was she busty?' asked Vanessa, the question materialising out of the blue.

'How would I know…' replied Sophie, looking down at her chest.

In unison the two friends looked on demurely, fluttering their eyelids. 'We just wondered only he seems to have his hands full with you.' It had been well rehearsed.

Sophie snubbed her nose into the air. 'Jealousy will get you pair nowhere!'

They laughed. 'Dave says window shopping is all part of a man's sex education. He claims it's a healthy occupation guessing a woman's bra size.'

'Don't they ever grow up?' Sophie sighed.

'Probably not,' Vanessa injected. 'I remember seeing Jonathon on sports day at school in his running shorts. As the saying goes from little acorns comes big oaks!'

'You are perverse, no better than old man Kinslade and size isn't everything.'

Jane created an offensive gesture with her fist and forearm. 'It helps Sprigg and what they do with it matters!'

Sophie changed the subject. She was not to tell all regarding Matt.

'Are you still running a stall at the auction?' she asked.

'Yes, something spicy!' It was inevitably typical of Dave and Jane.

'I'm adding a couple of pieces of art and Matt has agreed to give some bits as well.'

For once Jane was complimentary. 'And about time Sprigg. Your work is good and wasted hidden in that studio of yours. I tried putting some of mine in two years back under an alias, but Ralph Jackson gave it back.'

'Why?' Vanessa asked.

'He told Dave that he needed something that could raise honest cash not award money for charitable causes. Dave couldn't stop laughing when he brought them back home, I put the paintings in the bin along with his dinner. He had a takeaway that night. What made me even more annoyed was that Dave is colour blind.'

When the laughter stopped Sophie was curious to know just how spicy the fast food stall was likely to be.

'Dave's decided on going with a Mexican theme this year. He reckons on inviting the boys along from the rugby club, plus the lifeboat crew. We can save some back and have ourselves an evening meal after the fete, what do you think?'

Both screwed up their noses, unsure about a Mexican. 'As long as it's not like his Spanish dish last year. Jonathon didn't get off the loo for two days, after eating from your stall.'

'That's because he has a sensitive stomach and you don't look after him,' replied Jane.

Sophie sensed the discussion was hitting on sex again so she decided to butt in. 'We discussed children last night.'

Both Vanessa and Jane stopped to stare.

'Wow Sprigg, that's heavy and a bit soon isn't it?' Jane exclaimed.

'Maybe, maybe not.'

'You are taking precautions?' Jane asked.

'You sound like my mum.' Sophie admitted nothing, whether she was or not.

'So how many are you having?' Vanessa asked.

'Two, one of each preferably, like Annabelle and Scott.'

'Christ, you can have mine now if you want a ready-made family, call it my contribution to your future hell.'

Sophie rounded on Jane. 'That's an awful thing to say, they're angels and they love you and Dave to bits!'

'I know that Sprigg, but children are a big commitment and remember, I didn't get it right with Annabelle. It's not that we didn't want our children, it's just that we would have liked to have picked the time and date rather than have conceived our daughter behind the coastguard station.

'I remember my mother preaching making it sound like it was the divine prayer for having children. She would constantly tell me that, *'when the time was right, he above, who sees and hears all will provide for the righteous'*. If I believed that old bollocks, I'd also believe that the pope was a virgin.'

Vanessa crossed herself and looked up to the heavens.

'That is sacrilegious Jane. In some country's blasphemy is a cardinal sin. You should be more respectful about what you say about the lord and the pope.'

Jane laughed. 'Next to our priest, Dave is god and as for the pope, he's just a man. *Fuck* me, if I was a man and had that much power over two thirds of the religious world, I'd certainly be putting it about.'

Vanessa crossed herself again and told Jane that she would pray for her at confession. 'See you don't go to hell for saying such a thing Jane Aldridge.' Vanessa picked up the empty mugs and took them through to the kitchen leaving Jane alone with Sophie.

'Listen Sprigg, basically what I'm saying is have fun, but pick where and when you want your children. Dreams do come true, but only when the time is right.'

'I didn't think you believed in fate and destiny?' replied Sophie.

'I believe in what will be, will be - que sera sera.'

Sophie wanted to tell Jane about the dragon, but it was better that Jane saw it for herself when she had the chance to visit.

'Has Jonathon popped the question yet?' she probed.

'Strange you should ask that, Dave saw them standing outside the jeweller's in Ashburton Grange the other evening immediately after work. It looked as they were choosing from the ring trays.' Jane shot a quizzical look Sophie's way, 'why do you think she's pregnant?'

'No, I don't. Jonathon does everything as though it were a marketing strategy. Everything has a number and a flow chart. He reckons peaks and troughs have to match the right time of the month. Don't you remember last Christmas when he tried to help Scott put together his Lego set, he had trouble putting together the pieces. Jonathon needs a planned strategy.'

'So what are you two laughing at?' Vanessa asked.

'Nothing important, we were only reminiscing when the boys did woodwork at school.'

Vanessa eyed them suspiciously. 'I remember that, Jonathon was given a project to make a fishing box. When he showed it to me, it looked like a fall-out shelter for mice. I would never buy him a tool kit for Christmas or his birthday.'

Friends they were and friends they would always be. They would be there for one another whatever the problem, including Anna Van Janssen. Lunchtime Sophie accompanied Jane to the bakers to get in some cakes for afternoon tea. Coming out of the bakers they bumped into a pair of contented young mother's, happily walking by with a pair of toddlers, one only just about managing to waddle having learnt to walk. Sophie smiled and watched. One day she would have similar and wherever her children were conceived they would be because she and Matt had wanted them.

Chapter Twenty Seven

Walking around the moulded metal Matt casting his eye along the sides, the hull and stern finally arriving at the bow. He nodded approvingly, *'I like it'* he muttered.

It was the first time that he had ever sculptured a fishing boat, but the result was pleasing. Cutting to shape and welding the sections together had taken just over an hour and a half. He added an extra thirty minutes for the mast and rigging, giving authenticity to the sea going craft.

In the flickering light of the brazier the fishing boat looked as though it had returned after a night's catch to greet the new dawn. *'The Cockleshell Dogger'* he said, to himself stepping back to admire his latest creation. 'I hope they like it.'

He could so easily have fashioned a small anchor as they had suggested, but a trawler was in keeping with the town. Attaching two small brass plates to either side, he carefully etched the name of the boat into each screwing them into place. Then with one final application of lacquer it would stay rust free.

He had just taken a photograph of the Old Dutch fishing boat when his mobile rang.

'Hi Matt, am I interrupting anything?' Sophie asked.

'No, in fact I have just finished.'

'I meant to call earlier and see that you were okay, only Jane paid us a visit at the shop and when she gets going, not a lot else gets done.'

'The centre piece for the window display is finished.' He overheard Sophie tell Vanessa, followed by a whoop of delight.

'We never meant for you to put everything else on hold Matt. Vanessa said to say thank you and she can't wait to see it.'

'Getting my head around something else was an ideal tonic and just what I needed today.'

Creating the Dutch trawler had given Matt a lift and he felt better, more alive than when he had dropped her off at the shop. Matt wanted to tell her how much, but he decided that it would be better face to face.

'Any sign of Rosie yet,' Sophie asked, adding, 'and what did the nurse say?'

'Nothing yet and the nurse applied a fresh dressing. It's okay, but the bandage gets in the way when I'm working.'

Sophie was insistent, 'keep it on Matt as it will protect you from infection and especially when you're in the workshop. We can go look for Rosie later if you like?'

Closing the lid of the oil can, he went to the front lobby to take a look outside.

'Knowing Rosie, she's probably gone to ground to be safe. Cats are instinctive creatures and will do almost anything to defend themselves.' He thought about the raking scratch down his sister's arm.

'And anything from the police?' she asked, not really wanting an update although feeling it was polite to ask.

'They called soon after I got back from the surgery. There was no news, which means Anna's also gone to ground. Sooner or later though she will make a mistake and then hopefully the police will catch up with her. They need too, only without medication she could become more aggressive.'

'From the tone in your voice, you think that she'll come back tonight don't you?'

Matt wanted to say to reassure Sophie that she wouldn't, but he could give no such assurances.

'There's every possibility she will. Anna has no respect for any kind of authority. She's attacked the police before so even they don't scare her. Did you want to leave tonight?'

Sophie wasn't in the least surprised that he had suggested she stay away. 'Maybe that's wise Matt. Had I not been there when Anna arrived during the night, you might not have been injured!'

Although she couldn't see his reaction Matt was shaking his head.

'That would still have happened whether you were there or not. What about tomorrow,' he asked, 'if nothing occurs tonight, I can deliver your centre piece and pick you up at the same time?'

'How about you deliver our surprise package then spend the night at my house. Think about it, you'll keep Edith entertained and I can cook us dinner, I even have wine.'

He sighed, 'I am beginning to despise compromises, although it does make sense.' Matt heard Sophie tell Vanessa that she would have to wait a day for the delivery of their show-piece.

'There's something else. Carlos called to make the arrangements to have the bird collected by special courier tomorrow. Generally they collect around two, take maybe an hour to load the piece onto the truck. If I add another to tidy up, shower and change, I could be at the shop by four thirty, perhaps a quarter to five. Does that sound satisfactory?'

'The times are good with us Matt and Vanessa's promised to behave.'

She wished that she could be with him later, but staying away for a night was a safe option.

'Be safe tonight Matt and no matter how strong you think you are, please bolt down everything. Anna's probably still angry.'

'I'll be thinking of you!' he said goodbye, closing down the call leaving the line dead.

Looking at the mobile where the screen had gone blank Sophie would send a message before she went to sleep telling Matt that she loved him. She loved Rosie too and was equally worried that having promised to go looking for her that evening, Matt would go by himself.

*****

With a powerful torch he searched the bushes and cast his beam across the headland calling out her name to which there was no response. Taking the search down onto the beach below he checked the inside of the caves that had been forged deep into the side of the hillside by the waves.

On the rocky walls were traces of paraphernalia suggesting that the caves were also the haunt of local teenagers, it was highly unlikely that Rosie would take shelter where they had been.

There were so many crevices that had been cut into the rock and overshadowed by dark shadows that it was virtually impossible to see anything. Rosie could have been lying dead in any one of them having been caught out by the high tide. Matt tried not to think of the possibility. He had to stay focused and positive. An hour later having done all that he could he trudged back to the lighthouse where he sent Sophie a text.

'*No sign of Rosie. Starting to believe that she's never coming home. Miss you being here. Glad that you are safe. Will call to say goodnight xx.*'

Sophie was disappointed to read that Rosie had not been found. On the television in the background the outside reporter was babbling on about increasing austerity, but she wasn't paying attention to his broadcast.

'*Don't give up hope on Rosie. I miss you too xx.*'

A minute before eleven Sophie grabbed her mobile expecting the call to be from Matt. She was pleased that she had a call, although a little disappointed to find Jane calling.

'I thought that I'd catch up Sprigg, only a certain little bird tells me that you've spent the evening on your lonesome.'

'Vanessa's got a big mouth!'

Jane chuckled, 'we're only looking out for you and have your best intentions at heart.'

'Oh yeah, well where was you Aldridge when I was in London and needed you both then?'

Jane sniffed. 'That was all your doing Sprigg and we didn't find out that you were bonking the frog until you'd been ditched. Anyway, a night in to do nails or wash hair is quality time. Men have to respect that,' said Jane, painting her toenails on the bed. 'No doubt the hunk is doing his smalls tonight?'

'I wouldn't know and it was Matt who suggested that I stay away in case Anna came visiting once again.'

Jane sucked in through her front teeth, 'ah yes, loony tunes, I'd like to meet her somewhere quiet.'

'No, you wouldn't Jane. Anna's quite scary and she made the hairs on my back rise.'

'Okay, so I need to go armed!' Sophie knew Jane would if an opportunity presented itself. 'And the cat has she come home?'

'Not yet, Matt has searched the headland and woods, but there's no sign of her.'

'Cats can disappear for a week at a time sometimes, maybe even longer and then out of the blue they simply saunter back in, as though nothing important has occurred. You know you can stay with us if you would rather. We always have a room ready for a guest and Dave would rather have you here than my mother.'

'No, I'm fine, thanks Jane, but I am worried about Matt. Last night was scary and maybe it's good that we're spending time apart to help clear our heads. Anna has this overpowering ability to *fuck* with anything.' It was extremely rare that Sophie used such terms.

'And your heart,' Jane purred, 'does that need sorting as well?'

'No, my heart's just fine.' She listened, only hearing nothing. 'How's things at home, it's unusually quiet in the Aldridge household?'

'Good thanks. Dave's so different, much more attentive and tolerant, even towards my mother. She thinks he's going through some sort of the male menopause, although I've tried to explain that it's a bit too early. She replied, telling me that my father suffered the same problem around Dave's age. Truth known, I think what my father suffered was an incurable desire to throttle her, if only to have some peace and quiet.'

'Has Dave been on any shouts with the lifeboat?'

'Three to date. A dog that went for a paddle getting caught out by the strong undercurrent. Poor thing ended up a mile off-shore. It was lucky somebody on the harbour wall spotted her bobbing up and down and that the sea was very calm. The second was some damn fool, local drunk who had consumed a skin full during the afternoon. He decided to sleep it off in a rowing boat only in his restless slumber he had somehow kicked loose the mooring line. Dave said the young man was still unconscious when they towed him back. The last call involved some idiot entrepreneur from London who thought that he could hire a day boat and go fishing for oysters. Inevitably he got into difficulty not far out. He was given suitable advice and told that this is the Jurassic Coast and not the Persian Gulf.'

'So, no naked mermaids yet?'

Jane laughed, 'Dave wouldn't tell me, even if he had rescued one!'

'I think he's brave Jane, I couldn't go out in the dark and battle the elements like he does.'

'I think so too, only don't go overboard on the subject if you see him, it's bad enough that the kids call him 'hero' every time he walks through the door.'

'Oh, that's nice that they think of their father like that.'

'Yeah, I know and it's good to hear it. He has changed so much though Sprigg and for the better. Talking about mermaids do you know the other night the saucy sod asked if I would like to go to a fancy dress party, he suggested that I go as a female pirate and wear a tight short dress and fishnet stockings. Next thing you know the dirty bugger will be asking me to dress-up for bedtime.'

'I would be horrified if Matt asked me to do that, Antoine never did.' The vision of her standing in front of Matt dressed like a tart made her fan her face cool. 'I don't mind undressing, but not accessorising!'

Jane laughed.

'You wait until you've a son. I was making Scott's bed the other day and I found a girlie magazine tucked between the mattress and the bed base.' Sophie giggled, if she ever encountered a problem like that, she would make Matt deal with it. 'Did you tell him that you'd found it?'

'No, of course not. I've not even told his father, only no doubt the little sod took it from the pile that Dave had stashed in the garage. I thought he'd got rid of them before Scott came along.' Sophie was laughing uncontrollably. 'It's not funny Sprigg, the little bugger's not even ten!'

The laughter however was infectious making Jane join in. Annabelle called out from her bedroom along the landing informing Jane that she had been woken from her sleep by her laughter. Jane apologised and lowered her voice, 'I suppose that he'll end up taking after his father, god help me!'

Jane ended the call stating that she would call Sophie the next day.

*****

Almost immediately that the call ended with Jane, Matt called.

'This lighthouse seems bigger without you here and the dragon's missing you too!'

'And you,' she asked, 'are you missing me?'

'More than you know.' She closed her eyes and imagined him next to her, it was the right answer.

'You could come here tonight Matt, if you wanted. I promise that I'd prime Edith so that she didn't call the police.'

'It's a really nice idea, although I had best stay here tonight just in case Rosie does decide to come back home. I've distributed food around different locations in case she needed an incentive. You never know it might work.'

'I understand.' She missed the little black cat as much as he did and tonight she'd pray for Rosie.

They talked for half an hour about nothing in general that would interest anybody else, but themselves. When they did say goodnight it was because both felt the effects of the night before washing through their body.

When the call ended Sophie realised that she hadn't told Matt that she loved him.

*****

Where the path curved leading up from the beach Anna sat watching until the bedroom light went out. There had been no sign of the whore who had been visiting the night before. She smiled to herself, it was just as well. Now all she had to do was convince her brother that he should take her in and care for her instead.

Grinning lasciviously she jumped up from the path and onto the grassy bank imagining that she and Matthew were in bed together making love under the stars. Approaching the lighthouse, keeping to the cliff edge she suddenly stopped and listened. Something in the nearby bush moved, she was sure of it.

Clutching the knife she steadied herself. Anna was about to move forward when from out of the darkness came a sleek black shadow running straight for her, hissing it had its mouth open wide baring two rows of sharp pointed teeth. Anna saw the cat's eyes, rounded and deep set like her own.

Standing her ground she baited the approaching cat, *'come on then you fucking flea ridden piece of shit, I'll gut you and leave you for the fish!'*

But the cat moved fast, incredibly fast and the closer it got, the less brave Anna felt sensing that something was wrong. When Rosie leapt with claws outstretched she collided heavily with Anna raking her chest, but fortunately Anna's clothes prevented any injury. Slipping back she lost her footing. She tried to grab a tuft of long grass, but it came away in her hand. Anna screamed then fell.

In the bedroom above Matt stirred from his sleep thinking that he had heard a noise possibly a scream. He listened intently for a moment longer dismissing the scream, believing it was only the waves. After the attack Rosie victoriously went back into the bushes where moving amongst the shadows she quickly disappeared.

On the rocky outcrop below the cliff Anna groaned as she righted herself. Her saving grace had been a grassy knoll that had broken her fall. She checked herself, checking the head, neck, shoulders, arms and back, her hands and her legs. She was lucky that nothing was broken. Battered and bruised she crawled away to safety, to rethink her strategy. One day she would kill that black cat.

Chapter Twenty Eight

Matt woke just before dawn surprised that the night had passed without incident, although he could not remember anything from the moment that his head had hit the pillow. He recalled hearing what he thought was a scream, blaming the sea crashing down on the rocks below.

Taking his first coffee up to the lamp room he sat and watched the motion of the water, gathering his thoughts together, planning his day. He considered sending Sophie a message, but it was still very early and it was highly unlikely that she would be awake. He decided to call later.

Hitting the shower before grabbing the leftovers of last night's supper he went down to the workshop to occupy his mind rather than constantly wonder about Rosie. Calling had been futile, although he had a strange feeling that she was close by.

Illuminating the workshop, the first thing that caught his attention was the Cockleshell Dogger. Leaning slightly to one side it resembled a fishing boat riding the swell of the waves. He decided to give it one more application of metal polish, if only to make it shine.

Around eight thirty Sophie phoned Matt, she was running late so the call was quick with a promise that she'd call again later that morning. Telling her that he'd had an uneventful night Sophie sensed she could relax.

Around midmorning as he was making coffee Matt took another call, a very surprising and unexpected call which was full of remorse and pain. It was the only time that Matt had been caught out and unable to speak, instantly recognising the voice at the other end of the line. Stunned he didn't know whether to hit the reject mode or accept the call. After a few moments of indecision, he let his heart rule his thoughts begging him to be benevolent towards the woman at the other end of the line.

'*How did you get this number?*' he asked, his voice was slightly unfriendly and rather sharp.

'I found it searching through your grandmother's letters. I am very sorry Matthew, I truly am. Several days now, I've been anxiously gathering together the courage to call you and all I can ask for in return is your forgiveness. I've called, so that I can help your sister.'

Swallowing his pride and the lump in his throat, it was the first time that he had heard his mother say that she was sorry. He did not ask about his father.

'What will the authorities do with Anna, when they find her?' she asked.

'Send her back to the hospital where she belongs!'

His reply was less harsh, although still somewhat without compassion. Calling from Holland his mother felt her stomach knot with the pain of her guilt.

'Has she really become that dangerous?' she asked. He looked at his arm having removed the bandage, the cut was now an angry pink.

'Anna carries a knife with her most of the times and she is not afraid to use it mother. Several times now she has attacked me, cutting me twice with the knife and the other time hitting me over the head.'

'I should come to England and fetch your sister. She should be back home here with me.'

It was the first time ever that he could recall their mother wanting to take one of them home. Matt swallowed the saliva caught in his throat.

'Maybe when the authorities find her,' he suggested, clearly hearing his mother cry, 'maybe when she's been in hospital for a short while longer, they will allow her to travel.'

The longer that she was on the phone the more he felt his resolve breaking, diminishing. Gone was the hard shell that had protected him for so many years. It was good to hear her voice, he wondered what she looked like, older and perhaps lonely. She sucked up her anguish to continue.

'I have spoken with your father and we have agreed that I should give up my work to care for Anna. She should no longer be your responsibility Matthew, but ours. We have been unreasonably selfish for far too long and now the time has come for you to have your own life.' Murielle Van Janssen continued to wipe away her tears as she listened to the silence. 'Have you settled once again?' she asked softly.

He told his mother about the lighthouse, the peace surrounding the headland and the rocky beach below. He made no mention of Rosie going missing nor did he talk about Sophie, perhaps later he would tell her about his love for the artist. As with most mothers Murielle Van Janssen possessed an inherent quality of recognising when a son was holding something back, something important to him.

'And love Matthew, what of love?'

She had known about Helga and why he had left for England, but never questioned his motives. She wanted her son to be happy. She wanted him to love his mother.

'Are you asking me mother because you want to mock me or hurt me?' he asked. 'I am a man now and I have learnt many hard lessons. The most important lesson is that love only ever comes to those that deserve it!'

'I ask Matthew because you are my son, my first born and as your mother I am genuinely interested. I want you to be happy. I want your sister to find peace. I know that you won't believe this, but I love you both. Regrettably, it has taken me almost to the end of my life to realise just how much.'

He felt the invisible blade slice through his heart, severing the hatred from within. In his head he heard his grandmother's voice, it was soft as always and reassuring. She told him to be kind.

'There is someone, but we're taking things slow.' It was as much as he was prepared to reveal at present.

'I am pleased for you my son,' her reply was indeed genuine. 'And your work, is it going well. Your father and I, we have heard of your many achievements. We are very proud of you Matthew.' It surprised him that they should have kept track of his work and his success. Although Murielle Van Janssen could not see it, her son smiled.

'Thank you. Yes, my agent Carlos keeps me very busy. It pays the mortgage and I enjoy what I do.'

In the intervening moments she felt her voice begin to break once again. Her son had found it in his heart to be benevolent. Murielle Van Janssen wanted to hold her son so much and feel the man that he had become. Looking out of the kitchen window he thought of the dragon, had it somehow worked its magic again.

His thoughts were confused and yet he knew that it was up to him to be kind, to show mercy and prove that he was a good man. If not just for himself, he had to consider Sophie as well, if there was to be a future with her and children.

'You've done very well my son and I am so proud of you.' She was losing the battle as her tears fell uncontrollably down her face, not that it really mattered. His mother had expected her son to put the phone down upon hearing her voice, but that had not been the case.

'You were always a strong little boy Matthew with such a determined spirit that nothing was likely to stand in your way. Perhaps if we can settle things with Anna, you might allow me to come and visit you. Maybe also you would let me meet the woman who has captured your heart?' She broke down, unable to contain her control any longer.

Unable to suffer his mother crying any longer, he felt his own resolve dissolve. 'I would like that and so would Sophie,' it was the first time that he had referred to her by name. He wanted to reiterate that he and Sophie were taking things slowly, but he knew that to say so would have been a lie. 'We would like that very much!'

It was a good minute before Murielle Van Janssen could compose herself again, sufficiently enough to talk again, wiping away her tears with a lace handkerchief she breathed heavily.

'Thank you Matthew, you don't know how long I have waited to hear you say that. You have made an old lady very happy.'

He asked about his father and she told him that ill-health was taking its toll on his body and his mind, but like father like son, his father refused to slow down and bow down to the ravages of time. She was sad when she explained that so many years of working apart had taken its toll on their relationship. They were still legally married, but the spark of their love had long since been extinguished. It made sense now as to why she had said that she would come for Anna and visit the lighthouse by herself.

'Don't ever make the same mistake Matthew, because you can never get back the love and the years once they have gone. And the special moments that should be treasured simply vanish without trace. Time has no mercy where greed creeps in.'

He wanted to say that he was sorry, but he remembered how his father had shouted at Anna and him when they had been young. Anna had cowered in fear of being hit as Matthew had stood in front of their father and received the punishment instead. 'And what of the future?' he asked.

Murielle Van Janssen could only say that were no guarantees, only dreams. Eventually the clock would run down on them both. He ended the call promising to make contact should there be any update on Anna. He ended by saying *'Ik hou van je moeder'*. Murielle Van Janssen broke down a final time sobbing out her heart and replying, *'I love you too, my son!'*

Around four that afternoon he moved the fishing boat onto the front seat of the Chevy and headed into town stopping at the florists to buy flowers. The journey had been delayed a quarter of an hour by a local farmer struggling with a large bull, transferring the creature between fields. Matt had helped, although having showered he wasn't keen on turning up at the shop smelling like a fresh cut field.

Jumping into the vacant space outside of the shop Matt waved at the two faces that peered back at him from behind the sales counter. They looked pleased to see him and excited at what he was delivering. Vanessa was keen to hold open the shop door as Sophie passed through with a hand trolley to see if she could offer any help.

'That's ideal,' said Matt, as he lifted the boat from the front seat, concealed under a dust sheet, 'it's heavier than what I imagined it would be!'

He kissed her and standing behind Vanessa swooned.

'Thank goodness you're here,' Sophie grinned, 'Vanessa's been back and forth to the shop window almost every hour.' It was a slight exaggeration, but Matt knew what she meant.

'Do I get one of those?' Vanessa asked, as he passed through the open door. Matt obliged by kissing her on the cheek with Sophie following behind.

'Goodness knows what she'd be like if I wasn't here!'

He looked at the dress that she had changed into lunchtime, liking it. 'What do you think?' she asked.

'It's great, it's err...' He was choosing the right words when Vanessa finished the sentence for him. 'Revealing!' Matt laughed, 'I was going to say very nice, different.'

With a shake of her head, Sophie quickly added. 'Blame Vanessa, it's her latest marketing drive.'

'I am sure that it will be an instant hit.'

Matt manoeuvred the trolley into place and pulled back the dust cover. They both stood open mouthed in amazement. Vanessa moved forward. 'Can I touch it?' she asked.

'Sure, it's yours.'

Standing at his side Sophie was astonished at how much he had accomplished in such a short amount of time. 'It's beautiful Matt, really beautiful thank you.' She ran her finger along the top of nameplate, 'The Cockleshell Dogger', what's a dogger?' she asked.

'An old dutch term for a fishing boat and created in Cockleshell Cove the two went together nicely.'

Vanessa suddenly launched herself at Matt, hugging him tight, planting an appreciative kiss on his cheek with Sophie looking on and laughing. Reluctantly Vanessa had to let go.

'It's brilliant Matt and just what we wanted, actually better than what we wanted. Thank you. I think the boat will draw in a crowd, just to look at the dogger.'

Sophie was immensely proud that Matt had put the boat together and made it look so weather beaten. With both helping they hoisted it from the trolley and manoeuvred it into place in the centre of the window.

Savouring his coffee, he watched as they added small shells from the beach before setting Sophie's paintings as the backdrop to the display. Jiggling ornaments, books and a few cards about the window looked staggering. Vanessa took photographs from all angles including one of Matt standing beside the front window. She would have it copied and framed by Jonathon as a tribute to the creator, it would also serve as a good advert should they decided to place an advertisement in the local evening paper.

Over the coming weeks locals and visitors flocked to the shop as word got around about the window display and one particular holidaymaker, an American wanted to know how much they would take in exchange for the boat. Vanessa told him that it wasn't for sale, but instead Sophie gave him Matt's card. He left with a smile, stating that he would be in touch. Every morning Sophie would plant a kiss on the bow of the little metal fishing boat for luck.

That afternoon the shop was late closing because Vanessa had signed Matt up for the auction cajoling him into making donations for the forthcoming auction. Astonishingly, she refused his offer of a ride in the Chevy to take her home, stating that she had to meet Jonathon as they had something special to collect.

Before she disappeared Matt took a photo of Sophie and Vanessa together outside of the shop entrance saying that it was for posterity. Before departing Vanessa hugged him again, planting another kiss on his cheek.

When she let go, she sighed. 'Right, Jonathon!'

Chapter Twenty Nine

'What could be so special?' asked Matt, as they waved goodbye as Vanessa turned right at the junction and disappeared.

'Possibly an engagement ring only Dave saw them looking in the jewellers. It's about time that Jonathon made an honest woman of Vanessa, they've been together for a long time.'

Matt didn't make any comment, but instead he buckled up his seat belt, inserting the key in the ignition.

'And has the bird of peace flown the nest?' Sophie asked.

'Yes, it should have arrived at Dover Docks on the first stage of the journey. The next will be by boat and then train. Carlos will take delivery of the wooden crate around breakfast tomorrow morning.'

'At least we have the dragon,' she reminded herself.

'The dragon,' he said changing gear, 'has already been working miracles.'

Matt told Sophie about the phone call with his mother. She listened without interruption knowing how important the call had been. Silently she was pleased, pleased for them both. Whatever happens in a single lifetime without mutual love, an individual could struggle to exist. Sophie only made comment when he was done telling her.

'That took a lot of courage for her to call. I am so proud of you for reacting the way that you did. You're a good man Matthew Van Janssen.' She placed her hand on his forearm as he drove through the streets of the town. 'Maybe one day I will get to meet your mum.'

'Maybe, one day soon.' He replied.

She squeezed his arm reassuringly. 'It's been a long time Matt and sometimes change puts things into perspective. Perhaps it's time that deep rooted resentment and pain needed to be buried along with the past. For a future to be promising, you need to not look behind, but ahead.'

'I know.' He turned the Chevy into her road.

'When you unpacked, I didn't see any photographs of your parents amongst your belongings. Do you resemble either of them?' she asked.

'My mother probably, why?'

'Men normally do in some small way, either the eyes or the nose. There must be something else as well, but I think you'll find that's inside.' She touched his heart.

Stopping the vehicle outside of her house he waved at Edith. 'Im not so sure!'

Kissing him on the cheek, she smiled. 'Maybe, when you get to know her again, you'll probably find that you never left that place.'

Matt wondered, his heart felt as though it had somebody's hand holding on tight. 'What about you, what have you got of your parents?' he asked turning it around.

She waved at Edith. 'My mother's eyes and mouth, my father's nose and his patience. He needed lots of it with my mother!' Matt laughed, when he had met Sophie's mum, her dad had been absent attending one of his many activity clubs.

Edith watched the tall handsome man walk clear of his big American truck. She let go a memorable sigh, recalling the night many years back when an American Airman had come calling for her. Ignoring her parent's advice she had gone to the dance. Closing her eyes to capture the memory Sophie's date reminded Edith of her beau.

Seeing Edith, Matt recalled the night that Dave got pulled over by the police. He felt the grin crease his cheeks.

'What's amused you?' Sophie asked, pleased that he was in a good mood.

'I was just thinking, I would like to have been around to have seen Dave talk his way out of why he'd been looking through your window near to midnight in his pyjama's!'

Sophie chuckled. 'So would I.'

'Dave has always been so cock sure of himself, bragging to the other team members that he's never been caught doing anything wrong, not even when he was a teenager. In his teens, he described himself as a tearaway.'

Sophie nodded. 'We all grew up together. Dave, Jane, Vanessa and Jonathon, Penny and myself, so naturally we went around together. Dave is somewhat misunderstood. Outwardly he appears brash and knows everything, although he's really a big softie with a sensitive soul and gentle heart. There were times when he did get up to mischief, but Jane always reigned him back in before he got into trouble.'

Matt just smiled.

'As teenagers we'd meet over the park and try our luck with some of the less dangerous drugs and alcohol.'

She saw his disproving look.

'We were young and foolish Matt and lucky. The police never found out and none of us had any repercussions the next day. Nowadays, if we saw teenagers acting so foolishly, we would berate them. Dave always knew where to hide, so naturally he became our lucky charm. Looking back, had I not stayed with you the other night, he would not have been pulled over by the police so really it wasn't his fault, but mine.'

'And Jane keeps him under control?' the question was loaded with conjecture.

'Most of the time she does. Dave and Jane can be a formidable force. You'll see what I mean come the day of the auction.'

As soon as the front door was closed, she kissed him passionately letting him know just how much she had missed him.

'Is that how you see us, as a force to be reckoned with?' he asked, holding her close.

She looked deeply into his eyes. 'I see us not as a force, but a loving couple and no different to any other, with a promising future ahead. My motto has always been a little reserved. To let others duck and dive, facing the consequences, as I watch and learn. In reality, I am just a homely girl, who wants a man to love me and be there for me. I have only ever wanted to be happy, to share my love with a man that I love and respect and who wants to raise a family with me.'

She sent him upstairs to choose a painting that could be sent to Carlos while she started the dinner.

Sifting through the various paintings, some good, others exceptionally good, the decision as to which was the best was more difficult than he had imagined. Alone and by himself, Matt pondered over what Sophie had said downstairs, recalling the conversation that he'd had with his mother that very afternoon. She had got it so wrong, producing two children with whom she had no immediate bond of love and for the sake of a career, Murielle Van Janssen had abandoned her family. However years later, many years later she had come to realise just how wrong she had been. Matt did not want to make the same mistake, realising that he wanted what Sophie wanted.

When he returned to the kitchen he was holding a framed painting.

'For an unknown artist you have an exceptional talent Sophie, they're all very good, but this in particular stands out above the rest.' He showed the one that he had chosen. 'You should not be hiding them where they cannot be seen. They should be hanging in an art gallery, rather than the back bedroom of a house.'

Sophie continued to stir the ladle around the saucepan.

'That's been mentioned several times before Matt and no more so than my time in London.'

She added more spice to the saucepan.

'However, I am not like you, my art doesn't flow with as much ease as your creations and I'm hopeless at promotion. To be successful, you need bags of confidence and a little pot of luck on the side. I find criticism to be harsh and demoralising.' She added more herbs. 'You're the first person that I've ever told, but I gave up the opportunity to become a commercial artist, opting instead for the shop with Vanessa. I'm happy as I am Matt.'

'We all need a little pot of luck Sophie, mine was bumping into Carlos in Amsterdam. If fate had not intervened, I would probably still be a struggling unknown metal sculptor.'

He held the painting up to the light. 'I'm no painting critic, but this is good and if I like it, then I guarantee others will too. Think of Carlos as like our dragon, he'll make things happen.'

She stepped away from the cooker to look at the painting closely. 'Why this one?'

'It's contemporary and this art sells. I've seen similar paintings in prominent galleries. The image is eye-catching and funny, amusing.'

It had been a while since Sophie had finished the painting, an image depicting a nautical theme where various animated sea creatures sat atop a floating sea shell, clapping in time to the songs sung by beautiful mermaids. In the background a ship full of sailors were cheering and waving unaware of the danger that lurked beneath the calm waves. It was as Matt had said, colourful, full of life and humorous.

'I did this painting in my last year in London. Antoine didn't like it, he said that it was a ridiculous piece impressionism that would never get noticed. It's why it was at the back of the stack.'

Matt shook his head disapprovingly. 'Antoine was so wrong. There are others like this upstairs, perhaps with not so much detail, but equally as good. I like them and that's what counts.' Matt demonstrated a strong confidence needed to succeed. He made Sophie look again.

'Maybe you're right, the image does seem to grow on you.'

'The trick with any project Sophie is to capture the subject's mystique. You've done just that with this painting. The picture draws you in close, begging you to find more. Turner was a master at doing just that. If you study one of his works, you'll be forever looking, expecting something else to emerge from the painting, like a hare running from a speeding train. Not letting the world see your art is a sin. Let me send this one to Carlos, if it comes back without a comment, then we'll know that I was wrong. You can think of a penance to hit me with, for having encouraged you.'

'That could be costly,' she said, the glint bright in her eye. Taking a chilled bottle from the fridge she gave Matt two clean asking that he uncork the wine.

'I'd best stay tonight,' he said, filling the glasses, 'to make sure that Edith's safe next door!'

Sophie slapped him hard on the shoulder realising her mistake, Matt was solid and very strong. Following her back into the kitchen he came up behind her nuzzling her neck. Sophie enjoyed everything that he did to her, sending out the right signals, way down to her erogenous zones.

'You won't get dinner at this rate,' she murmured not really wanting him to stop, knowing that she wasn't the only thing coming to the boil.

*****

Wondering why the lighthouse was blanketed in darkness Anna prowled the exterior like a rabid dog, foaming at the mouth and snarling at the unknown.

Having survived on a meagre existence of scraps and wild berries she was long overdue her daily medication and cold-turkey was increasingly playing havoc with her moods. She had seen Matthew depart and head down the lane late that afternoon, expecting him to return before the moon had travelled south of the lighthouse.

Still aching from the fall, she was cut and bruised, not that her injuries would prevent her resolve. She was convinced that Matthew could help heal her wounds in a single night, if only he would trust her just once and allow her to show him how it was possible. Returning to the safety of the bushes she screamed, sending out a warning. *'I'll find that ugly bitch and when I do I'm going to cut her badly. I'll teach her to keep my brother away from me!'*

Drawing the blade of the knife across her forearm she sucked on the wound. The blood tasted good, but not as good as it would when she found out where the whore lived.

Chapter Thirty

The next morning Matt drove Sophie to the shop, stating that he wanted to get back so that he could contact Carlos regarding her painting. Parking the Chevy at the front door of the lighthouse, he immediately noticed the damage to the viewing panel beside the door, where the outer pane had been totally smashed. Lying nearby was a boulder, the type found down on the beach. There could be only one suspect, Anna.

Making sure that the painting was safely inside the lobby he fetched a crowbar from the workshop in case Anna was still close by. Locking the front door, he did a circuit of the lighthouse, but there was no sign of his sister anywhere. He was in the process of calling the police when he cancelled the call. There really was no point in reporting the damage, as Anna would be long gone, having appeared from goodness knows where in the night and vanishing before daybreak. Slowly, once again, Anna was becoming the painful thorn in his side.

Matt thought about his mother and that she would come and take Anna back home. He stood at the cliff edge holding the crowbar shaking his head. Not even his mother could cope with her wayward daughter. If and when the time did arrive when Anna could travel back home, it would have to be under sedation. Looking out to sea, Matt believed that Anna would never leave the hospital.

Finding a sheet of strong timber he shored up the damage. Banging in the last nail he felt a sudden change in the wind, a sure sign that things were about to happen. Before going back inside he called out for Rosie, but like the times before there was no response. Deeply saddened, he resigned himself to the fact that she was no longer around. He called Sophie, who told him not to give up hope.

Come Sunday and the day of the annual auction the weather was exceptionally warm with a blue sky and bright sunshine, the ideal conditions. Having consumed breakfast they loaded three of Matt's unwanted sculptures onto the back of the Chevy, the windmill, the dancer and a galloping horse. To the interior of the cab they added two of Sophie's paintings, which she believed were no longer attractive and should be hung in new homes.

Booking everything in with the auction team, they went around seeing how Vanessa and Jonathon were doing on their silk flower stall, Penny at the bakery counter and lastly Dave and Jane, together with Annabelle and Scott at the hot Mexican stall. In one corner of the stall was a round cake wrapped in cellophane.

'A special recipe?' Matt asked.

'A last minute donation from my mother,' replied Jane. 'Mother said that she didn't like anything Mexican, so traditional baked English would have to do instead. Where's Sophie?'

'At the auction tent sorting her paintings with the auctioneer.' Matt examined the cake, licking his lips. It was rather heavy, laden with fruit, but altogether very appealing and mouth-watering.

'What do you want for it?' he asked.

'You don't have to buy it Matt, really, somebody else will make an offer before the days out!'

Matt took his wallet from his back pocket. 'No seriously, I would like to secure the cake before Sophie gets here. A man has to have some little pleasures in life.'

With her children present, Jane was very reticent with her reply. 'Driving you nuts is she, with all this calorie counting?'

'Something like that although I'm not complaining. I eat badly, normally when the moment my stomach craves food and then it's always on the go. Having Sophie around has made me very health conscious, although a slice of cake every so often could be my secret indulgent moment.' He passed over a ten pound note to which Jane gave him five back in change.

'Five is enough and it will please my mother to know that you brought her cake.'

Dave who was standing nearby called across, *'and we don't accept returned goods, you buy and you cry at your own risk. There's no telling what my mother-in-law has put in the cake mix!'*

Dave offered a sample of his Mexican which Matt found too hot for his palate. Instantly fanning cool air into his mouth Jane rounded on Dave with the kids joining in as well.

'We told you not to marinate the meat overnight, at this rate nobody will enjoy the food on our stall.'

Unperturbed, Dave scooped a generous handful of grated cheese from a plastic container and added it to the mix. 'There, that'll cool it down sufficiently or at least disguise what's underneath. Mexican should be hot, whatever the weather.'

Matt laughed at Dave's flexible, easy approach. Sophie was right, nothing did seem to fluster his rugby team mate. Coming over from the auction tent he saw Sophie striding towards the stall with a smile on her face.

'What's with the red face?' she asked.

'An extra spicy Mexican.'

Sophie gave Jane, Dave and the kids a hug.

'So what did the auctioneer say?' Jane asked.

'He liked the paintings. They've been marked up with a reserve price, which I am not allowed to divulge. Ralph believes, that there's an art dealer down from Chelsea to watch the auction.'

Matt gave her an encouraging wink. 'You see, I told you opportunities happen. It only takes that one person to notice your work Sophie and suddenly a world of opportunity will open up before your very eyes.'

'Talking of opportunities Matt,' said Dave, 'the lifeboat coxswain is on the lookout for more crew members. Do you fancy applying?'

Matt watched Sophie playing with the children. 'Any other emergency service, I might have been tempted to say yes to Dave, but my sea legs turn to jelly on water. On a river, I'm okay, but not with a big expanse like the English Channel. Watching the sea from the lamp room is about as close as I want to get.'

Dave was thoughtful. 'It's a pity that old beacon lamp doesn't work,'

'Sophie and I were only saying the other day that we might try to get it working once again. Do you think it would help, if we did?'

'Would it ever Matt.'

'What are they talking about?' Jane asked.

'I've no idea,' replied Sophie, 'I'll drag Matt away soon as we should see Ralph Jackson before he starts the bidding.'

Sophie looped her arm through Matt's. 'I've invited Dave, Jane and the children back to the lighthouse for tea after the fete is that okay with you?'

'Sure, only don't forget to invite Penny and her new man, along with Vanessa and Jonathon. It would be a good test also for our new table.'

Sophie kissed Matt, making Annabelle and Scott cheer loudly, making Matt laugh into the bargain. 'They are so excited about the chance to see inside the lighthouse,' said Sophie, 'just like the time when I took Ollie for a walk, remember!'

Ralph Jackson took up position behind the old church pulpit where he used the tannoy system to announce the start of the auction in five minutes time. He watched as a decent sized crowd began to muster, some standing, others sitting on the grass. Looking resplendent, every inch the perfect master of ceremonies, Ralph banged his gavel down loudly on the wooden top.

'Today ladies, gentlemen and children, we have a number of very interesting lots that have been generously donated from new and old participants. Some items have been allotted reserve prices, but only because they deserve serious recognition. If we're ready to begin, I will start with lot number one, a charming Victorian chamber pot!'

There was a roar of laughter from the crowd as Jane slipped away leaving Dave and the children in charge of the stall, so that she could attend the bidding.

'I thought that we had agreed not to bid for any items this year!' Dave cried wistfully.

'I'm only going to watch and lend my support to Sophie and Matt.'

In rapid succession the lots were exhibited by an assistant, successfully finding new homes, adding much needed money for the running of the children's home. At the pulpit, Ralph Jackson's bone handled gavel banged up and down faster than an undertaker nailing down a coffin lid. By the time Dave had arrived to check on Jane she had already outbid two other buyers, securing an old wine rack and a metal horse.

'What in heavens name did you bid against them for?' he whispered.

'Not that much,' Jane replied, returning his wallet. She lowered her voice, to mumble 'besides which, you always record any purchases, I make in the works ledger under charitable gifts. The tax man will reimburse you come the end of the next financial tax year!'

'But a wine rack and a horse, what are we going to do with them?'

'Well we drink more wine than what the corner shop can stock and my mother can have the horse.' Dave Aldridge ceased discussing the matter, grinning at the fact that his mother-in-law was getting a horse for the garden.

Standing at the side of the crowd where she had a commanding view of the items coming under the hammer, Sophie watched with interest as Ralph Jackson skilfully encouraged, cajoled and enticed his audience into parting with their money. Looking her way, he gave her an encouraging smile.

'And now ladies and gentlemen, we have lot number fifty four, a beautifully painted seascape donated by our very own and well-known local artist, Sophie Sprigg.'

The announcement was met with a cheer, loudest coming from the members of the rugby club standing at the back. With a grin Ralph called the proceedings to order. Sophie felt her stomach knotting as Matt squeezed her hand. *'There's a lot of people here today, Matt.'* She whispered.

'That's a good sign, the more the merrier.'

'Have you spotted the dealer from Chelsea?'

He laughed. 'Do you mean the gentlemen with the straw boater hat or the lady wearing the big broach, dealers are just ordinary people Sophie. He or she could be standing next to you right now.' Sophie smiled at the elderly couple next to her, they didn't look like art enthusiasts.

'No...' she whispered, 'I don't think it's them!'

Ralph Jackson banged down his gavel as the auction assistant held aloft Sophie's first painting.

'Sophie Sprigg as many of you know already is a local resident and a promising artist with an extremely generous heart. I give you fair warning that this first lot is receiving a lot of interest not just here today, but from further afield. There is a rumour too that one of her paintings is on its way to a Venetian Art Gallery as we speak.' A buzz of excitement went through the crowd. Ralph had them in the palm of his hand. 'And so a purchase today could see you with a priceless heirloom for the future.'

'He's good,' Matt declared.

'Did you put Ralph up to that?' Sophie asked. Matt shrugged his shoulders, kissing the top of her forehead.

Checking his auction ledger, Ralph started the bidding. 'We start the bids at five hundred pounds ladies and gentlemen, who will give me five fifty?'

Several eager hands shot up from various factions of the crowd, including Jane's. 'What are you doing?' Dave asked his face draining of blood. *'Getting the price up you daft bugger!'* Jane replied.

With his brain calculating today's expenditure Dave's head was full of numbers. There were the ingredients for the Mexican, the stall and the kids printed tee-shirts. So far the stall had made around a hundred and twenty pounds and as far as he knew, Jane had spent more than that on her bids. Going through his fingers, he was at present fifty pounds down. He pulled her hand down. 'No more bids, my ulcer can't take it!'

On the far side of the crowd a man's arm shot up, 'eight hundred pounds!' There was an instant hush throughout the crowd, including Ralph, who stood with his gavel at the ready.

'Eight hundred is bid, any advance?'

Sophie looked at the young girl holding the painting aloft. The somersaulting crabs, crawling towards the sleeping sea turtle, unware that the crabs were about to hurdle over him looked suspiciously humorous. From a distance it looked better than it did up close.

'Nine hundred,' somebody shouted. Sophie felt her legs go weak at the knees. Supporting her arm Matt gave the air a short punch of triumph.

'Nine hundred and fifty!' called another bidder.

The gavel went down after the third call for more bids. Ralph looked Sophie's way and mimed *well done'.

Matt hugged and kissed her to the rapturous applause of the crowd, *you're an instant hit!'* he exclaimed. A minute later the assistant returned with her second painting.

'Lot number fifty five, another future heirloom painted by our own Sophie Sprigg. Now ladies and gentlemen, if the last bid was anything to go by this should be just as interesting.' Ralph ran his finger down the page of his ledger. 'I can start the bidding at seven hundred.' Sophie felt her heart leaping about inside her chest.

Held aloft for all to see the long trailing line of starfish, seahorses and hungry looking lobsters snaked their way up the path from the headland to the old lighthouse, a marine carnival possession arriving for afternoon tea. Matt had especially picked this image because he really liked it.

'Nine hundred,' he called out raising his hand. Completely taken by surprise, Sophie was dumbstruck. 'Matt… please,' she begged, 'had I'd known that you liked it so much, I would have given you the painting!'

A rounded lady with a funny hat added another fifty, which was immediately increased by another fifty, by Matt making a round thousand.

'Don't worry,' he said 'we can afford it, our *bird of peace* made a handsome profit.' Sophie was afraid to watch, keeping her focus solely on the painting. Matt had said *'we and our'* was there something that had happened at the lighthouse, something that she didn't know about. With her eyes shut and unable to watch, the gavel came down on the bid.

'Sold to the gentleman at the front.'

Ralph banged the pulpit so hard it left the echo ringing in Sophie's ears as well-wishers on either side, including the elderly couple congratulated both she and Matt.

'And that ladies and gentleman concludes our sale for today. The committee would like to thank everybody for participating and especially the contributors. We will soon announce how much the auction has made!'

A moment later Ralph Jackson stepped down from the podium coming over to where they were both waiting, he kissed Sophie on the cheek and shook Matt's hand, his smile full of joy. 'Thank you both, you've made the home a vast amount of money. I would say with the money from the stalls, the auction and the gate receipts, that we have far exceeded last year's tally.' Before departing he wished Sophie every success with her Venetian venture.

Unable to comprehend what had just happened Sophie could only stare at the auctioneer's tent. Her artwork had made almost two thousand pounds. 'Why didn't you tell me Matt, that you were intent on bidding?'

'Would you have kept them in the auction, had I said that I was going to bid?'

She hugged him, feeling the tears welling in the corner of her eyes.

'I couldn't just let that painting go to anybody Sophie. This bid was about the lighthouse and our future.' With big wet tears running down her cheeks she agreed. Matt added, 'we need to find a suitable place to hang it later, where it can be seen, always.'

'But Matt, you paid so much!' she sniffed.

'Think of it as an investment. I have something created by you and you have the dragon. It was only right I had the painting.' He wiped away her tears. 'We need to share everything from here on in.'

Sophie felt dizzy with success, she felt the sea breeze touch her face. Whatever had changed, had made a big difference and Matt seemed very happy. She believed it was talking to his mother, but whatever it was, it felt right. 'Thank you Matt, I love you!'

He responded was instant. 'And, I love you too!'

Coming towards them was a middle-aged Asian man who was gleefully holding under his arm a large brown wrapped package.

'I thank you most kindly dear lady. This painting is truly most pleasing to the eye. I will be enjoying it for many years to come.' Holding the painting under his arm, he templed his palms together, 'one day soon your talent will be recognised by many from distant shores. I pray that when it does, it brings you much happiness.' With that the funny little man bowed graciously, smiled before turning around and leaving.

'There you go,' said Matt, 'one happy customer and a painting of yours is heading abroad!'

'Not to Chelsea?' Sophie asked.

'Perhaps who knows, he was certainly taken by your work. Come on, I want to collect my painting.'

They were on their way over to the auction tent when the mobile in his back pocket activated. Matt read the text message, then showed it to Sophie. *Fax sent to Angelo Corelletti. He wants to see the real deal. Promising. Carlos.'*

'Who is Angelo Corelletti?' Sophie asked.

'One rich millionaire. He owns a string of galleries in Venice, Paris and New York. If Angelo wants to see your paintings Sophie, then I would definitely jump at the chance. With men like Angelo Corelletti, you only get the one break.'

Sophie felt her head spinning, the day was fast becoming surreal. Firstly, two of her paintings had just made short of two thousand pounds and now a multi-millionaire, gallery owner was interested in seeing more of her work.

'Jesus Christ,' she cried, reeling from the shock, *'I'm just an ordinary girl from Cockleshell Bay not some globe-trotting entrepreneurial artist from Milan or San Francisco. The international art world scares the hell out of me Matt!'*

Matt soothingly placed both hands on her shoulders. 'That's probably what Rubens, Rembrandt and Monet said when they started out on their travels. Ordinary people like you and me have dreams, big ambitions, but very few actually happen. It's not about the fame that matters, but how you as an individual react.

'You can stay as the lovely Sophie Sprigg and become a local household name, content to be a shop owner, painting for the annual children's home auction or alternatively you can become a household name. A celebrity known around the world and hope that you stay as lovely as the Sophie Sprigg, that I admire and love.' He paused momentarily, pausing for thought.

'What makes the difference is you as an individual. My work sells all over the world, but buyers only know me by name. I am nobody famous and having my name out there hasn't changed me, probably because I have not let it happen. My sculptures, like your painting is just art to be admired and purchased by people like that Asian man. We make it fun and in return it can give you a comfortable existence.'

Sophie nodded, believing she understood. 'Promise to be there Matt,' she asked, 'and if I do travel, will you come with me?'

'Whatever it takes, we'll do it together Sophie, I promise!'

They sensed a movement approaching from their side, turning they saw Vanessa coming armed with two flutes of champagne. She gave them a glass each.

'To celebrate your success Sprigg, you're amazing, both of you!' They chinked glasses, thanked Vanessa then looked at one another, *'always'* Matt uttered.

'Are you and Jonathon coming back to the Lighthouse for tea?' he asked.

'Try keeping us away, Jonathon is already like a dog with two tails. I'm not quite sure who is more excited Jonathon, Annabelle or Scott.'

The stalls were dismantled and Matt collected the painting, giving Ralph Jackson a cheque. Dave and Jane had some of the Mexican left over and Matt had his cake much to Sophie's amusement. Sitting Annabelle and Scott between them they drove back to the lighthouse in the rusty blue Chevy with Sophie holding onto Matt's painting. Sorting the boot, Dave and Jane managed to get everything in, including her mother's horse.

*****

Standing alone, where she could not be seen Anna watched the vehicles leave the car park, driving beyond the gate of the children's home. She was only really interested in the adult passenger in the Chevy. It had angered her having to watch the two of them toast their future, hug and kiss.

Soon however, Anna vowed that she would wipe that sickly smile from the face of the whore. Having heard Ralph Jackson tannoy the name Sophie Sprigg, Anna now had something more tangible to work with. The standing around had proved not to be a complete waste of time.

203

Chapter Thirty One

Annabelle and Scott had climbed and come back down the lighthouse stairs so many times that eventually their energy levels were beginning to sap. They loved the old beacon room and the dragon, believing that it did possess a magical power and that it would make dreams come true.

The afternoon tea with added Mexican, cheese and pickle sandwiches, plus fruit cake was a success ending a wonderful day. Matt had put the painting to one side where it was safe, but could be seen. Later with the lighthouse to themselves it seemed immensely quiet, blanketed in only the last rays of the evening sun.

'Annabelle, Scott and everybody else had a great time, thank you Matt.' She knew that they would be excited, but had not been prepared for just how much. Sophie hugged him tight. 'I liked having them here, it gave the place life. One day the lighthouse will have children of its own.'

'I have never had people around before, there was always a complication.' He didn't spell it out. 'But I did like it and hearing Annabelle and Scott play was nice.'

'You might get unexpected guests every so often, you do realise that don't you!'

Matt brushed his hand encouragingly up and down her back.

'I'm sure that I could find them something interesting to occupy their time in the workshop, which they could do. They're very intelligent and well behaved, so I would have no problem with them coming here and helping me. Children like Annabelle and Scott need to stimulate their minds and be creative.' She was pleased Matt was keen to have them come, knowing it would be a coffee stop for Jane as well.

'Vanessa has offered to open the shop tomorrow and take in the delivery. Are you okay for me to stay over tonight?' He stopped rubbing her back.

'I presumed that you would. Was that wrong?'

'No, never Matt, but respecting one another is good!'

They decided that the best place to hang the painting was on the wall in the kitchen, near to the window where looking out to sea you could image the procession making its way back to the shore. Stepping back Matt admired his purchase. 'The painting will forever remind me of this day.'

His auctioned creations had also done well with each finding a new home in and around the town, becoming another good advert for his creative abilities. They held one another for a long time settling into one another's bodily contours. The lighthouse was becoming special for each of them.

'If only Rosie would come home, it would be the end to a perfect day.' Sophie felt the disappointment as it reverberated through his chest. She closed her eyes and breathed in the ambience of the room.

'She's close by Matt, don't ask how I know, but I feel her heartbeat and hear her purring. She's safe, but maybe waiting.'

'Waiting for what?' he asked.

'I'm not sure. When I close my eyes I can see her, but I get the distinct feeling that she's waiting for a something special to happen.'

Admiring the painting Matt went over to look closer as something had caught his eye. There in the window of the lighthouse was a little black cat, he pointed it out to Sophie.

'Goodness, that was a long time ago that I painted that, I didn't even realise that there was a cat in the picture.'

'It has to be a good omen,' he claimed. Looking again he saw a man looking out from the old beacon room. 'That could very well be me Sophie.'

'That's spooky. It was finished a long time ago. Who knows Matt, maybe my destiny was known long before I ever took Ollie on the walk along the beach.' Sophie remembered how she had felt things had changed back at the auction. 'Somehow Matt, you must have featured in my destiny.'

Even more bizarre was the workshop at the side of the lighthouse depicted in the painting. Matt asked when the painting had been created, Sophie thought at least ten years back. He looked at the painting again and then her.

'The owners didn't add the extension until six years ago, it's as though you subconsciously looked into the future, knowing that someday you would be standing in the workshop choosing the sleeping dragon.'

Sophie didn't have the answer. Things happened at the old lighthouse that was inexplicable. She wondered why the previous owners had moved out. Matt thought it was because they could never settle. 'It wasn't meant to be theirs Matt.' Was all she could offer.

So much had changed, since he had talked with his mother, as though hearing her voice had calmed the storm brewing on the horizon. With the stars appearing they were content just being with one another. Love could be a very usual emotion, filled with sadness and happiness at the same time. Sophie sensed that each moment spent together would eventually become a memory that she would treasure for the rest of her life.

'So where do we go from here Matt?' she asked, shutting her eyes again.

'How about setting up an art studio in the lamp room?' he suggested. She looked at him, her eyes searching, was he serious. Matt continued, before she could respond, 'the light is amazing up there, better than anywhere else in the lighthouse.'

'Live here, with you and Rosie?' she asked, making it sound exciting. He liked the fact that she had included Rosie, even if she was still missing.

'Would that be such a bad thing?' he asked.

Shaking her head decisively Sophie's mind was a mix of dreams and promise. 'I couldn't see anything bad in being with you Matt. When was you thinking?'

'Whenever it suits you.'

'And what about Anna?' she asked, not wanting to spoil the moment by bringing his sister into the equation, but she was a consideration to factor in. Sophie needed to know that she was going to be safe coming and going each day.

'Anna doesn't feature into this arrangement.'

'I know that Matt, but I meant she's not been found!'

He wanted to say that they would deal with Anna as and when the moment arrived, but it wasn't fair to subject Sophie to another dangerous ordeal. 'She will be and soon.'

'How can you be so sure?'

He placed his palm on his chest. 'Because, I feel it in here. I had hoped that her visit had been made when you weren't around. If she turns up again, I am not going to stand for any more of her nonsense. Anna has the offer to go back to Holland to live with my mother, however, if she cannot accept help from anybody then she will spend the rest of her life in a locked ward. I am not being insensitive, cruel or even harsh, but we've a chance to build on something here and I am not prepared to have Anna destroy us. This is Anna's journey of self-destruction, not ours!'

'In the meantime I'm the one in danger Matt. I heard what Anna said the other night and what she intends to do with me.'

Matt was cornered and he admitted it. He did not have a convincing reply. 'I guess so.'

'I really do want to be with you Matt, but maybe we should wait awhile until Anna is out of harm's way.' She tried to let him down gently, knowing it would hurt however it was said.

'I wasn't suggesting that you give up your house, only maybe consider renting it out and saving the additional income.'

It was obvious to Sophie that Matt had given the matter considerable thought. She put her hand on his forearm. 'When the time is right, I would still need to explain to Edith the reason why. I've a feeling that she'll be disappointed not having you come to visit next door!'

His grin wasn't convincing. 'Is Edith the only consideration?'

'More or less.' She replied.

With a cloud of uncertainty hanging over their heads Anna was becoming a thorn in both their sides. Sophie partly wanted a confrontation so that the matter could be settled once and for all. Matt wanted to hate his sister, but somehow he couldn't, he smiled as a sly grin creased her face.

'What?' he mused.

'You do realise that if I move in with you, you will have Jane, Vanessa and Penny calling to visit. You'd have a home full of gorgeous women to contend with, I might be jealous with all that competition!'

The idea made him chuckle, 'I would struggle along bravely, somehow finding the willpower to control myself.'

'You'd better control yourself Matthew Van Janssen.'

They planned the lamp room, where she put her easel and paints, store her canvasses and where best to keep a space for them to sit in the evening, as there was still a view to be enjoyed. Sophie went over to where the dragon was keeping watch of the drive. Beyond the rolling hills of the Dorset landscape the sky outside was dark and the treeline in the distance was just barely visible. Every so often the dark was punctuated by an illuminated farmhouse light. With her head on his chest she listened to the heart pumping blood around his body.

'Ignoring Anna, I could begin getting my effects together after work each day and if things prove not to be too risky, I could move in sometime the following weekend. Would that suit you and any plans that you might have?' she saw him nod.

'That would give me time to tidy the place.'

'It is tidy Matt and I don't want you doing anything out of the ordinary because I am moving in. I like you and the lighthouse the way that you both are. I could however do with some help with the heavier boxes.'

He looked over at the sleeping dragon then at the ground below believing that he saw a sudden movement, although he did not mention it. Was it Rosie, he couldn't be sure. He was still in the habit of leaving out food in the hope that she might come back. Of course the movement that he saw could have been a hungry fox.

'Skyhort and me, we discussed you moving in the other night. He told me that you'd need help!'

'You discussed it with the dragon,' she replied, slightly bemused, 'and why Skyhort?'

'Skyhort was the name of a dragon from a fictional story book that my grandmother would read to Anna and myself before we went to sleep. And like most dragons Skyhort would emit huge plumes of fire from its mouth terrifying the villagers in the valley below the mountain, until one day when he was confronted by a small girl. The dragon was so taken aback by the girl's courage that he vowed to change his evil ways. Hence from that day forward Skyhort protected the villagers rather than scare them. I thought Skyhort was an apt name as the dragon watches out for us.'

Sophie leant across and rubbed her hand over the dragon's tummy. *'Hi Skyhort,'* she murmured, *'please cast one of your magic spells for us and bring Rosie home again safe and sound.'*

Chapter Thirty Two

Lying together naked under the quilt they talked for a long time making plans for the future, needing the luxury of sleep although fighting hard the effort to stay awake wanting everything to be just right. They were still talking when Matt suddenly sat bolt upright in the bed with his finger pressed against his lips.

'What is it?' Sophie whispered, the hair on the back of her neck bristling.

Matt went to the window to look down expecting to see Anna outside. Slipping on his jeans and tee-shirt Sophie did the same, her heart beating fast beneath her blouse.

'Did you hear it,' he asked, 'the scratching?'

'Oh no, not again Matt, please don't let it be Anna, not tonight!'

'No, I don't think it is her,' he said, 'the scratching, it's different not feral.' He started to descend the stairs down to the kitchen below.

'Are you sure it wasn't the branches from the rose bush beside the front door?' Sophie asked.

Matt gave a shake of his head knowing that the only way to expose the origin was to go and look. Sophie was right behind him. Picking up the wooden rolling pin she armed herself, going down the last flight down to the lobby. It was impossible to see beyond the door because of the board across the broken window. Momentarily, they stood and listened, suddenly picking up the plaintive sound of a cat crying.

'Rosie...' Sophie called loudly, making to unlock the door, but Matt grabbed her arm in time to stop her from releasing the bolts.

'Wait,' he suggested, 'it could be another of Anna's tricks.'

Sophie felt the anger rise in her. 'Alright, when I raise the rolling pin you open the door, if she has a knife, I'll knock it out of her hand!'

With his foot and leg against the base panel Matt cautiously pulled the door open a few inches, enough for Rosie and her four kittens to pass through. Rosie waited until her brood was safely inside before she circled Sophie's ankles.

'*Oh Matt,*' shrieked Sophie, as four adorable bundles of fur cried out hungrily for warm milk. '*Rosie stayed away because she needed to find a safe haven to have her kittens.*'

Huddling together the four kittens looked lost in the interior of the lobby, it was so different from the barn where they had been born. With more plaintive cries they appeared exhausted. Matt gently scooped Rosie up into his arms and hugged her affectionately, as Sophie knelt down letting the four kittens wriggle and vie for her attention. She stroked and caressed their tiny heads with her outstretched fingers. 'Skyhort heard our wish Matt, she brought Rosie home safe and sound.'

'So it would seem,' he went down on one knee, allowing Rosie to drop down to the floor again so that she could be with her kittens. 'I wonder who's the father?'

Sophie looked up smiling, 'now that could remain a secret, that only Rosie knows the answer too.' She stroked the back of the cat's head, 'sometimes we girls have secrets that have to stay secret, don't we Rosie.' The cat purred loudly in agreement.

Scooping two tiny kittens each they went back upstairs with Rosie following closely behind. Sophie made warm milk adding the contents to a cereal bowl, where immediately four tiny mouths began devouring the warm liquid. She gave Rosie her own bowl. 'She will need this and more to rebuild her strength and especially as the kittens begin to grow.'

Rubbing the pinkish line on his forearm he remembered Anna having similar. '*So that's why you scratched my sister,*' he said. '*Well done girl, she probably deserved it!*'

When the kittens had finished their milk they went over to join their mother.

'Natural instinct kicked in Matt. Rosie would have protected her young at whatever cost to herself. She must have known that she was pregnant when Anna took her, having found her wandering about outside. It might also account for why Rosie was so restless before all this kicked off.'

They opened and crushed several tins of pilchards together placing them on a small platter. Tiny paws clambered over each other to fill their stomachs, but with a natural display of motherly skill, Rosie stepped in amongst the eating confusion and made sure that they each received their share.

'They're absolutely divine Matt, although obviously hungry.' Rosie made a fuss of Sophie, pleased to see that she was back at the lighthouse. 'And you,' stroked Sophie, 'are one very clever mother Rosie for keeping your little ones safe.'

Finding some old towels they made a bed for the kittens to lie in. One by one with their stomachs full they began shutting their eyes. Washing would come later. When they were asleep Sophie

210

checked their markings. Surprisingly each had a white tuft on the ear and a similar speck on the end of their tail.

'You would be hard pressed to find the father going by the lack of markings.' She said.

Matt laughed, although not overly loud. 'I'll still be asking around, only you never know one of the local toms might come forward'

'I know it's early to be thinking about it, but what are you going to do with the kittens when the time comes to leave their mother?'

Matt rubbed his chin. 'Well for a start, they'll need their inoculations and in the meantime, I suppose they'll have the freedom of the lighthouse to play in, until such time that we find alternative homes!'

Sophie was pleased to hear that for the meantime they would be safe inside. 'I know at least two, possibly three good homes that would take a kitten each.'

'Who precisely?' Matt asked, seeing Rosie's ears prick up.

'Annabelle and Scott for one, Vanessa another and quite possibly Edith the other.'

Matt had thought of the first two possibilities, but not the third. 'Isn't Edith getting a bit past it to take on a kitten only they can be quite a handful when they are so young?'

'She lost her tabby to a delivery van six months ago and has pined for Suzy ever since. Replacing her dead cat would be hard, but a kitten could possibly be just the pick-me-up that Edith needs.'

Matt nodded, the proposal sounded good. 'And Dave and Jonathon, they'd both be okay with an addition to the household?'

'I'll ask Jane and Vanessa, but I can almost guarantee they will say yes. Around here we call it girl power.'

Matt saw the boy kitten look up at him with one eye open, the other closed. 'Look, listen and learn little one,' he advised, 'once these women get their claws into you, life can change very quickly.'

Stroking the top of Rosie's head, Sophie bent down even lower, 'if it wasn't for us girl's Rosie, these men would be lost!' The cat lifted her head and looked at Matt, purring.

The little boy with the flecked white tail ignored his sisters as he stretched. Matt picked him up and placed the kitten in the palm of his hand. 'I think that whatever we decide, we should keep this little one here, if only to balance the gender ratio.'

All of them slept in the bedroom that night and had an undisturbed night. Rosie slept in her basket surrounded by her brood. On the floor above Skyhort kept watch.

Whatever the reason that Rosie had arrived with her kittens it was a good omen and had been an end to an amazing day. With the moon moving to the far side of the bedroom Sophie was soon asleep nestling comfortably in the crook of Matt's shoulder. Every so often she would wake, hear a murmur coming from the basket, then settle again believing that everything was going to be alright now that Rosie was home.

Looking up at the full moon, Matt was very grateful for Rosie being back, accepting that the wind of change was undeniably inevitable. He sensed too, that there was more change to come and that it would arrive when least expected. When the time was right Sophie would move in and begin painting again and later that morning, he would call his mother, just to hear her voice.

Chapter Thirty Three

Several hours later Sophie was the first to wake hearing the sound of little thuds outside of the basket as the kittens explored the upper floor wanting to make their way down to the kitchen and morning milk. Easing herself silently from the bed she slipped on Matt's tee-shirt, going down, carrying the kittens in the crook of her arm. Waiting beside the bowl Rosie sat licking and cleaning her paws.

'Busy night girl?' Sophie asked, as she filled the kettle, not knowing how many times the kittens had suckled their mother. She refilled the bowls and spooned into the mugs two heaps of coffee for her and Matt. Hearing footsteps move across the floor above Sophie added the hot water to the mugs. Moments later he reached around, pulled her in close and kissed the back of her neck.

'Good morning, I was wondering where my tee-shirt had gone.'

Sophie turned around so that she could respond, suggesting that he could have the tee-shirt back, but it would leave her naked and she wasn't sure what time the postman was due. With a smile Matt told her to leave it on.' He sniffed, 'coffee smells good.'

Looking down at the kittens they were far too busy filling their stomachs to notice that he'd come down from the bedroom. Reaching over, he gently stroked Rosie's head, 'busy night girl?'

'I've just asked that,' Sophie looked at the spill of milk at the side of the kittens bowl, 'they've certainly got an appetite.'

Matt pulled Sophie over so that she sat on his lap. They could drink the coffee together and watch the kittens together. 'I'll ring the vet later and arrange to have them inoculated. Maybe then they'll give Rosie a rest, she looks exhausted.'

Sophie agreed Rosie was a little listless. 'She's had a traumatic experience, she needs to recuperate!' Sophie didn't elaborate, but Matt understood the inference.

Having done at the bowl the boy kitten padded over where Matt sat drinking his coffee.

'It seems that you two have formed a bond.' Sophie reached down and picked up the kitten. It promptly opened its mouth to yawn. 'It looks like you too!'

Matt grinned. 'Quite possibly.'

Mid-morning the vet gave Rosie a clean bill of health. Examining the kittens she held them in the palm of her hand looking adoringly at the bright eyed little balls of fluff, with their distinctive blue eyes. Updating the records the vet asked, 'do you know the father?'

Matt shook his head. 'No, he's not presented himself yet!'

'Well, going by the colour of the kittens eyes, I would say that his are blue too.'

Matt smiled. 'That's something to go on.' He turned to face Rosie, 'she's saying nothing!'

The vet stroked Rosie affectionately, 'don't you tell him girl,' she laughed. 'I'll give them their inoculations and then you can take them home Matt. Have you decided what you'll do with the kittens after they've been weaned from their mother?'

'The girls are already spoken for and the boy is going to live with us.' Matt responded taking hold of the boy. 'We thought Edith Dawson might like one of the girls.'

Alison Branford smiled approvingly. 'That's a nice thought. Edith was devastated to lose Suzy.'

*****

Sophie sent Jane a text telling her that she had something to show her, suggesting that she met them at the shop. Jane was there before Sophie and Matt arrived. They left Rosie asleep in the Chevy taking the four kittens inside in a little cardboard box.

'I'm afraid that the boy is not for adoption,' explained Matt, as Sophie, Jane and Vanessa played with the kittens lifting them from the box.

'Oooh, they're gorgeous,' Vanessa cooed, as she held up a little bundle of black fur. 'When can we take one home?'

'Not for another ten weeks,' Matt replied, 'sorry, that was the vet's instruction.'

Both Jane and Vanessa took photographs on their mobiles of the kitten that they had chosen, identifying each by the white tuft, marking the tip of their ears. Ten weeks was going to seem like a long time and especially for Annabelle and Scott. To make the time go by easier Matt suggested that they both come by the lighthouse after school or at the weekend so that they could see the kittens.

Vanessa was already on the mobile to Jonathon telling him the news, when she came off she was grinning like a Cheshire cat. 'He has strict instruction to make the kitten a bed this weekend.'

Sophie smiled, it was just as she thought it would be. Vanessa would tell Jonathon that they were taking delivery of a kitten, not ask him and Jane would undoubtedly do the same with Dave, although in her case she had the children to support the argument. Matt took the kitten's home promising to call Sophie later. He kissed her goodbye stating that he had an important call to make. She wished him luck and made him promise to say hello from her to his mother.

With the kettle on Jane went to the bakers to buy the pastries. When she got back Sophie suggested that they invite Penny along as well. Ten minutes later Penny arrived leaving Ollie tied to the post outside.

'So come on Sprigg what was so important that I leave my work at home and come here, the suspense is killing me?' asked Penny.

'Matt has asked me to move in with him!'

Jane slumped. 'Is that it Sprigg, we knew that was inevitable, it was just a case of when. You made poor Penny leave her drawing board to hear that. For a moment we thought you'd announce that you had given up family planning!'

Penny gave Sophie's arm an encouraging squeeze. 'Don't pay any attention to Jane and the drawings can wait. When Sprigg?' she asked.

'End of this week, maybe next depending upon how quick I can pack and...' she didn't finish. Jane however did, '... when they find loony tunes, right!' Sophie nodded.

'So what are you going to do with the house?' Vanessa asked.

'I'm not really sure, either sell up or rent it out. The market is strong for either option at present.'

'I would have to ask Jonathon of course, but I'm almost certain that we would be interested in whichever option you decide, although selling would be preferable. Our present accommodation is far too small and we could do with the extra room.'

'Why, are you pregnant as well?' asked Jane.

Sophie sighed. 'Not everybody is as loose or sex mad like you Aldridge.'

Jane screwed up her nose. 'Then you lot don't know what you're missing. When the engine needs a retune and the mechanic finds that it hasn't been turned over in while, it's not the engine that's at fault, but the spark plugs as well. Keeping everything lubricated and in working order is what keeps it from going to the knacker's yard.'

All three hung their heads in despair, Jane really was impossible.

Trade was good during the morning, but like an ebbing tide come the afternoon the shop had very few customers. Around four Vanessa suggested that Sophie cut away and begin her packing. Walking the back streets to her house she noticed that everywhere appeared unusually quiet. Sophie was almost at her front door when Edith caught her attention banging on the window to attract her attention.

'Are you okay?' Sophie asked, concerned that Edith had suffered a fall or some other mishap.

'I'm fine dear, it's just that I wanted to catch you before you went inside. I had hoped that you would come home with that nice young man!' Sophie immediately perceived that something had upset Edith as she appeared very edgy and agitated.

'Why is there something wrong Edith?' She ushered her elderly neighbour back inside, shutting the door behind her and following Edith into the front room. Edith sat in her normal chair breathing in through her nose.

'Most of the afternoon, there's been a stranger lurking about, constantly going up and down looking at your house in particular.' She touched the side of her nose. 'I can tell these things.' Edith nodded at Sophie. 'Oh, I know you young people think that I'm past it and a little screwy, but my marbles are still rolling around inside my skull, without any help from medication!'

It wasn't unusual to see a lost holiday maker walking up and down, confused and bewildered by the maze of back lanes and alleys. Unless you were familiar with the town and the peculiar layout you could soon become disorientated. In bygone days the lay of the old harbour and arched beach had once become the haunt of resident smugglers.

'Are you sure that it wasn't just some poor soul who had got themselves lost Edith?'

'No, I would swear that this person was looking for something in particular. She made me shudder every time that she walked past. She had wild staring eyes, you know like them druggy types. She looked like she should be in Ashburton Grange rather than out on the streets!'

Sophie felt a shiver run down her spine. She asked Edith to describe the woman.

'Scruffy, very scruffy like one of those homeless types, hair all wild and unkempt, dirty clothes and not washed for days, maybe weeks. Down and outs they call them.'

'Anything else?' she prompted, hoping that Edith might remember something else.

'No, not really although I couldn't see too well, I blame the sun over the top of the roofs opposite,' she stopped, then remembered, 'although, at one point, I thought I saw a knife in her hand!'

'Have you called the police?' Edith shook her head.

'Why not, you normally do?' asked Sophie.

'She frightened me. It was the way that she looked at me. I thought that if I did phone them and she escaped, she would come back when it was dark and knock on my door.'

'Whose door did she knock on Edith?'

'Yours, several times. I am sorry Sophie, I know that I'm being silly, but I'm not as brave as I used to be.'

Sophie gave her a hug and said that she'd done her bit by just watching. If it was Anna, she had first-hand knowledge how terrifying she could be. Sophie thought about calling Matt, although until she verified that it was Anna she didn't want him driving through the lanes at speed to get to her.

Edith felt more composed sitting alongside Sophie. 'She peered in through your front room window and tried the bell several times before she vanished. At first, I thought it might have been the lady with the dog, what's her name…?'

'Penny and Ollie is the dog.'

'Yes, that's her. No, it wasn't Penny, she's much, much prettier and her hair is always so nicely brushed.'

It would amuse Penny that she'd been described as a wild woman.

'After looking through my window, what did she do then Edith?' Sophie asked.

Edith mimed the lifting of a letter box. 'She said rude words through your letterbox, terrible disgusting things. I didn't want to listen, but I felt compelled to hear what it was that she had to say. She called you a whore Sophie.'

Sophie felt the tightening in her chest, it was Anna. How did Anna find out where she lived and how did she know her name? Like a bad dream, Sophie suddenly remembered the tannoy announcement at the auction. Having registered her interest with Ralph Jackson the application form would have recorded her home address. It was possible with Ralph busy with the auction, Anna would have had ample time in the tent alone to have gone through his briefcase.

She went over to the window keeping hidden behind the curtain, there was nobody in the street. Sophie called Matt and told him what Edith had told her. He immediately arrived at the same conclusion, especially when calling through the letterbox that she was a whore.

He advised, 'stay at Edith's where you're safe, I'm on my way. Have you called the police?'

'No, that was my next call.'

'I'll do it from here. They know me and they know my circumstances, it will save you time having to explain. Be safe. I love you!' The line went dead.

Sophie made Edith a strong cup of tea to calm her down, with two chocolate biscuits for a quick injection of glucose. She had only just sat back down herself when the sound of glass breaking echoed through from the back of the house.

'That, I believe was my kitchen door!' whispered Sophie. 'Call the police Edith and tell them that I'm being burgled. I'm going to have a look.'

Edith surprisingly was out of her chair and had hold of Sophie's wrist with a firm grip. 'Please dear stay here, where you're safe. Let the police deal with the intruder!'

When the wall shook, rattling Edith's hanging ornaments and pictures, Sophie realised that the vibration was coming from her house. Whoever was inside was smashing and trashing the house. Sophie stood and put her hand on Edith's shoulder.

'That's my home Edith, I am not going to stand by and have somebody smash it up for fun!'

Edith nodded, as she reached for the phone, she dialled asking the operator for the police.

Slipping the key into the latch Sophie pushed open the front door, making sure that once inside the catch was down so the door remained open to provide a quick exit should she need one. Stepping into the hallway there came the continued sound of more ornaments being smashed against the fire surround. Sophie hunted around quickly for a weapon, finding only a metal drip tray that her planters stood on. Putting the plants to one side she took up the tray.

Standing in front of the fireplace, Anna Van Janssen was gleefully removing and breaking up Sophie's treasured possessions. Either side of the chimney breast she had already slashed two of her paintings, not her best work although Matt had liked them.

Instinctively Anna sensed she was being watched. She turned with the knife pointing at her guest. Crunching underfoot broken glass from the mirror that had hung over fire she grinned, the smile of a mad woman. Her eyes were as Edith described wild and untamed.

'I guessed you'd come home sometime soon you filthy, ugly whore.' Spreading her hands wide she indicated that the room was spacious. 'Nice little house you have here. It's just a pity that you didn't fucking stay at home, instead of worming your way into my brother's bed.'

Anna licked her cracked and bloodied lips. On each of her forearms there were fresh cuts, knife wounds. Keeping her eyes focused solely on the knife Sophie was careful with what she said. 'You're not well Anna, I can help you!'

Anna Van Janssen laughed hysterically, stroking the blade of the knife across her tongue.

'My brother doesn't really like you, you do know that don't you whore. Matthew's only using your body until he can have me again. He likes fucking me. He did it, when we were teenagers and he misses me, I can tell that he does.' She touched first her breasts, then her vagina.

With the back of her hand Anna wiped the drool of saliva from the side of her mouth wincing slightly where they had been cracked by the salty sea air. She had spent the last few nights hiding in the cliffside caves avoiding the police who were out to recapture her. She winced when she moved from the bruising, where she had fallen, having lost her footing when the cat had attacked her. Anna blamed Sophie for Matthew having not returned to the lighthouse, another good reason to cut her badly.

Sophie took a good look at Anna, she was as Edith had described. Anna's clothes were dishevelled and no better than rags. She did smell and her hair was a matted mess with bloodied smears nearly everywhere. How she hadn't been spotted before today seemed almost inconceivable. Sophie reached forward, holding out her hand. 'Please Anna, let me help you, let us be friends. Matt is on his way, he wants to help you.'

Anna waved the knife left and right preventing Sophie from advancing any closer. Retreating back into the doorway of the living room Sophie knew that to her left and only two metres away was the dining room. Had she turned right she doubted that she would make it to the front door before Anna plunged the knife into her back. With a low growl, like that of a dog about to strike, Anna realised Sophie's intentions. It was enough to make Sophie turn and run towards the kitchen. Anna was close behind.

Scraping the tip of the blade along the plasterwork of the passage wall Anna left a deep damaging rent in the decoration. 'That's it pretty slut, run like the whore that you are. I once made Helga run, but after I caught up with her, she did everything that I asked her to do. By the time that my brother gets here, you will look no better than dog meat in a tin!'

Anna was beyond being pacified, instead she was hell bent on killing Sophie, her hatred of other women coming to the fore. Taking a step back at a time Sophie stepped on broken crockery, crunching and slipping beneath her feet, the bone china set that her mother had brought for her daughter last Christmas.

Anna kept advancing slashing and breaking everything that she could lay her hands on. She stopped at one point to pick up a framed photograph that had fallen to the floor, she licked the glass pane then smashed it against the wall. It was a photograph of when Sophie had been at school.

'Poor little Sophie Sprigg, all demure and pony tails. You did look all prim and proper in your uniform. Tell me, was you the class whore with your pert little breasts tempting the boys to touch you, fuck you. After school did you take the boys around the back of the sports sheds?'

Finding a frying pan on the side Sophie grabbed the handle, making Anna laugh.

'Look at you whore. Holding a metal tray in one hand and a frying pan in the other, who do you think you are, fucking Joan of Arc?'

Sophie glared back, 'If you recall Anna, she won her battles.'

Anna snarled. 'I'll gut you like the cat and leave you dying before my brother gets here!'

Oddly enough Sophie thought of Skyhort sitting in the lighthouse and watching, looking towards the town, towards her house. 'Rosie came home last night Anna, she's safe and sound and where you cannot get to her.'

Anna momentarily stopped advancing, she lowered the knife down to her side. The fact that the cat was safe seemed to register something in her twisted mind.

'So the flea-ridden creature survived did she. Well, after I've taken care of you, I'll pay the cat another visit, only next time I'll make doubly sure that she never walks or runs ever again.'

Without warning Anna suddenly cut herself on the forearm drawing blood. She sucked on the wound like a banshee. 'She will never see another sunrise, just like you won't Sophie Sprigg, the whore of Cockleshell Cove.'

Anna was a crazed psychotic maniac and no amount of talking was ever going to change her future, stepping over broken glass from the back door where Anna had gained entry into the house Sophie backed away towards the garden out back, playing for time, knowing that Matt and the police were on route, she tried one last ploy.

'We could have been good friends Anna. I realise that will never happen, not now, not ever. When the police arrive, they'll take you back and throw away the key!'

Taking another step backwards Anna realised Sophie's intention, she rushed headlong at Sophie thrusting the knife at her chest. Using the drip tray and the frying pan together Sophie lashed back with every ounce of her strength, connecting heavily with the side of Anna's head, using the frying pan as a weapon of her own. Sophie watched in horror as Anna fell to the ground, the side of her head bleeding from the cut. Anna however wasn't down and done, spitting blood she howled revenge. Within seconds she was rising.

Sophie fled to the garden running towards the back gate, but it was bolted top and bottom, there would not be time to release both bolts. Kicking open the shed door she hastily barricaded herself inside. Where were the police and where was Matt, she thought, if they didn't arrive soon Anna would surely find a way to get inside. Howling from pain or madness Anna repeatedly crashed against the shed door splintering the thin timbers slats. Inside, Sophie was almost out of solid things to stop Anna getting in.

'I'm going to tear the heart from your chest you fucking whore and give it the pigs back at the farm where I slept when I escaped. When I get in, you'll squeal like the piglets did.'

The tip of the knife crashed through a middle slat narrowly missing Sophie's hand where she was holding the door fast. With each threat and knife thrust Sophie could feel her fate coming. Through the tears she closed her eyes and thought of Matt, her mother and father, Jane and Vanessa, Penny and Ollie. None of it seemed fair. Just when she had found love, real love her life was going to be cruelly snatched from her by a mad woman. Thinking of Matt she prayed that the police got to Anna before he arrived. Despite her promises, there was no telling what Anna would do to her brother. Tearing a hole in the door panel, Anna poked her nose through.

'Come outside you whoring bitch and face me, I promise to make the end swift!'

Suddenly everything went silent, the demands, the shouting, the screaming and the abuse. The blade of the knife was still stuck fast in the timber slat, but instead Sophie could hear the birds singing nearby. All that she remembered hearing was the sound of a dull thud and something falling against the shed door. The next voice that she heard, belonged to Edith.

'You can come out now dear,' said her elderly neighbour softly and reassuringly. 'That crazy bitch won't no longer be a threat to you!'

Sophie cautiously removed the barricade and pulled back the shed door, Anna was surprisingly nowhere to be seen.

'Oh don't worry about her,' Edith said, with a smile. 'I expect she'll be over the wall at the end of the service alley and on her way down to the harbour. She scarpered good n' proper, like they used to say in the movies.'

Proudly standing astride of the wooden cold frame in Sophie's garden, Edith was brandishing a very heavy looking saucepan and affectionately rubbing the base.

'How?' Sophie asked, her mouth agape and her heart thumping inside her chest.

'An old trick that I learnt some time back when I was a bit younger than you my dear. With a girlfriend we would go fruit picking in the fields of Kent, spending every summer holiday on the same farm, where the days were long and hot, sunny and so romantic. Trouble was some of the men could get affected out in the fields all day long under the hot sun and come the evening with a couple of cold beers inside of them, the passion in their loins would be positively running wild. Walking out they would get over amorous, expecting a little bit too much of a young lady. A good whack to the back of the head with a heavy object soon put paid to their advances.' To demonstrate she gently hit the back of her hand with the saucepan base. 'It soon put paid to their ardour, so to speak.'

Edith craned her neck over the adjoining garden fencing, but there was sign of the mad woman. Out front they heard the sound of a cars arriving and screeching to a halt. Dropping the saucepan back over the fence Edith prepared herself for the police.

'Having said that, had they given out free contraceptives like they do today, things might have been very different when we'd gone walking!'

Calming her beating heart Sophie lay against Edith and let the tears flow thick and fast. Edith had saved her life. Coming through the house, avoiding the broken glass and china Edith had reached the back garden just in time. It had taken a great deal of courage to attack Anna and have her run off. Holding her gently Sophie did not want to let go.

'I don't know what to say Edith, other than thank you, you saved me from a terrible fate.'

Whispering gently in her ear Edith replied. *'That's what I used to say to myself, when I had whacked one of them over the head. They'd lay on the hay bales with such an astonished look.'*

Shoving the damaged kitchen door aside Matt arrived closely followed by several police. He was surprised to see Edith in the rear garden consoling Sophie.

'Are you both okay?' he asked.

'I am now, thanks to Edith and an old contraceptive substitute.'

Matt looked puzzled. 'I'm sorry, I would have been here sooner, but that damn bull got loose again and wouldn't budge from the lane. It took an eternity to coax the beast back inside!'

Sophie looked at the two officers talking to Edith. 'And the police,' she asked, 'what took them so long?'

'You wouldn't believe it, they were detained down at the harbour dealing with a fight in a pub. They arrived the same time as me.'

The back gate suddenly crashed open as a fierce looking police dog arrived. 'Where is she?' asked the handler.

'She went that way,' Edith pointed, 'although by my reckoning young man, she's probably heading down Stalwart Avenue and heading for the harbour.'

The dog handler let the dog sniff the handle of the knife then turned the dog around. Both man and beast heading down the alleyway.

Edith invited Sophie and Matt in next door asking the police to delay taking any statements until later. She feigned being old and that she needed a cup of tea to calm her nerves. Sophie smiled to herself. Edith was as fit as a fiddle and her nerves were as strong as the bull that had got loose again.

The police and the dog searched for almost two hours, but they found no trace of Anna much to the dismay of Matt and Sophie. Sophie was checked by an ambulance crew and Edith quite rightly became the focus of attention. She had surprised them all with her gallantry and resourcefulness.

'I was only saying to my friend this morning that I needed something exciting to happen to galvanise myself into action again and rouse the old spirit within in me. I'd long forgotten the things that I could do, but this has taught an old woman a valuable lesson. It's time things changed around here and starting with today.' She rubbed her hands together determined to make it happen.

Instead of taking tea at Edith's, they invited her to the lighthouse for supper where they told her about the offer of a kitten. Matt secured the back door as best he could promising that he would do a better job the next day. Sophie said she would contact the contact the insurers and they could begin assessing the damage.

Standing by the front door, they were waiting for Matt to start up the Chevy. With a nudge of her elbow Edith came in close to whisper. *'Now that's a real man that you've got yourself there my dear.*

Had Matt been a strapping farm hand back when I was young girl picking fruit, I would have tossed aside that tractor brake handle and let him had his wicked way!'

Sophie felt the laugh come from deep within. Edith was a real dark horse and underneath that demure exterior was a basket full of shenanigans, wanting to be re-released. Before the evening was through they would tell Edith about her moving in with Matt, a move that could not come soon enough for Sophie. Although disappointed, Edith would be pleased for them both.

Nestling herself between Matt driving and Sophie, Edith closed her eyes and remembered a time when she had sat up front of an apple lorry going to market with the farm boys. Smiling to herself the memories came flooding back, good times and probably the happiest of her life. She turned to Matt and asked if she could switch on the radio as she wanted music, any kind of music. She found a station playing contemporary dance tunes.

'This reminds me of when I was courting,' she hummed, 'we'd go down to the beach in his grocer's truck and find ourselves a quiet place to take in the breeze. We would sit there all evening with the windows open, watching the sunset before we found a nice pub to finish off the date.'

She touched the leather of the long bench seat in the Chevy, 'it was very much like this,' she said, winking at Sophie, *'blimey did that seat see some action some nights!'* She turned, smiling at Matt resting her hand on his forearm.

Listening to the music the mood was relaxed, despite the trauma of the afternoon. Sophie let the late afternoon breeze wash through her head wanting to forget everything. With Edith at her side she felt a connection, a spiritual bond and there was so much more that she wanted to know about her elderly neighbour. Surprisingly, Edith laid a hand on both of their wrists.

'Love is like a thick book. Sometimes the narrative loses it way and struggles to get back on track, but when you pick up a damn good read, one that you never want to put down, not until you reach the end, then that is the book worth keeping.'

Edith sighed, recalling how she had let her best book go a long time ago.

'However, should you reach the last, but one page and you feel that you've exhausted all the love and fun that you can experience together, don't despair because by beginning to read the book again, you'll soon see a different story appearing the second time around. My advice to you both is go and write your own story and let destiny decide the ending.'

After that Edith rocked gently to the music humming to herself and admiring the leafy lanes, lanes that she had not been down in years.

She fell instantly in love with the old lighthouse, understanding why Sophie wanted to move in with Matt. Edith was given an open invitation to visit whenever she wanted, which she gladly accepted, providing Matt collected her in the Chevy and that they had the radio on.

Beyond the headland the evening breeze was gentle, still warm and relaxing. Changes had taken place and mostly for the good, but not all had been experienced. Some were still lingering in the soft curve of the cove.

Chapter Thirty Four

Anna found a large smelly fish tarpaulin under which to hide concealing herself from sight as the police searched the harbour. Lapping gently against the harbour wall the fishing boats were resting having been out all night.

With the police foot patrols nearby she could just about hear them talking to one another, as they overturned crates and lobster pots close to where she was hidden. Repentant that she had to leave the knife embedded in the door of the garden shed, she looked around for something else to use as a weapon.

They were almost upon her when a radio message announced another disturbance at the harbour pub. Within seconds the patrols were running back to their vehicles.

Anna stayed put another five minutes before she pushed aside the tarpaulin. The air smelt salty, but fresh, more appealing than it had beneath the fishy sheet. Rubbing her head the bleeding had stopped, although an aggressive bump was quickly forming. She remembered seeing something large and black looming out of the corner of her eye, but when it connected everything went black. Recovering seconds later, she was in no fit state to remonstrate with the old woman who had hit her. Forgetting about the knife, Anna's instinct was to escape. Frustratingly she clenched her fists, once again the pasty faced whore had escaped her wrath.

Lying at anchor a short distance from the harbour wall a group of fishermen were busy tending to the nets, as the lone woman hurried along the stone walkway, searching for a suitable boat that she thought she could manage. One of them saw her looking, but he assumed that she was just another tourist interested in everything nautical and smelly.

'There's an unusual amount of police about today!' one of them mused, as he cast his needle through the blue twine for the umpteenth time.

Sat next to him the coxswain sucked on an empty pipe, observing the woman as she went from boat to boat. 'Aye unusual,' he muttered, 'I wonder what she's about?'

'Summit n' nothing I expect,' remarked another. His interest already at the pub and what was on the lunchtime menu. 'Them there boys and girls in blue are always racing around, pretty soon they'll be disappearing up their proverbial, if they don't watch out!' The group laughed going about their repairs.

The coxswain however wasn't entirely sure, something about the women suggested that she was up to no good. Pulling tight on his thread, he kept a watchful eye on her movements. When she took the stone steps down from the walkway to the small wooden jetty below he stood up, wanting a better look. Anna saw him looking, she waved a moment before she jumped into the small motorised dingy.

'That ain't right,' he called out to the others, pointing over to where she was trying to start the engine, 'that's Dick Berrand's boat.'

'Oi...' yelled another, 'what's your bleedin' game?'

Anna ignored the men as they continued to shout. Moments later the engine spluttered into life. Casting off the jetty line she steered the dingy away from the harbour wall, as the coxswain called the harbour master's office.

Pushing the handle down hard on the throttle Anna increased the revolutions of the engine, coursing the bow through the mouth of the harbour and out into the open sea. By her reckoning she would need to turn east once she was clear, taking the south coast up to the Channel and across to Holland. Home was a short distance away. She vowed to come back one day and sort the whore and the old woman.

Chapter Thirty Five

Supper was a relaxed affair, after which Matt and Sophie gave Edith a guided tour of the lighthouse, she especially liked the old beacon room and the workshop.

'This is magnificent,' she said clasping her hands together, 'so big and I would never have imagined that it would be here.' She walked around touching heavy tools, feeling the smooth lines of the metal in awe of his creations, still to be sold.

Standing alone on the gallery balcony Edith breathed in the salty air. As a girl she would walk to the end of the beach and look up at the tall white edifice wondering what lie beyond the front door. Towering above the rocky headland, she looked at the sea ahead, taking in Cockleshell Cove to her left then the harbour. Edith had never seen anything so beautiful.

'I have only ever seen the beach and the town from way down below. It all looks so different up here!'

Inside, Matt and Sophie smiled. Matt took out a glass of wine and handed it to Edith. 'It can get a bit fresh out here sometimes. I find this helps!'

She took the glass and thanked him. It had been a long time since she'd had wine.

'I could sit here all day and night, just watching the world go by.'

'We do that a lot,' Matt admitted, holding onto his own glass. 'Is the wine okay?'

'It was once my favourite tipple.' She nudged his arm, 'and one never forgets how to ride a bike!'

Sophie joined them closely followed by Rosie, the cat made a fuss of Edith much to Sophie's delight.

Matt went back downstairs retuning with a cardboard box, where inside four inquisitive and wide-eyed kittens looked up at the lady cooing overhead. They closed the balcony door and let them run loose in the lamp room. The boy kitten immediately made a bee line for Edith. She gasped, clasping her hands together, looking across at Sophie. 'They're absolutely divine, oh my goodness such a difficult choice.' She picked up the boy.

Sophie looked at Matt, who put a finger to his lips. The little bundle of black fur gave Edith a knowing cry of contentment. In that single cry the choice was already made.

'Oh my, you are the cutest little thing that I have ever seen.' She put the kitten on her chest where he purred. 'He's so handsome and so strong.' Edith remarked.

Matt sat himself down next to Edith. 'He's very lively and from I've seen without any fear. This little one has been leading his sister's on a merry dance all day. He'd be good company for you Edith!' Sophie sat next to Matt looping her arm through his.

'Together we'd have lots of fun, wouldn't we Harry.' Edith had already named the cat.

Matt nodded, it was a good name, vibrant and had strength. Sophie laid her head on his shoulder, Matt was an extremely kind understanding man. She knew that he had chosen the cat for himself, but was willing to put up with another female in the home instead.

Edith let Harry down so that he could play with his sisters. She watched them tumble then chase one another's tail as Rosie sat on Sophie's lap.

'I know that I am knocking on in life and I am nobody's fool, but there's something special about this old lighthouse. You feel it as soon as you walk through the door.' She looked down to where Skyhort was sleeping. 'Did you know, the Chinese believe that dragons are the symbol of good fortune?' Edith touched the top of the dragons head for luck. 'Although this creature looks like he's had a very tiring day.'

Haven't we all, thought Sophie, remembering the level of aggression dispatched against her by Anna. It was strange why she had thought of Skyhort. She wondered, that if by some quirk of fate the dragon had prompted Edith into action.

'We're thinking of making part of the old beacon room into an artist's studio for Sophie that is until we get the lamp working again.'

Edith nodded approvingly, looking about the room. 'The natural light would be ideally suited to your painting. I've seen the two in the shop window. You really are very talented Sophie.'

Matt had already thought of a way that he could shield one side of the lamp room so that they could still sit and enjoy the view without being blinded each evening. He watched Harry nibble the end of Edith's finger with his milk teeth. 'Of course, there'd still be enough space left for us all to sit up here, when you come to visit.'

'With wine and supper thrown in, plus a ride in the Chevy there and back, you'd never get rid of me!' Edith replied.

'I think that I had best come along too for the ride and keep you two apart.'

'You're learning fast Sophie Sprigg, remember to write that book one day!'

Edith continued to play with the kittens as they crowded around her.

'You might wonder why I called him Harry. He was a young man that I met one summer on my Kentish escapades. In the hot sun we had ourselves some fun I can tell you. Time however moves on waiting for no man, or in my case woman. We lost touch with one another down the years. Sadly, two years back a letter arrived one day from a niece of Harry's. She had been looking through his personal effects and found our letters. She very kindly wrote to tell me about how Harry had passed away peacefully in his sleep. As a favourite niece, he had told her about me. My little Harry will help keep those cherished memories alive.'

The sound of a wailing shrill from the siren of the lifeboat station cut across the cove sending a dread through the hearts of those that heard it.

'Some poor soul needs help!' Edith remarked.

Awash with light the lifeboat station doors were opened. They saw the lifeboat drop down the slipway and crash into the water. Touching the top of the dragon's head, Sophie whispered. 'Keep whoever safe Skyhort.'

'I do hope Matt that I didn't hurt your sister too badly this afternoon when I hit her, my only intention was to stop her from hurting Sophie.'

Matt put his hand reassuringly on her forearm. 'We're glad of your intervention Edith. I dread to think what would have happened had you not taken the appropriate action. At some point, today, tomorrow or whenever, it's inevitable that Anna will get hurt. Anna will not go down without a fight, whatever the circumstances. My only worry is who she hurts doing so. Thank god that you were there, we'll be indebted to you now and forever.'

'I hope the police do find her Matt and that she gets help. It must be very hard for you!'

Leaving the safety of the harbour the familiar red and orange boat headed out beyond the harbour wall to a sea that had many undercurrents and was no friend, day or night.

'Will you sell the house?' Edith asked.

'You know Vanessa, my partner at the shop. She and her boyfriend are keen on either buying or renting the house, they would be ideal neighbours Edith.'

Edith seemed happy to hear that somebody she knew might be her new neighbour.

'You do know Edith that there's nothing to stop you visiting the shop during the afternoon. We generally make coffee or tea and have a slice of homemade cake around three.'

Matt's eyes lit up, it was news to him. He gently nudged Edith's arm as she sat beside him. 'I'll pick you up in the Chevy and we will both visit the shop!'

Some way out, some distance from the Dorset coastline a bright green flare suddenly lit up the late evening sky. Edith felt the hairs on her neck rise.

'In all the years that I have lived in Cockleshell Cove I have never liked seeing the lifeboat launched or that green flare. I think of the crew risking their lives to rescue a poor soul, stranded and possibly frightened. It turns my heart icy cold to think what might happen if the weather is really bad.'

Sophie smiled, she dare not tell Edith that one of the crew could possibly be the prowler that she had reported to the police the night that she thought Dave Aldridge was a pervert.

An hour later they both took Edith back home, but not before she had kissed the dragons head, said goodbye to Rosie and the kittens telling little Harry that she was going home to get his bed ready.

Just before midnight, looking up at the stars Edith experienced an odd, although wonderful feeling pass through her thoughts, bringing with it a mindful peace. Looking at the night sky a vision appeared. She didn't need telling who the face belonged too. Blowing him a kiss, Harry smiled back.

Pulling up the duvet cover, she whispered gently. *'Goodnight Harry,'* then as her eyes started to close, *'one day, I'll take you to see the lighthouse.'*

Clutching his letters close to her chest she sighed just once, fell asleep and walked into a lovely dream, sitting alongside Harry as they watched the sunset go down.

Chapter Thirty Six

Immediately beyond the safety of the harbour wall Anna hit the fury of the English Channel where things changed dramatically. Bouncing over the waves she found it difficult to steer and power the tiny dingy, the undercurrent pulling her one way then another. Pushing the engine full throttle she powered the little craft to maximum efficiency, but the further out that she went the more dangerous it became.

Gritting her teeth she was determined to reach Holland and safety. Some way behind her she heard the siren of the lifeboat.

Watching the small dingy power its way through the harbour gateway Bertrand Trent, the harbour master continued to stare incredulously at the woman that he had in the sights of his binoculars.

'Where in blue blazes does that fool of a woman think she's going, there's a south-easterly whipping up all along the coast, in that dingy she'll never ride the waves.' He shook his head in disbelief. *'The waves will cut through Dick Berrand's boat as though it were made of butter!'*

With the police cars screeching to a halt Robbie Croton had climbed onto the cabin roof of the trawler, pointing in the direction that the woman had taken in the dingy.

'I hope she knows how to swim,' he yelled, *'that sea is getting real choppy.'*

It was a minute later that Bertrand Trent hit the button to alert the lifeboat crew. Jumping down from the cabin roof Robbie knew that his services would be needed.

Coursing her craft over the waves Anna struggled with the rudder fighting the incoming squall, but the force of the sea was much stronger than it had looked when she had passed through the harbour entrance. With each wave the dingy engine seemed to slow. Anna began to cry despairingly wishing that Matthew was with her. Why could he not accept her for who she was and live the rest of their lives together in peace.

Leaving his office Bertrand Trent ran to the lifeboat shed to give William Harland, the Coxswain, as much information as he could about the woman in the dingy. He also had a weather projection of the incoming storm.

Working late in his office, a short drive from the harbour, Dave Aldridge heard the siren. Within seconds he was through the door of the factory and heading down to the lifeboat station.

Abandoning his car at the rear he joined others arriving. They dressed quickly and stood ready for the launch. In under five minutes the rigid hull lifeboat was dropping down the slipway and heading for the harbour mouth.

'Time's not on our side,' Harland called out, as he steered the craft towards the unforgiving swell of the Jurassic coastline. 'We'll need to catch up soon, otherwise the more distance that she puts between us, the more perilous our task will become!'

Checking the fluorescent lifejackets strapped to their chests each of the crew pulled the safety harness in another notch tighter. The swell was increasing and effecting a rescue was going to be tough going. With fingers clamped tight around the safety bar Dave Aldridge, Robbie Croton and Shelia Swanson from the butcher's shop knew what to expect. Relentlessly lashing their faces with salty spray the sea was ready to do battle. Over the noise of the engine and the sea William Harland informed the crew that the female in the dingy was a young woman named Anna Van Janssen. Dave Aldridge tensed when he heard the name. From Matt and Jane he knew all about Anna.

'She's volatile and extremely dangerous,' he warned, 'I know her brother!'

Taking a handful of extra strong plastic ties from the equipment box Robbie slipped them into his pocket, 'these might come in handy, if she causes us any trouble!' Dave nodded, Robbie was right to be cautious.

Bobbing high above the crest of a wave the bow of the lifeboat dipped once again. In the distance they spotted the small craft struggling as she took on water. William Harland's keen seagoing mind quickly assessed the situation.

'I'd say her outboard motor has stalled in the water, we had best get alongside soon otherwise she'll overturn or sink.' He turned to look at each member of his crew, 'remember no heroics, safety first at all times. It won't do her any good, if we find ourselves in difficulty.'

William had been battling this stretch of coast for a good many years. He knew the waters, the tides and where the sea was most dangerous. The English Channel had to be respected.

'As soon as we get alongside, see if you can secure the dingy to our craft Shelia, although if you can't leave it. In this water a strong wave will flip us both over.' Harland kept an eye on the gathering of grey clouds overhead searching for the sign of a rescue helicopter. With patches of black amongst the grey the sky looked menacing. 'If they've launched a chopper from one of the shore bases it could be at least twenty minutes before they get here and I'm not keen on being rescued by the Weymouth lifeboat!' he grinned, light heartedly although the crew knew that he meant it.

Coming alongside the drifting dingy Anna was lying motionless against the small bulkhead where the constant battering of the waves had knocked her unconscious and sapped the last of her energy. The palm of her right hand was bloodied and blistered where the skin had been shredded trying to restart the engine. Drifting hopelessly in the water the little dingy wasn't going anywhere and Anna would not be landing at the Hook of Holland.

With her first attempt Shelia successfully managed to lash together the two crafts as Robbie skilfully slipped into the sinking dingy.

'Get her aboard as soon as you can,' William Harland called out as steadied himself for the next incoming wave. Conditions were getting worse and he didn't want to be out any longer than absolutely necessary.

At the bow where the inflatable was attached, Shelia watched the incoming wave, letting the line go slack through the cleat. It was a manoeuvre that had been practised many times, although conditions were never quite the same. Lifting Anna across Dave Aldridge waited until Robbie was safely aboard before tapping William Harland on the shoulder signalling that they could leave. Swinging the lifeboat about with the dingy attached both vessels headed back to the safety of Cockleshell Cove.

'Slip a tie around both wrists, just in case,' advised Dave to Robbie, 'and add another around her ankles. If Anna comes too, she'll be like a caged tiger.'

Shelia was about to question why Robbie had applied the ankle ties, but Dave had anticipated her doubt.

'Matt, her brother is built like a goliath and yet twice she's attacked him resulting in him receiving medical treatment. Anna was recently a patient Ashburton Manor until she escaped!' She approved of their caution.

Robbie put his finger through the ties. 'They're set real loose, so they won't hurt even if she does wake, although they'll keep her restrained until we reach the harbour wall, from there the police can take over.'

Forty five minutes later William Harland manoeuvred both crafts alongside the harbour wall where an ambulance and sufficient police were already waiting. Strapped to the stretcher Anna was lifted into the back of the ambulance and left with a police escort. She remained unconscious for the journey back to the hospital and would not gain consciousness until the next morning by which time her medication had once again been intravenously administered calming her tormented mind.

Chapter Thirty Seven

Sophie and Matt were on the return journey to the lighthouse having made sure that Edith was happily settled back at home when they received the call from the sergeant at the police station. He informed Matt of his sisters attempt to escape capture. Matt turned to Sophie, his expression one of shock and disbelief.

'The lifeboat was launched because of Anna. She stole a motorised dingy, heading out in the English Channel.'

Sophie put a clenched fist to her lips. 'Oh Matt, we need to be down at the harbour when they bring her back. I hope that she's alright.'

Despite the horror of that afternoons attack Sophie's first instinct was to know that her future sister-in-law was safe. Thinking about the attack she had realised that Anna's vile temper and violent actions were the work of the voices inside her head and without the necessary medication she was unable to supress the evil that had long taken over her mind. Sophie felt only sorrow for Anna.

Matt brought the Chevy to a halt, spun the wheels round and headed for town. Sophie sat very close by his side as the vehicle increased in speed.

'Stay positive Matt, they'll bring her back safe, I know they will.'

Turning the wheel one way then the other Matt looked at Sophie, unable to comprehend how she could be so sympathetic and understanding.

'She tried to kill you earlier, why in heaven's name would you say that she'll be alright. Perhaps the kindest thing would be for Anna not to survive!'

She made him stop the Chevy. Applying the brake, she took his head in her hands.

'*Because I love you and one day Matt, whatever the circumstances Anna will still be my sister-in-law and your family will mean as much to me as my own. Anna needs help and in time she will get better!*'

Far out to sea the clouds were black, interspersed with grey and foreboding. Instinctively, Sophie kissed Matt to have him know that she would be there through good and bad times. Moments later she made him restart the engine. 'To the harbour. Remember we have Rosie, Skyhort and a little kitten to keep us safe.'

They arrived shortly before William Harland brought the lifeboat alongside the harbour wall. Matt and Sophie stood at Anna's side, where her eyes were shut, her injured hand and arm bandaged.

'She looks peaceful,' Matt said, 'if only she would remain like that.' He kissed his sister lightly on the forehead and Sophie heard him whisper, *'I love you, please get better.'* Anna was then lifted into the ambulance.

'We need to go home,' he said, 'I need to call my mother.'

'Will she come over to visit?' Sophie asked.

Matt nodded. 'Yes, I believe she will.'

'That's good, because then I get the chance to meet your mum. I'd best improve my cooking skills.'

She put her arm through his and pulled him in close as they walked back to where he had left the Chevy. Not so long ago he had seen a beautiful woman waiting at the junction. He had driven by and waved, but she'd not returned the gesture wondering if the wave had been for her.

*****

As the days and the weeks rolled into one another life settled back into the slow easy pace in Cockleshell Cove. Edith divided her leisure time between visiting the shop and the lighthouse, spending the hours that she was not with little Harry with Sophie discussing art and loving every moment of her new found lifestyle.

She also had made significant changes, enrolling in the towns over seventies club and taken up dancing again twirling not only herself around the dance floor, but most of the retired male population of Cockleshell Cove.

There was one man in particular who had caught her eye, not as dashingly handsome as Harry, but he did possess a certain smile that was remarkably like that of a young man with whom she had known a very long time ago. When the time was right Edith would slip into the conversation that she lived alone and that she was available, only keeping the saucepan handy just in case.

Matt helped Sophie move her belongings out of the terraced house and into the lighthouse, leaving it up to her as where she thought it best to put everything, including her artwork. As the weeks rolled on by it was as though it had always meant to be. The lamp room would always be her favourite place, come early morning, midday or last thing at night when the stars were at their best.

Sophie loved being in the workshop just watching Matt create things for Carlos, photographing each one which she added to his portfolio. Several of her paintings had been sold abroad and gradually her name was becoming known both at home and overseas, but keeping herself very grounded, Sophie Sprigg would rather remain just a local girl, donating the odd painting to the children's home annual auction.

As a way of saying thank you and a tribute to their bravery Matt invited the lifeboat crew to supper at the old lighthouse. Also present were their many good friends.

Midway through dessert Dave Aldridge suddenly tapped the rim of his wine glass and asked for a moments silence as he had an important announcement to make. Standing with his glass in his hand, he created an enormous smile. Buttoning their lips together the faces around the table waited in anticipation of what he had to say.

Edith and her new beau. Penny without Ollie. William Harland, Shelia Swanson and Robbie Croton, sitting alongside Vanessa and Jonathon, Annabelle and Scott, their grandmother and Sophie's mum, who looked quizzically at Jane was unusually silent for once. As guest of honour and sitting at the head of the table was Murielle Van Janssen, between her son and Sophie. Asking them to raise their glasses, Dave began his prepared announcement.

'Not only have I recently become part of a very important family of volunteers, extremely brave men and women with whom I hold each in such high regard, I have also recently gained a new black cat courtesy of Rosie, Sophie and Matt. She is aptly named Pickles, why I'm not entirely sure, although I believe because I find myself in some occasionally.

'There is however something very important that I wish to announce in the presence of our many friends, something of which you will all be part of in the future.' He looked at Jane and raised his glass. 'My beautiful wife and I are pleased to announce that come spring of the next year we will have another addition to our family, less furry than the last, but loved as much.'

The cheer almost took the glass panels from the old beacon room as it reverberated through the lighthouse, which fortunately had thick walls. Sleeping alongside Skyhort, Rosie raised her head, opened one eye to give a cursory nod of approval before she promptly went back to her slumber. The winds of change had long gone, but she was sure that they would be back one day.

Sitting between her son and future daughter-in-law, Murielle Van Janssen held their hands. 'One day soon that announcement will be yours to make.'

Looking back at them both, Sophie smiled, knowing that it would be sooner rather than later, although as promised, she would tell Matt first. Holding his mother's hand Matt wasn't particular which, whether it be a boy or a girl, although if pressed he would say a son to even up the balance of gender in the home.

Standing on the gallery balcony Sophie, Jane, Vanessa and Penny looked up at the stars.

'There's one for each and every one of us up there,' announced Jane.

Standing at her side Sophie grinned. 'And you three were the one's looking out for me!' She looked at Jane accusingly when she said it. 'Was it planned?' she asked.

Jane chuckled. 'What like my first, don't be bloody ridiculous Sprigg, other than Scott when have I and Dave ever planned anything together!'

She placed her hands over her abdomen. 'Anyway don't put the onus all on me, blame that bloody lifeboat. Since becoming part of the crew my old man is all fired up when he comes home after a shout. He nudges me in the back to see if I'm awake and as soon as I murmur he's at me like a rampant ram.' She gently stroked her abdomen again. 'And unlike the occasion behind the coastguard station this baby is all his doing!'

The echo of their laughter went down to the headland below and across the beach to the town.

Later that night when they were alone, when the moon was high in the night sky keeping the stars company, Sophie would tell Matt that soon the patter of tiny feet would fill the old lighthouse and that a baby would seal their happiness.

There would be many friends to choose from for the role of godparent, but one in particular that they would both want first would be Edith. Jane, Vanessa and Penny would have their turn in the years to come.

*****

When at last the lighthouse went completely silent leaving only Rosie, the kitten and Skyhort alone in the old beacon room, the trio looked out across the cove where everything seemed to be at peace. In time Rosie would have more kittens, although the mystery of the father would never be known.

Sophie and Murielle Van Janssen became good friends and vowed to help one another with regards to Anna. Matt proposed to Sophie and she said yes. Their baby was due a month after

Jane's. Matt had found forgiving his mother easier than he had expected and in time it would never be mentioned ever again.

With the kitten sleeping by her side Rosie looked out of the lighthouse window and wondered what had become of the crazy woman who had never returned. Change was inevitable as was time itself and over the six months that they had been at the lighthouse it had seen its fair share of change. At present however life at the lighthouse and Cockleshell Cove was better than it had ever been.

About the Author

Known more for his criminal, psychological and suspense fiction writing Jeffrey Brett was asked by a female friend if he had ever considered writing a romantic novel aimed for the female market. Believing that he might have a story in mind, he asked for the title, whereby the friend gave him 'Looking for Rosie'. Living not that far from the English coastline the author set about creating the old lighthouse, names and faces, not forgetting of course a black cat, called Rosie.

The writer lives in Norfolk, having previously lived in London and Hertfordshire, where he served professionally in two of the front line emergency services from the seventies through to the end of the century. Now in his mid-sixties and soon to be retired Jeffrey has been gathering together literary ideas for almost four decades. With the luxury of time now available, these ideas have at last been put into books.

Current fictional publications include:

Looking for Rosie

Leave No Loose Ends

The Little Red Café

Beyond the First Page

The Road is Never Long Enough

I Was On That Train

Printed in Great Britain
by Amazon